THE HEAT OF THE MOMENT

Just when Xander thought Cleo's resistance would crumble and she'd slip from his hold, she came up on her toes, leaning into his body, her mouth inches from his, the scent of her making his head swim. "Would a simple kiss for the spies be too much to ask?"

"A simple kiss?" Not really a possibility, but Xander would let her discover that. He pulled her up fully against him and held her, letting her absorb the way they fit together. "You think you know desire because some lordling politely groped you in a garden, put his tongue in your mouth, and popped your stays." He shook his head. "You don't know the first thing about desire."

He lowered his mouth to hers, just to show her how uncomprehending she was, or maybe just to nudge her onto that path where he was already waiting leagues ahead of her.

She made a small sound in her throat as he joined their mouths . . .

To Tempt a Saint

KATE MOORE

B

BERKLEY SENSATION, NEW YORK

THE BERKLEY PUBLISHING GROUP
Published by the Penguin Group
Penguin Group (USA) Inc.
375 Hudson Street, New York, New York 10014, USA

Penguin Group (Canada), 90 Eglinton Avenue East, Suite 700, Toronto, Ontario M4P 2Y3, Canada
(a division of Pearson Penguin Canada Inc.)
Penguin Books Ltd., 80 Strand, London WC2R 0RL, England
Penguin Group Ireland, 25 St. Stephen's Green, Dublin 2, Ireland (a division of Penguin Books Ltd.)
Penguin Group (Australia), 250 Camberwell Road, Camberwell, Victoria 3124, Australia
(a division of Pearson Australia Group Pty. Ltd.)
Penguin Books India Pvt. Ltd., 11 Community Centre, Panchsheel Park, New Delhi—110 017, India
Penguin Group (NZ), 67 Apollo Drive, Rosedale, North Shore 0632, New Zealand
(a division of Pearson New Zealand Ltd.)
Penguin Books (South Africa) (Pty.) Ltd., 24 Sturdee Avenue, Rosebank, Johannesburg 2196,
South Africa

Penguin Books Ltd., Registered Offices: 80 Strand, London WC2R 0RL, England

This is a work of fiction. Names, characters, places, and incidents either are the product of the author's imagination or are used fictitiously, and any resemblance to actual persons, living or dead, business establishments, events, or locales is entirely coincidental. The publisher does not have any control over and does not assume any responsibility for author or third-party websites or their content.

TO TEMPT A SAINT

A Berkley Sensation Book / published by arrangement with the author

PRINTING HISTORY
Berkley Sensation mass-market edition / January 2010

Copyright © 2010 by Kate Moore.
Excerpt from *To Save the Devil* by Kate Moore copyright © by Kate Moore.
Cover art by Phil Hefferman.
Cover design by George Long.
Cover hand lettering by Ron Zinn.
Interior text design by Kristin del Rosario.

ISBN: 978-0-425-23306-1

BERKLEY® SENSATION
Berkley Sensation Books are published by The Berkley Publishing Group,
a division of Penguin Group (USA) Inc.,
375 Hudson Street, New York, New York 10014.
BERKLEY® SENSATION and the "B" design are trademarks of Penguin Group (USA) Inc.

PRINTED IN THE UNITED STATES OF AMERICA

10 9 8 7 6 5 4 3 2 1

For Pamela Ahearn,
an agent with a silk suit,
a BlackBerry, a sense of humor,
and endless faith in her authors, with thanks.

"I will that every child be his father's heir after his father's day."

CHARTER TO THE CITY OF LONDON
FROM WILLIAM THE CONQUEROR

Prologue

THE fight was not a fight, just a brief, bloody proof that title trumps presumption. Still, Xander Jones had to admit that nothing united a London crowd like shared delight in violence. Dukes and draymen roared with one voice when the champion's fist leveled the challenger. Boxing's famed Fives Court, and possibly all Leicester Square, rang with the sound.

Within minutes costermongers and Corinthians, in perfect amity, began to jostle their way into the night, oblivious of rank. Only the Marquess of Candover failed to catch London's new democratic spirit, stepping back with a contemptuous curl of his lip from a near meeting with his bastard son.

Some lines were not meant to be crossed.

Xander kept his brother Kit in front of him, his hands

on the boy's shoulders, steering a path away from the marquess. No sense in spoiling a brotherly outing.

"Did you see his left, Xander?" Kit jabbed the air, mimicking the champion's trademark move. "The champion planted him a real facer."

"*A facer*?"

"That's what sporting men say."

"As long as you don't say it at home." Xander turned Kit's shoulders, directing an awkward but earnest blow away from the purple silk waistcoat of a stout gentleman engaged in settling a side bet. The man gave them a fixed stare.

Xander waved off friends headed for further entertainment. Their evening would likely start in the public rooms of a well-known establishment in Piccadilly and end in the private ones of a more notorious place in Covent Garden.

Xander found he preferred his plan for supper with Kit. Beef pies and porter had been mentioned. Not that Kit was ready for spirits, but Xander smiled at the idea. A year ago he would have resented having the charge of his youngest brother. Now he didn't mind their London rambles even though they inevitably ended in maternal reproaches that Xander was far too old to endure. He thought his mother a fearless woman, but lately she imagined footpads or worse lurking in every dark lane, waiting for boys not tucked in bed by ten.

The crowd bunched up ahead of them at the pavement, where it split undemocratically into two factions—men with waiting vehicles and their inferiors. Xander steered Kit away from a pile of steaming dung, and in deference to his mother's fears, headed the boy toward a side lane that skirted more dangerous streets.

"Mother doesn't like you to take me to mills, does she?"

"Best to keep it our secret."

"May not gentlemen enjoy boxing?"

"Many do." No use denying what Kit himself could see. The cabinet could have settled the business of the nation at tonight's match.

"But not our sort of gentleman?"

"Exactly." Their sort of gentleman, the well-bred bastard, had to be a social contortionist, fitting himself to his company.

"Because our fathers did not marry our mother?"

There it was, out in the open, the reason behind Kit's new passion for boxing. In school a boy could fight till his knuckles were raw, and there would always be another sapskull to make a remark about Sophie Jones. Kit, fair-haired and small for his age, would find it rough going to defend their mother's honor.

A familiar anger gripped Xander. He shook it off as nothing more than a delayed reaction to the chance sighting of his father. Neither the gods nor the British legal system was likely to stand up for bastards. A cool head and quick left hand would be of more use to Kit than cargo holds of anger at the going rate. "A lucky thing for us that our mother doesn't marry her lovers, infant."

"Not if we can't go to mills."

"Ah, but if *my* father had married *our* mother, then she wouldn't have met *your* father, and then where would you be?" They halted to let a lumbering cart pass ahead of them in the narrow lane.

Sophie Jones had had three lovers that Xander knew of in her career as a courtesan. Each had given her a son; the "Sons of Sin" their brother Will called them. Made by wickedness for wickedness, a theory Will meant to prove among the paid-out soldiers of several armies in the most debauched hells in Paris.

Sophie's efforts to make gentlemen of her sons were laughable, Xander supposed, when she herself knew better than most how gentlemen behaved in London. Still, being a bastard son of a notorious courtesan had its advantages.

Their mother had taught them how to handle money. No banker had a surer grasp of investment. Her lovers' gifts of jewels, carriages, horses, and extravagant gowns had become a tidy empire of investments, a comfortable house off Berkeley Square, a gentleman's education for her sons, and now a snug cottage between the Surrey Hills and the Thames, where she meant to retire in widow-like respectability once Kit was launched in the world. A boy could do worse in a parent.

Her affair with Kit's father had scandalized London when Xander was seventeen and making his way through university. Then somewhere in India under Wellesley, long after the man's folly had ceased to be the latest London gossip, the poor fellow had died. Sophie Jones was doubtless the only one who still wore black for him. She had taken no new lover.

Fog as murky as the Thames itself swallowed the huge cart ahead of them. Its rumble faded, and Xander and Kit walked on, only a few stragglers in their wake. "Most fellows don't look at it that way, do they, Xander?"

"Most fellows don't have a pair of first-rate brothers." A man couldn't choose his connections, but Xander preferred his Jones brothers to his father's lofty family. He had long ago cut short the one name his father had been willing to give him. Alexander had become Xander at school.

Kit tugged his sleeve. "You know what makes a first-rate brother?"

"Enlighten me."

"One that'll take a fellow to mills and teach him to use his fives."

"That bad at school, is it, infant?" Xander hadn't seen any marks on Kit, but he, too, had been good at concealing the evidence of his schoolmates' assaults.

Kit kicked a loose cobble. "Not so bad. But a miller gets respect, you know."

"Then we'll make you a miller."

Kit gave a leap and shot a fist into the air with a triumphant cry. The sound echoed in the fog. "You taught Will, didn't you, Xander?"

"Everything he knows." *About boxing.*

They left the thinning crowd behind, turning up a narrow street of cook shops, cheap stationers, and secondhand clothes dealers. Watchful proprietors pulled in goods hanging from doorways and canvas awnings and put up shop shutters, cutting off what light illumined the way. No oil lamps had been lit, and darkness closed off all the adjoining lanes and courts. This was the edge of the London their mother feared—crumbling, stinking, disease ridden, and vermin infested—where gin was the purest substance a body could find and survival meant preying on others.

Elsewhere in London, Xander's London, the London of the future, the Gas Light and Coke Company was lighting up the night with miles of gas lines and new streetlights. Xander had joined the admiring crowds at each new illumination, caught by the Promethean promise of banishing darkness. He counted himself among the new breed of men who envisioned a city with wide thoroughfares to replace narrow, stinking lanes, and efficient channels of commerce flowing with clean air and water. He had staked his small fortune on that vision of a new London.

Here was a reminder of the work to be done. Decaying buildings sagged against one another, and the dark felt coal-bin close and heavy. They were far from the boxing crowd now, but for a moment Xander thought footsteps trailed them. He steered Kit northward. Rumbling wheels on stones and a confused murmur of sound, distorted in the fog, told them they were nearing one of London's main east-west thoroughfares.

They turned a corner and stepped into chaos. A mob of men with blackened faces and ragged sailors' uniforms rained stones and offal on a pale yellow carriage at the center of a milling detachment of Life Guards, their scarlet coats lurid in the light of flaring torches. Giant shadows of the combatants writhed on walls and shuttered shop windows.

Xander needed only one glance to know the carriage with the royal crest on the door panel. *Popularity was never the prince regent's strong suit.*

A pole wedged in the spokes of the coach's rear wheel

had disabled the vehicle. Its windows were cracked. The liveried driver held his hands up to ward off stones while the horses reared and backed, tangling their traces.

Xander yanked Kit back against the shop fronts. This was not their fight.

The guards, outnumbered three to one by Xander's count, drove their mounts into the mob, swords drawn, flailing at the circling men while the officer in charge fumbled with his shining helmet. A bloody gash on his cheek showed where the strap had been cut. *Bloody hell! Men were going to be skewered or trampled because the damned idiot couldn't get his hat on.*

Three men reached the prince's coach. It rocked viciously on its springs as they scrambled aboard. A hatless scarecrow with a beak of a nose drew a pistol from the band of his trousers and waved it in the air, swaying with the violent motion of the coach. Xander decided he had had enough of being a bystander. Riot was a fine London tradition, but regicide was too French for Xander's taste.

He pressed Kit deep into a shadowed doorway. "Don't move," he ordered. He shoved his hat on Kit's head and flung himself into the mad surge.

The gun had his undivided attention.

Churning knots of men and soldiers blocked his path. He plunged forward, dodging elbows and feet, knocking skulls together, and pulling men off the struggling guardsmen. He reached the carriage just as Scarecrow cocked the gun and tapped the dark barrel against the cracked window. Xander heaved a last man out of his way and leapt, knocking Scarecrow's pistol arm skyward.

The gun went off next to Xander's ear, and the crowd roared. Scarecrow howled and struck Xander's temple a glancing blow with the discharged weapon. Xander seized the man's pistol arm, twisting it back and up. His ear rang painfully, and the sharp scent of powder burned his throat. Hands pulled at him from behind. He held his writhing victim until the gun fell from the man's grip.

With a splintering crunch the carriage jolted forward, and Xander grabbed for the top rail. Released, Scarecrow dropped to the street. As if a signal had been given, torches hit the pavement. Men scattered down a half dozen dark streets. The guards at last formed a circle around the prince's vehicle. Xander leapt down, turning for Kit, slapping the rump of a riderless horse to clear his path.

He could see the doorway. *Empty.* He glanced at doorways to the left and right. Nothing. His gaze swung back to the first doorway. His upended hat lay on the pavement. *Where was Kit? Hell, he had not joined in, had he?* Xander spun, looking for a downed body. Two soldiers had been unhorsed. Not one rioter had fallen. He shouted and couldn't hear his own voice.

From somewhere in the dark came a wavering cry that made his gut twist. He spun toward the sound.

In front of him were fog and shadows and the hiss of expiring torches. His ragged breath roared in his head. Only his left ear seemed to be working properly, filled with shouts and pounding footsteps and jingling harness. Xander wanted to demand light and silence. He edged toward the lane where he thought he'd heard the frightened cry.

"Halt," a voice shouted. He ignored it, moving toward the vanished cry. Behind him a pistol fired. A bullet grazed his right ear in a fiery streak of pain that made him turn. The helmetless officer covered him, a weapon in each hand.

Warm blood caught on Xander's collar. He forced himself to speak slowly and clearly. "They've taken my brother."

The idiot officer scowled.

Xander swore. The man's incomprehension was costing him time. He backed away, hands raised. *He'd made a grave mistake, a wrong turn down the wrong street. This moment should not be happening. He and Kit should be having beef pies and porter.*

Maddening voices filled his good ear. His senses strained toward the dark while a knot of soldiers surrounded the royal carriage. One opened the crested door. Men came to stiff attention. From inside Xander heard the regent's voice, "Where's the fellow who saved my life?"

A soldier broke from the ranks around the coach, hastening toward them, and Xander's hatless officer glanced away. Xander whirled and sprang toward the dark.

"Kit," he shouted. He hit his stride when something caught him hard in the back of the head. His knees crumpled, and darkness took him.

Chapter One

❧

A T four and twenty, Cleo Spencer could measure how far she had fallen in the world by entering Evershot's Bank on Cornhill Street. No heads turned in the bank's columned interior, vast as a ballroom. Instead Tobias Meese, Evershot's clerk, darted out of the hole he inhabited, intent on blocking her way.

She headed straight for the president's office, surprised she had not worn a groove in the marble from the regularity of her visits. Once a quarter for nearly four years she had come begging for her own money, and the practice was wearing as thin as her cloak.

At sixteen she had had thick cloaks to burn. With green eyes and chestnut curls, she had entered her first ballroom and turned the heads of all the available gentlemen. Her partner for the second set, a dashing, red-coated lieutenant, had whispered, "You have dancing eyes," and the compliment had, she supposed, set her on a reckless, giddy path to this moment.

Now she slipped past a group of bewhiskered gentlemen engaged in conversation, putting them between her and Meese and gaining a couple of yards on her adversary. Gold gleamed on the heads of their walking sticks and watch fobs and winked from the rings on their pinky fingers. They were men who could smell money in the air, hear its song in the wind, and see its glint on the horizon, and they shifted to let Cleo pass without so much as a glance.

Meese stopped her at the president's door by the simple expedient of stepping on her hem. Flounce parted from skirts with a distinct rip.

"Miss Spencer, Mr. E is in a meeting."

Cleo summoned her haughtiest look. "Impossible, Meese, he has an appointment with me at this hour."

Meese pinned her in place with his foot, an oily gleam in his eye, three wiry hairs bristling under his lip. "For a consideration, Miss Spencer, I can show you to an antechamber, where you can wait private-like." He rather emphasized the word *wait*.

Cleo lifted her chin. She would step out of her skirts before she gave Meese a penny. Her fragile hem parted another inch, and she considered braining Meese with her reticule, heavy with a half dozen precious potatoes from her neighbor Farmer Davies. Reason prevailed. It would be a shame to sacrifice the potatoes.

Smiling, she held up her bag. "Let me see, Meese. I may have something for you."

Meese extended an ink-stained hand and stepped back to allow her to reach into the bag.

The instant he removed his foot from her hem, Cleo grabbed the knob and swung the door open on an empty office.

"Miss—" Meese gaped at the unoccupied room, and Cleo flashed him a quick grin as she stepped inside. Evidently, Evershot was elsewhere.

His Axminster carpet was thick underfoot, and a fine fire blazed in his grate with an absolute indifference to the price of coal. Paintings, marble busts, leather-bound books, and rich damask drapery all spoke of expensive tastes indulged. A huge black desk with a vast gleaming surface, on which the little, wheeled inkpot could go skating if it had a mind, dominated the far end of the room. In the near corner a lacquered oriental screen depicted an eastern emperor and his fawning court, concealing those necessities gentlemen could avail themselves of in a way not permitted to ladies.

Directly in Cleo's path a small tea table had been set with a steaming silver pot, a pile of biscuits, and pale white cups and saucers for two. "My compliments, Meese. You've outdone yourself."

The tea set provoked a worried crease on Meese's narrow brow. "You can't wait here, missy." Meese wrung his hands. "Mr. E won't like this, won't like it at all. No unaccompanied women in Mr. E's bank."

Cleo stripped off her gloves. "Evershot's Bank has had the keeping of a substantial sum of my money for nearly four years. I think I am well within my rights to expect Mr. Evershot to keep an appointment with me." She was early, but she would not let Meese tuck her out of sight in some closet.

Meese shook a finger at her. "You're a bold baggage,

miss, but you'll not get a farthing more out of Mr. E."
With a parting glare, he scuttled out.

Cleo removed her bonnet. Meese was probably right,
but on the whole, she thought the tea was a good sign.
Evershot had never provided tea before. He was her best
hope. Stingy he might be, and set in his opinion that
women and lunatics could not manage money, but of her
two trustees he was the honest one. A delicate thread of
steam carried the scent of rich black tea her way. The
biscuits added a faint buttery note, and her stomach
rumbled appreciatively.

She settled herself to wait, draping her cloak over her
knees to conceal the torn flounce. Sadly, the arrangement put the tea out of reach, and she felt ridiculous, as
if she were poking her head out of a shabby tent. The
fine silk frogging on her cloak, all the rage four years
earlier, was its last pretension to fashion. She lifted the
edge to inspect the torn flounce.

It was worse than she thought. A late summer rain
had made a mire of the lanes. Muddy straw clung to her
drooping hem, and her half boots would disgrace the
lowliest private. She had saved a shilling six riding in
Farmer Davies's cart only to look as if she were collecting for a Bonfire Night effigy.

The privacy of the men's corner beckoned. If she
were quick, she could repair her skirts and meet Evershot with some dignity. With a burst of resolution, she
tore her glance from the tea and ducked behind the
screen.

The private area was as rich as the rest of the president's office, with a tall cheval glass, a leather-covered
bench, and a handsome commode. Cleo ignored the

glass, knowing what she would see. A torn flounce was the least of her problems. She was thin and brown and looked ready for the parish workhouse, not the ball-rooms of Mayfair in which she'd danced away countless evenings. She should slip out the door with her bag of potatoes, find her coach before it became a pumpkin, and get home while there was still light in the sky. *Too bad she had no coach.*

She dropped down on the bench and pulled her bedraggled skirts up over her knees. Trying to move Evershot to generosity was one of those impossible fairy-tale tasks like spinning straw into gold.

At least she had the straw. She had only to pick it out of her skirts.

She bent to her work, her mind taking up familiar and dismal calculations. If she simply did nothing, in time, six years to be exact, things would right themselves. In six years she would turn thirty and have access to her money with no interference from her trustees. In eight years Charlie would come of age. Though he was now the Right Honorable Lord Woford, as a minor, he had no access to his fortune.

At the time of her father's death, his half brother, Archibald March, had come to their aid when every-thing seemed most difficult and confusing. But Uncle March had had shocking revelations to make of the circumstances of her father's death and the size of his gaming debts. Cleo had agreed immediately to the strictest economies. She had signed the documents put in front of her, believing them necessary to protect her father's reputation and the inheritance he left for her and Charlie. She had believed then that they would remain in their own home, and have enough to eat and decent clothes to wear, and the company of friends. Only later did she understand how she had played into her uncle's hands.

Now she simply had to convince Evershot to give her a more substantial allowance. A single woman of four and twenty should have control of her own purse and not live at the whim of outmoded ideas of female capability. It was intolerable for the bank to keep *her* money, while she and her brother lived like parish paupers on relief.

At thirteen Charlie was a tall, gangly young man whose wrists and ankles stuck out comically from his coats and trousers. He didn't complain, but he was becoming dreamy and absentminded. Cleo was convinced he would become a hermit if she didn't get him to school among boys his own age. Worse, lately, her Uncle March had sent letters hinting that he could take Charlie from her on the grounds that she was not able to support him properly. By her calculations they needed five hundred pounds to set Charlie up in school. Without the bank loosening its hold on their funds she could not even hire a proper tutor for Charlie's entrance exams.

A rumble of voices outside the office gave a brief warning of someone's approach. She plucked out more straw and jabbed another pin through the worn fabric as the door opened. A flirtatious feminine voice, not at all the voice of a bank president, announced the newcomer.

"La, sir, you are so clever to arrange this assignation! Papa will never think where we are, and we will be quite alone."

"Quite," came the reply in a grim baritone.

Oh dear. Cleo froze. *Where was Meese?* The door closed with a discreet click. A long silence followed, giving her time to wish she had helped herself to the tea.

"Miss Finsbury," the baritone finally said. "Let me be plain with you."

Cleo was not leaving, but politeness dictated that she should stop her ears. No doubt she was about to hear some private discourse, though taking a woman into a bank president's office to make love to her struck Cleo as a poor romantic strategy even to avoid a disapproving papa. The man must be very sure of himself to attempt wooing without the aid of moonlight or music or the sweet air of some garden.

She gave her gown a quiet shake and let the folds fall back into place. At least the lovers did not seem interested in her tea. She had only to wait in perfect stillness for the affecting scene to play itself out. She folded her hands in her lap.

The gentleman cleared his throat. Another dreadful pause followed. Cleo hoped he was thinking the better of his plan. She considered whether she could see beyond the screen without being observed and decided not to risk detection. *Blast Meese!* Now she understood his peculiar alarm about letting her into Evershot's office ahead of her time. He had obviously pocketed a tip from Sir Baritone for the use of the space. Perhaps he had thrown in the tea.

"Miss Finsbury," Sir Baritone began again in that deep, assured masculine voice, a voice that made Cleo's skin stir as if he had touched her. "Your fortune has drawn the attentions of many suitors."

Miss Finsbury tittered. "I am sure, sir, I never dreamed of your particular notice."

The gentleman took a deep breath at that bit of falsehood, and Cleo shifted ever so slightly toward the thin crack where the panels of the folding screen met. Did he actually mean to *propose* in a bank office?

"Miss Finsbury, we are both of an age and time in life when the world expects us to marry, so it will not surprise you to be addressed on the subject by me."

Not surprise her. Of course, it didn't surprise her. What female with half a brain was ever surprised by a proposal of marriage? Really, it took very little to bring one about. Cleo herself had received four proposals in her first season alone. And, unless she missed her guess, Miss Finsbury had angled assiduously to bring Sir Baritone to the sticking point. Cleo leaned a bit more to the right toward the crack above the panel's hinge. A quick peek would give her a better idea of the two parties.

"Miss Finsbury, I am prepared to offer you a comfortable home, freedom . . ."

There was a pause Farmer Davies could drive his hay wagon through. *Why couldn't the poor man get on with it? Was he hopelessly shy? And why did he insist on repeating his beloved's name?* Cleo adjusted her position slightly.

". . . And children, should you desire them."

Oh my. Would poor Miss Finsbury have to lead him to her bed? Cleo had a feeling the girl was hardly expiring from strong emotion, unless it was frustration with the pace of the gentleman's proposal. *Really, did men never read novels? Did they have no idea how to proceed?*

Cleo let herself lean that final fraction more, so that one eye looked out on a thin slice of the two people in the center of the carpet. The main object in view was the gentleman's back, the powerful back of a tall, athletic man. He wore a dark blue coat and gray trousers perfectly tailored to his form. He did not look like a man who would feel unduly shy at the thought of the marriage bed. He had thick black hair and broad shoulders in that excessively fine coat—oh, how she would love to put Charlie in such a coat—a narrow waist and long, lean legs.

The girl, whom Cleo could see rather better, was hardly a girl even with her mass of golden curls and pink cheeks, and entirely too many bows. She appeared to be a few years older than Cleo herself and confident of the charms of her bosom, the white expanse of which swelled appreciably above her bodice.

"I don't understand."

Of course you don't, poor dear.

"You will have a house in Mayfair, and you may visit your family and friends in Cheapside as often as you like. I will never reproach you for those connections."

Generous of you, Sir Baritone. Did you notice, you idiot, that she isn't exactly swooning with delight?

"And you need have no fear that I will be reckless with your dowry. I am no gambler, whatever you may have heard. The bulk of your money may be settled on any . . . progeny that ensue from our union."

Ensue! Does he imagine that children will turn up in the kitchen garden like turnips? Cleo watched the girl's expression falter. Miss Finsbury's eyes were big and round in her pink face.

"You don't love me?"

Sir Baritone seemed not to hear. "All I ask is the immediate use of a portion of the thirty thousand pounds to invest in an enterprise that will change the face of London."

Cleo had to clap a hand over her mouth. Tears welled up in Miss Finsbury's blue eyes and spilled over. It would have been tragic except that she looked as if she were playing a part in a bad farce.

"Oh, I should never have come here. My papa said that you, sir, were a common fortune hunter and, and . . ." Miss Finsbury produced a lacy handkerchief from between her breasts and dabbed her eyes with it. ". . . Lord Candover's . . . *bastard*."

The awful word in the cloying voice hung in the air. For a moment Cleo feared that she had actually gasped. Surely no sound had escaped her. She felt the change in Sir Baritone. *Run*, she urged the girl.

"I could never marry such a man." Miss Finsbury's tremulous voice caught, and she dashed for the door.

It banged shut behind her.

Cleo held her breath. The very air in the room was motionless. No coal on the fire dared to crumble.

Her nose itched and her stomach threatened to complain about having nothing to eat since before dawn, but she didn't stir.

As long as he didn't turn, she was safe, but the crack compelled her to watch him standing with his back to her. The stillness of his person suggested a man of iron will composing himself, holding his energy in check.

No doubt he was shocked to be rejected. Really, Cleo could explain it to him. It had nothing to do with his flawed pedigree, although she was sure that, at the moment, his pride stung from the unexpected attack of an enemy at whom no gentleman could strike. Cleo was equally certain he never permitted a man to say that word to him.

At last he moved, reaching down and picking something up from the chair where Cleo had been sitting moments earlier. Slowly he turned until he faced the screen. Cleo's black bonnet dangled from his long fingers like something offensive that he wished to keep at a distance from his immaculate person. Her wretched stomach sank alarmingly.

"Are you coming out?" he asked in that deep baritone. His voice had the dangerous edge of controlled rage. His gray gaze, cordial as steel, met hers through the crack in the screen, and alarm like a chill draft rippled over her. At the same time she wanted to shake him for letting that pudding-faced snob get to him. She preferred his arrogance.

She stepped from behind the screen. "Well, that could have gone better, don't you think?" She lifted her eyes to his and halted, instantly making a series of mental corrections. She was wrong to think his proposal marked him as awkward, shy, or inexperienced in any way. Wrong to think Miss Finsbury could wound his self-assurance. And most of all wrong to think any woman could take the lead from him in the marriage bed.

Cleo could not take another step or say another word. She was not prepared for the man's looks at all. He was taller than Charlie and broader in the shoulders than Farmer Davies. Not that he was so very handsome, but the angular symmetry of his face mixed with the leashed sensuality of his limbs had a devastating effect on her senses.

"You want to offer advice?" He might have been asking if she wished to die. She should beg his pardon for eavesdropping, but she had the feeling it would be fatal to do so. At the least sign of fear, he would drop a smoking thunderbolt at her feet and send her ragged cloak up in flames.

"Oh, you are quite beyond advice, I'm sure. A sheep driver could have done a better job."

He tossed her bonnet aside. "Familiar with the amorous practices of sheep drivers, are you?"

She forced herself to move toward the tea table and chairs and desperately tried not to think about anyone's amorous practices. "I know the female mind. I daresay Miss Finsbury's a novel reader."

"I didn't investigate her reading habits."

"I rather think you didn't investigate anything about her besides her bank account." Cleo took a seat before her knees could give out. Her stomach clenched again. "Tea?"

His face hardened, the darkness of the brows becoming more evident. He had a terrifying frown, and it was really all because of that unflinching gaze. She suspected that he was not a man who readily admitted errors. Still, there was a sensual jut to that lower lip.

"How did you get in here, Miss . . . ?"

"Spencer, Cleo Spencer. And I am here by appointment." Really, he was the interloper. She looked away and steadied herself by concentrating on filling the two waiting cups with the lovely steaming brew. It was a rich amber, and the heady steam made her mouth water.

"Appointment with whom?"

"With Mr. Evershot, of course." Cleo could see him assessing her, a cool, dispassionate judgment that weighed her purse and found it wanting. She had to stay on the attack. She set the brimming cup on the table, opposite her own position.

"Since we are being frank, Miss Spencer, if that is your name, you appear to be a stranger to banks and their contents."

She was right about one thing. He had an instinct to go for the throat. She stirred a bit of cream into her own tea. "You judge by appearances, do you? Now, Miss Finsbury, she might have been taken in at first by your splendid tailoring, but when push came to shove, she saw through you perfectly. You want the use of her fortune for some purpose of your own."

"I admitted as much. Should I have lied and declared passionate love?"

"Of course not, but perhaps you should have taken the time to become acquainted with her. She seems to be of a more romantic disposition than you anticipated. Did you observe what she was wearing or compliment her on it?"

He made a strangled reply and took a seat opposite her.

"Did you take her hand? Drop your voice to a husky whisper?" Cleo shook her head. "You don't have a sister, do you?"

"If you think my understanding of the 'female mind' might be improved by a sister, you are way off the mark. Believe me, I have ample experience of the female . . . mind." He leaned forward, and his dark, bold hands closed around the cup. It was her first glimpse of those hands, corded, lean, and strikingly male in contrast to the pale cup nested in the curve of his palms.

Cleo blinked. She had the most disturbing image of herself standing naked before him.

"Females may fancy themselves in love as much as they like, but I have yet to see one forget her pocketbook in the process."

"And so, you chose a bank office to declare yourself?" She thought her voice sounded remarkably calm.

His glance shifted away. His profile was handsome in a stern, carved stone sort of way. "It was difficult to arrange to see the lady."

"Were you thinking that you could draw on the bank directly for your beloved's fortune once she swooned at your feet?"

"My proposal was honest."

"Admirable, I am sure, but clearly Miss Finsbury was not moved by your devotion to her thirty thousand pounds." Cleo took a fortifying sip of the heavenly tea.

He set his cup down without tasting his. "She would have what most women want from marriage."

Cleo looked at him, at the uncompromising cut of his jaw and the full curve of his lower lip. The stretch of his fine trouser fabric outlined one muscular thigh. He clearly didn't understand a woman's reasons for marrying a man like himself. "Yet here you are, not a quarter of an hour later without your potential betrothed or her fat dowry. May I tell you how it sounded to me?"

Their gazes crossed and held, and Cleo recalled an errant lesson of childhood, *in flint is fire*. An awkward realization hit her. He was way ahead of her. He had *wanted* Miss Finsbury to refuse him. He had encouraged her rejection. Whatever his reason for courting her in the first place, he had changed his mind.

Cleo wondered when he had realized he could not go through with it. She gave him credit for bearing all the humiliation of the moment and sparing that beribboned twit her share.

"Why hesitate now?" He made an offhand gesture and leaned back in his chair.

Cleo gave up on her tea and stood. *Oh, she could play his game. She would be glad to catalog his follies for him.* "You began by telling her that her fortune was her great attraction. You took no notice of her person when she had troubled to dress with such care for you. All those bows took time to arrange. Next you pointed out that she is getting rather long in the tooth."

She began to pace, warming to her subject. "Then you offered her things her papa already provides—a comfortable home and freedom. Furthermore, in case she missed your first mention of her fortune, you then suggested that while you were busy spending her money, she might occupy herself with her socially inferior connections and such children as will magically appear." She came to halt opposite him. That hard slate gaze was fixed on her, not in anger now, but in amusement. "Even turnips require planting, you know."

"You are outrageous. You are what, twenty? How is it that no one has strangled you?"

Cleo sat down again. She felt inexplicably deflated. "I am frank, I admit, but your next proposal shall undoubtedly go the better for my advice, and since you seem to have a pressing need for someone's dowry, I take it you will propose again."

"Perhaps you can direct me to a more accommodating heiress." It was mockery she saw in his cool, gray gaze. He could enjoy the game, sitting there in his fine tailoring while the mud dried on her ragged hem.

Something wild flashed in her brain. Suppose he transferred his proposal to her? She felt like Charlie's hero, Ben Franklin, with his kite, trying to catch lightning with a key. She took hold of the teacup again, but the lovely liquid had cooled, and the idea in her head was unstoppable. "Well," she suggested, "you could propose to me. Unlike Miss Finsbury I am of a practical turn of mind."

Again he made a swift, hard-eyed assessment of her person that started that little tremor going in her belly. He leaned down and plucked a piece of straw from the carpet, laying it on the silver tea tray. Cleo felt instant heat flash in her cheeks. "And your dowry, Miss Spencer? What is the going rate for black silk frogging in the secondhand shops?"

She clasped her hands together in her lap and willed herself not to answer. He had spotted her one remaining vanity and her desperate economy. She should let it pass. No one knew the size of her fortune except her trustees.

Easy for him to tease about money. Whatever need he had for Miss Finsbury's dowry, he felt no pinch in his purse for daily life. But oh, he tempted her. The chance of getting access to her own money dangled there like a ripe plum to be snatched.

When she lifted her gaze, he was watching her

closely. A reckless laugh bubbled up inside her. "My dowry? Why, I have seventy-five thousand pounds in this very bank."

She caught the flash of surprise in those cool eyes, immediately subdued. Then his glance returned to the piece of straw, and the curl of his fine mouth said he did not believe her.

The door opened, and Mr. Evershot entered, chuckling and rubbing his hands together with a banker's gleam in his eye. Thin gray strands of hair barely concealed his pink scalp. He looked straight at Cleo's companion. "Your business is concluded? Everything satisfactory?"

"Thanks to this lady." Sir Baritone rose, a slow unfolding of his tall person. "Apparently, Evershot, you should beg her pardon. She claims she has an appointment with you."

"Miss Spencer? An appointment today?" Evershot frowned at Cleo. "Jones! I beg your pardon."

"His pardon!" Cleo had the satisfaction of seeing Jones register both Evershot's recognition and the truth of her name.

Evershot turned back to Jones. "You've not been inconvenienced, I trust?"

Cleo fumed. She had never seen Evershot grovel before. How lowering that a *Mr. Jones* mattered as a client while she did not. "Mr. Evershot, Mr. Jones has been kind enough to keep me company while you were delayed. He was just leaving."

Jones's stern mouth quirked up in a hint of a smile. "Evershot, Miss Spencer, good day."

Evershot's bow nearly scraped the floor. He would be picking carpet threads out of his linen all night. Cleo turned back to the tea. At least the wretched piece of straw was gone, lost in the carpet pattern somewhere.

"Clearly Mr. Jones knows the secret of receiving good service here."

"Not *Mr.* Jones, *Sir* Alexander Jones, the man who saved the prince's life."

Chapter Two

❧

CLEO returned to Fernhill Farm in the dark. She trudged up the boggy lane trying not to let disappointment slow her steps, and trying not to land in the muck. Her encounter with Sir Alexander Jones had been a disaster. In Evershot's view she had come between the bank and one of its *important* clients.

Evershot refused to help her without consulting her other trustee, Uncle March, and that was the very thing Cleo must avoid. If she could not find a way to get Charlie off to school, March would take him away from her. She didn't deserve that. She was sure that she had long ago atoned for any vanity or folly she had committed in those three dizzying years of her girlhood when she had believed herself untouchable by misfortune.

Her mother's death in childbirth had faded to a gentle sorrow by the time Cleo made her come-out. By then she had been so used to looking out for herself and Charlie with help from their childhood nurse, Miss Hester Britt, that she had not imagined needing any particular parental guidance in London. She had not imagined that her father would fall down a flight of stairs at a brothel and break his neck. She had not imagined that he had signed away his children's care to a half brother more interested in their money than their welfare. Nor had she imagined the power of a piece of paper to limit her freedom and her brother's.

What if Sir Alexander Jones had taken her up on her outlandish proposal and simply transferred his plans to her? Would she have said yes? She shivered at the thought. Once again she had to reflect on her great fall. No use recalling those seasons full of proposals from charming, half-sincere young men to whom she had said "no," believing eligible suitors would always be as plentiful as chestnuts in the fall.

If she had accepted one of those young men, however flawed her marriage might have been, she and her fortune would never have been under her uncle's control. And she had to admit that any of them would have been better than the husband Uncle March had chosen for her.

But those suitors were gone. Today she had all but proposed marriage to a hard-eyed stranger about whom she knew nothing except that he was willing to marry a complete ninny for money. Jones had had an unfortunate effect on her. She could only explain it as desperation for money. It was utter folly to reveal the amount of her fortune to a stranger. She was lucky Evershot had interrupted their conversation. With Jones out of the room,

Cleo had recovered her sanity. She didn't think Franklin had persisted in his dangerous kite experiments, either, or he would have been burned to a cinder.

Sir Alexander Jones had obviously come to his senses as well about Miss Finsbury, so he was unlikely to make another hasty proposal, especially to a ragged girl with straw on her skirts.

At the turning in the lane, she could see a light coming from the barn, which meant that Charlie was at his chores. Another few steps and Charlie's setter Bess raced to greet Cleo with a cheerful bark and much tail wagging. Cleo stopped to rub the silky head.

Then Charlie appeared with a pail of milk. Cleo's empty stomach made a desperate rumble. She watched her brother lurch toward her with the heavy bucket, making a thin shadow in the light from the barn door.

"What kept you? I worried some."

"Not too much, I hope. I've brought you a present, a real treasure." Cleo showed him the thin roll of draftsman's paper she had carefully protected on the stage.

"And didn't eat, I suppose?"

"I wasn't hungry."

"Liar."

"Till now, of course." She peeked into the pail. "Bless Agnes for giving us all that lovely milk. What shall we do with it?" She slipped her arm into Charlie's free one and tugged him toward the kitchen, trying not to notice that he'd done his chores in his one good shirt and pair of breeches.

"Well, if we had some eggs and flour and sugar and cinnamon, we could have a pudding."

"And if we had some potatoes?"

"We could boil and mash them." He said it dreamily. Potatoes were the main course of the imaginary feasts with which they planned to celebrate their return to Woford Abbey, now leased to a tenant. They would bake them with cream, brown them in roast drippings, and whip them into buttery mounds.

Cleo hefted her reticule. "We do have potatoes. Thanks to Davies. He gave me a half dozen this morning and I've lugged them about London all day."

"Potatoes? Seriously?"

"Seriously. Let's put the pot on."

"Cleo, you are a sister in a million."

"Perhaps, but I didn't persuade Evershot to give me a shilling more allowance." In spite of her best intentions the news came out sounding a bit gloomy.

It subdued their banter as they cooked and put a damper on the glory of the potatoes when Cleo put the steaming dish on the parlor table. Not all the reckless brilliance of four tapers lifted the mood, but Cleo savored every bite, and when the dishes were removed, she did not immediately put out the candles but brought out her gift for Charlie. She set the roll of thin paper in front of him and settled down to anticipate his pleasure. Charlie never dove into anything. If she had her way, she would give him endless gifts just to watch the thoroughness of his appreciation. Let the candle stubs burn on.

Charlie held the roll of thin paper lightly in his hands. "You're not going to tell me where it came from, are you?"

Cleo shook her head. "Guess."

Charlie's thin fingers moved lightly over the roll of paper and circled its ends. "Stanford's?"

Cleo could not deny it. She had stopped in the book and paper shop on Rose Street after she left the bank. "Not an entirely fruitless trip to town, after all."

"But what is it?"

"You have to open it to find out."

Again Charlie waited. His eyes shifted back and forth in the way he had when he was thinking. His hair, a shade more brown than Cleo's, stood out in thick waves from his thin face. "You know, Cleo, I could do more for us."

"No."

"I talked to Davies this week, and he's willing to let me have the entrails when he slaughters his hogs. He says if I scrape out the muck till they're white as snow, Mr. Hems the butcher will pay me a penny a pound for casings."

"Charlie Spencer, don't you dare think it. You have more than enough to do to keep this farm going and keep up your studies." Cleo was shaking. She thrust her hands into her lap and clenched them together. "We will have you in school by Hilary term. Now open it, open it."

Charlie pulled the ribbon off the roll with a sweep of one thin arm and spread the paper open. He could not resist the pleasure of the gift. "It's capital!"

In clear lines and wonderful detail was a diagram of a series of improvements to a Boulton and Watt steam engine. Charlie was instantly engrossed in figuring the math of each variation. "This one would double the efficiency of that one."

"I'm glad you like it. We're managing well enough, and only feel a pinch because we must get you to school."

"Before March takes me away."

"I won't let that happen, but let's try everything else before the pig entrails plan."

Charlie grinned. "You're sure?"

"If you are to be a great inventor, you need a scientific education, and we will find a way to get you one." It was a fine resolution, only a little diminished as one of the candles guttered and went out.

T HE administration of justice at Number Four Bow Street being one of the principal cheap entertainments of a London evening, a crowd packed the magistrate's room when Xander arrived. He worked his way through the mob to his brother Will, who cleared a space with a swift, sharp glance at a burly apron-covered fellow reeking of fish.

Xander leaned toward Will to make himself heard above the babble. "Anyone of interest in tonight's lot?"

"Nate Wilde, petty thief and informer. He's one of Bredsell's boys."

A member of the foot patrol in a black hat and blue coat with brass buttons hauled a short, wiry young person into the court by his manacled hands. The youth swore and resisted, but the officer paid no attention. Behind the youth a man in severe clerical attire whispered something and the boy subsided.

"A pony says he gets off." Xander offered more than his usual wager.

Will did not look away from the proceedings. "A pony? You're flush in the pocket. Ah, Miss Finsbury accepted your proposal."

"She did not."

"That paper knighthood Prinny gave you didn't impress your pigeon?"

"I was honest with her."

"Quaint. She saw through you, then."

"That point has been made." Xander had a vivid recollection of a pair of green eyes and a smart mouth.

Will grinned. "Good, we wouldn't want you to think that a tap on the shoulder from his royal fatness changes who you are."

Trust Will to remind him that his knighthood was a careless honor bestowed at the whim of an unpopular prince. Being Sir Alexander Jones did not change the facts of Xander's birth.

It was one thing for his brother to understand him so thoroughly, but it was unsettling for a bedraggled stranger to do so. She had made him realize what he'd been unwilling to admit to himself—how thoroughly reluctant a suitor he'd been. "In fact Miss Finsbury accused me of being a common fortune hunter." He did not need to mention the other accusation the lady had made.

"Ouch."

"I'll live."

"Of course you will. It wasn't a heart wound because you have no heart."

"An inconvenient appendage at best, prone to breaking, I hear." Xander ventured a quick look at Will and noted a fresh cut above his brother's right eye.

"The question is—will your bleeding partners wait for you to raise the ready?"

Xander shrugged. He had been invited to join the

newly formed Metropolitan Works Group, one more change in his fortunes since the night he had come to the prince's rescue. The MWG planned to transform London from an unhealthful maze of crooked lanes to a fitting capital for an empire. To launch the venture each member was expected to put up twenty thousand pounds of his own money. Xander had spent a great deal of his own money in the search for Kit. What he had left, a modest fortune, he kept invested, hence the great charm of Augusta Finsbury's substantial dowry. Ready money was what he needed at the moment.

"By the way, Brother, I have a letter for you." Will handed him a creased and well-traveled envelope covered in a lacy feminine script.

The letter's spicy perfume reached Xander even among the competing scents of heated bodies and well-aled breath. He tucked it in an outer pocket of his coat. He would have his man air the coat tomorrow.

"Not going to read it?"

"I'm assuming you did. Is she well?"

Will laughed. "You think I read your bleeding letters?"

"I wouldn't think much of your spying abilities if you didn't."

"Paris agrees with her."

"Good." He meant it. One member of their sorry family at least should find peace and a fresh beginning. Nearly three years of searching had not produced Kit. The restless pack of unanswered questions stirred to life in his mind. *Who had taken Kit and why? Was he still alive? Was he in London or in some wretched corner of the wide globe? What more could they do to find him?*

Attending these sessions was Will's idea of a search strategy. In Will's view London's vast underworld was a network as elaborate as any assembled by army intelligence. Toshers and mudlarks, prigs, drabs, and hired fists were linked to fences and abbesses and even more shadowy employers. The vilest wretch passed through the dark labyrinth of inner London and saw and heard its secrets. Slowly, Xander and Will were plotting these connections, following the threads that linked pickpockets and prostitutes and those that preyed on them.

The buzz in the courtroom ceased as the bewigged magistrate entered the hall and took the bench. An officer bid the onlookers come to order.

Xander studied the youth now leaning insolently against the iron-railed dock. His face had such a hungry, feral look, it was hard to tell his age. Xander guessed anywhere from twelve to fifteen. The boy had been groomed like a choirboy for his court appearance, but his features had the twisted quality of one hardened by life's blows. He caught Xander's gaze, and his lips peeled back in a snarl, baring strong white teeth. "He might know something."

"If he's one of Bredsell's boys, he knows all the rigs in St. Giles and more."

"What's his history?"

"Born in the Seven Dials, raised on drink, brawls, and thievery. Bredsell's only had him a year though, so he's not gallows bait yet."

Bredsell ran a school for boys in a warehouse off Bread Street in one of London's worst rookeries. "Receptacles," they were called, for boys in trouble with the law. If Bredsell wanted to get a young man out of the hands of the law, he generally managed. Xander scanned the crowd for Bredsell's aristocratic patron, Archibald March.

In the year that Xander and Will had been attending the night court sessions, Xander had come to expect the appearance of Bredsell and March.

The charges against the boy were read. The list was long, and the penalty for his most grievous crime was transportation.

The Reverend Bertram Bredsell rose, a pink-cheeked man with a head of close-cropped, yellow gold curls and a downcast gaze as if the wicked ways of the world grieved him, but Xander was not fooled by the angelic face. Bredsell, dubbed "the Moralist" by the papers, could get a crowd to believe almost anything.

"Your Worship, if I may speak a word on this young man's behalf."

"Mr. Bredsell, this court is not a pulpit. Speak briefly and to the point."

"Thank you, Your Worship." Bredsell then fell silent until the hum in the court died down and all eyes were focused on him. The man had presence. He looked up and spoke in a silken tenor. "The world judges Nate Wilde harshly, but he is not to blame for the darkness in which he lives. And that darkness will not be cured in the blackness of the hold of a transport ship or a cell. No, his spirit can only be cured if we bring him into the light. I appeal to this court to turn this young man over to me and my school so that we may bring light to his soul."

Xander swore and turned to Will. He doubted Bredsell had much spiritual light to offer the boy. "Better to bring light to his street than his soul."

"That is your plan, isn't it, Brother?"

It had been. With Miss Finsbury he believed he had found the perfect match for the sort of marriage he had in mind. Her father was a grazier whose fortune had allowed him to establish his family in fashionable circumstances among London's wealthy tradesmen. Miss Finsbury had been broad-minded in her taste in suitors. Xander's knighthood and the town house off Berkeley Square had been sufficient inducements to get her to that meeting in the bank.

His plan had suffered a severe blow with her rejection of his suit. Without her thirty thousand pounds he could not join the Metropolitan Works Group. His part in the partnership was an experiment in lighting the streets of St. Giles, the darkest rookery in London, where the likes of Bredsell preyed upon the hungry and desperate. He had lost a month courting Miss Finsbury. Now he had to begin again. He had only been half joking when he asked Miss Ragmanners to recommend an heiress.

Will nudged Xander as a gentleman ambled into the court and leaned down to whisper something in the learned judge's ear. Archibald March, the chief "patron" of Bredsell's school, was a man of lean, cool good looks. In his forties, he had a long nose made for sneering at the world and a thin slice of a mouth. His dark hair fell with careless abandon over his broad brow. For all the foundling schools and widows' societies that March supported, Xander could not detect a charitable line in the man's smooth face.

"Self-satisfied worm," Will grumbled.

March settled himself in a reserved seat with a

proprietary air. According to Will, March had endless funds to pass around to charities. Will suspected that he profited in unholy ways from Bredsell's school, by training boys as petty thieves and using them to peddle illicit materials and spy on men whose positions made them vulnerable to scandal. It was a monstrous accusation to make against a man with friends in high places, but it could not be denied that March always came to the proceedings when there was a chance of a boy being sent to Bredsell, and his word in the magistrate's ear was often sufficient to sway a case. Both March's unexplained influence in the court and his ties to the Home Secretary troubled Will.

Bredsell was still speaking about the power of his school to enlighten the souls of poor children, who would, without his guidance, surely end up leading the most degraded lives headed for a noose or transportation.

The magistrate cut him off. "Enough, Mr. Bredsell, you need not tout your school any longer. Young Wilde may remain under your tutelage at present, but if he comes before my court again, he'll see the shore of Botany Bay before he's sixteen."

Xander caught the look exchanged between Bredsell and March as Wilde was released from manacles and turned over to the reverend. The youth himself could not contain a sly smirk and a swagger as the manacles fell from his wrists. Now there would be no chance for Xander or Will to question him. Within minutes Nate Wilde would disappear into the dark lanes off Holywell Street. As he passed, the youth gave Will a cheeky salute. Will's hand shot out and clamped on the boy's arm, stopping him in his tracks.

"'Ey, beak, oi'm a free man now. You don't get to pump me no more." The boy flashed his toothy grin at Will.

Will leaned down to get in the youth's face. "Don't choke on your own sauce, Wilde. Transportation's your best hope. Let Bredsell and March give you orders and you'll end up in hell."

"Bugger off. Weasels like you got nowt to say to me no more." The boy shook off Will's hold and followed Bredsell out of the court.

"You owe me a pony," Xander told his brother.

Will stared after Bredsell. "I hate that bleeding maggot. If I could prove what he does, he'd swing for it."

"You got a lot of information out of young Wilde, I notice."

"Sod off. Wilde will be back in the dock in a month."

"When he returns, be sure to ask him about our brother's disappearance."

Will advised Xander as to some immediate forms of self-abuse he could practice and suggested a permanent address in the hereafter.

The next case, a carver brought up on a charge of wife beating, was creating a row. The brothers left the court, Will still grumbling about Wilde's release into Bredsell's custody. Xander listened to the angry voice with half an ear. Each of them had to deal with the loss of Kit in his own way. Anger was Will's way. Flight had been their mother's choice. Action was Xander's. Outside the court they paused. "I've got another investigation for you."

"What?" Will made the subtle adjustments to his dress that allowed him to slip into London's darkness.

He rarely came to the house on Hill Street but kept some mean apartments elsewhere, to which Xander had never been invited. *You don't want to know*, he once told Xander.

It was like Will to reject the gentlemanly trappings their mother had sought to give them. He refused to hide the stain of his birth. A baseborn fellow ought to live like a baseborn fellow.

"I need to know everything about Cleo Spencer."

"Who is she?"

"She's a chit not much above twenty, who claims to have a fortune in Evershot's bank."

"Ah, another shot at lighting the streets."

"Find out about her for me."

"You're going to try again?"

"I still need twenty thousand to buy into the partnership."

Will whistled, his transformation complete. His black staff of office tucked up his sleeve, nothing remained of the official costume of a Runner. "And Miss Spencer has it?"

"Apparently she needs a husband to get access to her money." Xander had figured that much out in the wake of her astonishing proposal. What he didn't know was why she hadn't found one.

"If she has twenty thousand and needs a husband, why should I call you?"

"Because, if anyone has less heart than I do, Brother, it's you."

A short, harsh laugh was the only reply as Will slipped into the darkness.

Xander didn't envy him much. Will seemed to seek

those roles that most hardened a man. As a Bow Street Runner he entered London's darkest streets, places that never saw another officer, without hesitation. His fellow Runners declared that he could see in the dark. Xander didn't credit that assertion, but he knew Will had uncanny abilities, honed as an army spy, to operate with swiftness and sureness where other people stumbled blindly. Sooner or later his brother would get whatever information Nate Wilde possessed.

Xander stood alone in the middle of Bow Street. Across the way the Brown Bear did a brisk trade in spirits, indifferent to which side of the law a man was on. Up the street, luckier souls streamed out of the colonnaded front of the Opera House, laughing and chattering about the evening's performance, climbing into carriages and hacks, heading for bed or assignations, or a club, people careless of the light, not imagining how quickly darkness could snatch away laughter.

Xander's search for Kit had been fruitless. First, injuries delayed him. Then the regent's fickle solicitude and his father's objection in the Lords to Xander's knighthood cost him precious days. By the time he recovered and Will returned from France to begin the search in earnest, London's darkest rookery had swallowed Kit deep into its fetid belly, and their mother had retreated into impenetrable grief.

Now he had a new chance. Lighting St. Giles meant entering the dark places at will, tearing down walls, tearing up streets, taking picks, axes, and shovels to all the district's secrets. Lighting St. Giles meant unlocking a dark closet in the heart of London and freeing those huddled inside.

A woman's high, brittle laugh caught his good ear, a false laugh of the kind he'd heard too often in the months after he'd been knighted. In those first months of searching for Kit, when finding him seemed possible, the exclusive ballrooms of London, and some of its still more exclusive bedrooms, had opened to Xander as they never had before, and he'd discovered he could draw on the vanity and self-interest of certain fine ladies to fund his search with no other price than his own body. And perhaps some pieces of his soul. The scent of his mother's letter caught his notice again. He reached for it, and his fingers encountered a piece of straw.

In the bank in that first moment of realizing he had an audience for his awkward proposal, he had expected to find Meese or some underling of Miss Finsbury's father paid to spy. Then he had seen the girl's wretched bonnet on the chair. Ironically, it was the straw on her hem that had convinced him she was no spy. Whether she proved to be an heiress or not, he had to thank her for making him understand his reluctance to marry Miss Finsbury. And for making him laugh. He would go home and put his mother's latest letter in a drawer with the others. He knew its message.

Leave the lamps burning. He will return.

Chapter Three

❧

XANDER found Fernhill Farm just where his brother's information had placed it, at the edge of the village of Woford in a low-lying set of acres along the river. The summer just past still had a grip on the fields and hedgerows, and the morning mist had burned off in the heat of a long afternoon. Nothing about the place suggested that its mistress possessed a fortune.

A plain brick farmhouse and barn stood at the end of a boggy lane past a pond. A few geese made a welcoming party, waddling away with unhurried arrogance as his rig approached. Xander tended to his pair, armed himself with the picnic basket he'd purchased from the local inn, and strode in the direction of the house.

A slight breeze carried the scent of washday. No one answered his knock, but from the rear of the house came the rhythmic thwack of someone beating the life out of a carpet. He followed a weedy path to his right toward the sound.

Cleo Spencer had squared off against a sorry rug of indeterminate hues draped over a sturdy line and was beating it with a broom. Her hair, coming loose from its pins and knots, dangled in coppery wisps about her face. He could see the pink flush of her exertions in her cheek. An unbleached apron covered a faded green muslin gown, hiked up around her waist, exposing a pair of coltish legs. She looked more like a laundress than an heiress, and Xander had to remind himself of what he now knew about his ragamuffin. She was a lord's pampered daughter. She might have fallen from fortune and grace, but he would be wise to remember that she was a London-bred blue blood of his father's ilk, and he would be better off keeping their relationship commercial.

He put the basket at his feet to watch her. She took a wide stance, hauled back her broom and let fly with a swing like the most determined of batsmen trying to loft a bowl over the boundary fence. Every line of her person was angry. *Take that*, her body seemed to say, *and that*.

"Taking aim at your banker?"

She spun toward him. The reach of her broom just missed his chest and sent a sweet stir of air wafting over him, filled with the scent of her. She wore no perfume that he could detect.

"You." She let the broom drop, and he could see in those green eyes the proud sting of being at a disadvantage. Will's report said she had only a meager allowance controlled by Evershot and March until she turned thirty. *Or married.*

"I've come to accept your proposal of marriage."

"You haven't." Her doubting gaze took in his whole appearance and the basket at his feet, stuffed by Mrs. Lawful, the very accommodating and openly curious proprietress of the Swan in Woford.

"You had the advantage of me the other day in making your offer while I was reeling from another woman's rejection."

"Reeling?" She put a hand to her brow, pushing aside damp curls of that brandy-colored hair.

"It was a low moment."

"You've recovered, I'm sure. Your heart did not appear to be involved."

"But my hopes were." He took a step closer now that the broom rested on the ground.

"Hopes that require a great deal of funding?"

"Twenty thousand pounds." He gave her credit for not gasping.

"So I'm to be your accommodating heiress?"

"You are twenty-four and have no access to your fortune until you reach thirty . . . unless you marry. Evershot is one of your trustees, and Archibald March, your father's half brother, is the other. He lives in your old home and has sole control of your brother's fortune, though not your own."

Will's investigation had been remarkably thorough and told him as much about March as the heiress herself. Her uncle had proclaimed her mad with grief over her father's death and incapable of managing her fortune. No wonder March had such deep pockets to fund charities.

Xander didn't say anything about March's character.

He doubted she knew anything about March's questionable connection to Bredsell's school. But it struck Xander as odd that the titled niece and nephew of a noted London philanthropist lived on a weedy farm.

The girl's frank gaze was fixed on him. "To think I accused you of not finding out more about Miss Finsbury."

"I have my sources."

"Well, it's a good thing that I proposed to you, for once again, you are making a mull of it." She wiped her hands on her apron. "You might as well drag me to the pond, shove my head under, and hold me down."

He had to laugh. "Until you come up spitting and swinging?"

"What woman wants to be told unpalatable truths about her circumstances as a prelude to seduction?"

His laugh faded at once. *Seduction* was an interesting choice of words. "I should follow your advice then and notice that fetching gown you are wearing."

She unhitched her skirts from her waist and let them fall. "You might as well admire the barn as this dress."

"The barn doesn't cling so well to your person or bring out the color in your eyes." He didn't lie.

She laughed, a fresh, spontaneous sound, dangerous to listen to, because he'd like to hear it again. "Stop. You mustn't think that I require false coin from you."

"I think what you require is cash." He meant to stick to his purpose. Any sexual interest in her would only complicate his plan.

Her lively glance sobered at once and fixed on him. "Is that what you're offering me?"

"I promise you I am a more generous banker than Evershot."

"I don't want a banker." She began to pace as she had in Evershot's office, as if the energy of her thoughts could not be contained, back and forth across the dry grass until she halted in front of him again. Her hands flew up in a quick gesture of disdain. "Why should men always be the bankers?" Another slash of the hands. "Why shouldn't I have charge of my own money and sit on a throne of golden guineas and let you come begging to me on your knees?" Those angry hands came to rest on her hips.

"In that case, you would be a most unaccommodating heiress."

The green gaze measured him, full of hostility and longing. "No." She turned away from him, and a startled thrush nearby took flight at her sudden vehemence.

Xander regarded the girl's profile. He could see the round curve of her cheek, a curl tucked in the hollow behind her ear, and the delicate ridge of her spine. There was not much to her, far less than Miss Finsbury offered. She was prickly as a holly bush and haughty to boot. He should have no sympathy for her, but he understood the desire to control one's own money. His mother had taught him how essential that control was to a woman's independence.

Cleo Spencer's arms were crossed in front of her, held tightly to her body.

One fist emerged and swiped at her eyes.

Hell! He stepped forward and took hold of her shoulders, turning her to face him. "Let's try again, shall we?

Miss Spencer, would you like to gain access to your fortune by marrying me?"

"What do you intend to do with my twenty thousand pounds, Sir Alexander Jones?"

Trust her to keep her mind on the money. "Purchase the East London Gas Company and restore its operations."

Eyes green and gold as summer, luminous with tears, stared at him, then she smiled and let out a brief hiccup of a laugh. "Your talent for flattery astonishes. I am a gasworks. It is a fresh comparison, not overused by poets to be sure." She stepped back out of his hold and dried her eyes with her sleeve. "What will you do with your gasworks?"

"Light St. Giles."

"No wonder you are looking for heiresses. No bank would fund such a venture."

"Just so."

"Paying your gaming debts would be more profitable. Why St. Giles? Why not some fashionable quarter of London where you could make a profit and a name for yourself?"

He didn't like that reference to making a name for himself. It meant she understood a bit too much of the scene she'd overheard. "Scores of investors are willing to light the palaces of the rich and titled. No one is quite so willing to bring light where it's most needed."

She studied him frankly, her head tilted to one side. "You don't look like a saint to me."

"Believe me, Miss Spencer, I am no saint."

"What sort of marriage are you proposing?"

It was his turn to pause. He had intended to bed Miss

Finsbury in the approved manner, but he was honest enough with himself to acknowledge that his conjugal visits were likely to have been few and far between. Maybe in the end that reluctance had been impossible to overcome.

Cleo Spencer presented a different sort of problem. Taking hold of her was like taking hold of one of those electrifying machines his friend Tom Ruxley set up to entertain dinner guests. But she was March's niece and as blue-blooded as they came. Bedding her was not part of his plan.

"The usual sort." He told himself the lie was justified. The partners of the Metropolitan Works Group wouldn't wait forever, and Xander wasn't going to let this opportunity slip away as the last had. His plan would do her no harm after all. She would have as much money as she needed now, and when their marriage ended, he would repay her.

She started her pacing again. "I suppose you want an heir, someone to carry on your name and fortune."

If she had a talent, it was for plain speaking. The last thing Xander wanted was an heir. "The Jones name is in no danger of fading."

"We could pretend to be married," she suggested, turning back his way, with a hopeful expression.

He smiled. Maybe he didn't have to worry about his plan after all. Women of her class generally found his person attractive enough, and his background—a definite inducement to sin. But Cleo Spencer's lack of enthusiasm for warming his bed meant his conscience could rest easy about their bargain. "Defrauding a bank, Miss Spencer, has penalties you probably don't want to contemplate."

"Nevertheless, marriage is notoriously permanent, a life sentence."

Not if you expected the marriage to be contested in court. He had already thoroughly investigated a way out. "Six years is a long time to wait for your money."

Her face assumed a bleaker aspect, and she looked away. "Do you intend to have a mistress?"

He could not fault her for vanity. Apparently she had none. "You underestimate the charms of your person."

"It's the charm of my purse that brought you here today. That you can't deny."

"A purse you can open only when you marry. Do we have a bargain?"

She faced him squarely then, a militant tilt to her chin. "I want a generous allowance and equal access to *our* money. If you go to the bank, I go with you. Every time. And I want an exact account of every penny you spend. I shall insist on receipts."

He regarded her coolly. Did she imagine that a man kept receipts for his mistress's services? "If you wish, but you will have to bring *your* receipts to our meeting as well."

Her haughty look came and went in a blink. "I must see it in the settlement papers before I wed."

"My solicitor will prepare the papers." He waited, undergoing another close scrutiny before she gave a barely perceptible nod.

"Where will we live? Or will we even live together?"

"I need to be in town to pursue my hopes."

"Town will suit me if I may have my younger brother with me. You know that I have a younger brother?"

He nodded. He knew little of the brother, the titleholder, a boy three years younger than Kit. "There's room."

"I wish to outfit him for school and provide tutors. Once he's settled, I can live anywhere."

"Then nothing remains except to set a date. Will Sunday be convenient?"

"This Sunday?"

"I have a special license in my pocket, and I am impatient to take a wife."

"Do I have to point out how abominably sure of yourself you are?"

"It may be that I am more sure of your desperation."

"Desperation!" The word came out on an indignant huff of breath.

"Isn't that what drove you to propose to me?"

She did not pretend to misunderstand him. Her face assumed an expression he was already coming to know. She was about to be frank with him.

"Maybe I simply saw Miss Finsbury's loss as my gain. And if you told me one thing about yourself, I'd have a reason for our bargain other than the obvious economic one."

He could not hold back a grin. "I am ten and twenty, weigh thirteen stone, and dislike peppermints."

"No one dislikes peppermints."

"Knowing me will enlarge your experience of men."

"Where will we be married?"

"The curate of Woford Abbey has agreed to marry us."

She looked at her faded dress, and he experienced a dangerous moment of sympathy for her. She had probably dreamed of Hanover Square.

"You do think me quite destitute."

He kept his face expressionless. "Do you require immediate funds?"

Her chin went up. "No."

She *was* stubborn. He withdrew his pocketbook and offered her two substantial notes.

"Really, I don't need your money."

His patience snapped. It was not his intention to turn his proposition into an actual courtship. That would not fit his plan. "We both need money. That's the point, isn't it? We'll get on better if we acknowledge that."

"Fair enough. It's all about the money." She took the notes. "You will have to meet with my trustees to gain access to my funds."

"And present our marriage lines. I know." He offered his hand to seal their bargain.

She looked at it, and after a pause, extended her own. There was a brief contact, her hand in his, small and rough and determined. He thought he detected a tremor in hers before she snatched it back. He opened and closed his fist, undoing the sensation of that hand in his.

"Well, I promise to hold my tongue occasionally even if you are about to make a terrible cake of yourself."

He grinned. He couldn't help it. "I promise not to strangle you."

Chapter Four

❧

CLEO watched Charlie slice another portion of Mrs. Lawful's best ham. He had been eating steadily for a quarter of an hour from the feast provided by her betrothed, and she judged it was safe to tell him her news. "I'm going to marry."

"I should hope so." He pushed a piece of ham across his plate.

"On Sunday."

He looked up, the captured ham hanging from his fork. "What?"

"On Sunday I'm going to marry Sir Alexander Jones." She pulled her shawl tight to cover a quick shiver. To speak her wedding plan aloud made it real, not some mad invention concocted in the heat of the afternoon's work. Charlie lowered his fork to stare at her.

"Cleo, what are you talking about? Did something happen to you?"

"It did. I met Sir Alexander last week at the bank. We . . . talked and realized that we could help each other by marrying."

"You mean he's a bloody fortune hunter, don't you?" Charlie was as versed in the details of Cleo's inheritance as she was.

"He's going to buy a gasworks and light St. Giles."

"A gasworks?" He was momentarily caught by the idea. Cleo could see him start to imagine it and stop himself. "With your money."

"Not all of it. There will be plenty for us. No more waiting and starving. We will buy cartloads of potatoes and have them three times a day. You will wear fine coats and go to school." She had rather concentrated on that part of the bargain since Jones left. She had wanted to ask Jones about his tailor, but thought the inquiry might be premature. Still, within a fortnight, she would be able to take Charlie to Bond Street to outfit him properly and engage a tutor to see that he passed his entrance examinations. And March would not be able to take him away from her.

Charlie pushed away his plate with a look of regret as if the food had suddenly become inedible because it was part of her bargain with Jones. "Cleo, you aren't making any sense. You can't marry just anyone to get your money."

"Jones is not just anyone. He's someone quite specific. He has dark hair and gray eyes and a direct manner. He's forceful. I think he can stand up to March." She did not mention that Jones was the natural son of

Lord Candover, as cold and powerful a lord as any in London. She could not guess what Jones's relations with his father were, but he did not like his position in society. Of that she was sure. He seemed a gentleman in every way except the one that counted. To marry him would mean turning her back on the world Charlie would enter some day. But really, that world had turned its back on her over her father's debts, his scandalous death, and her uncle's rumors about her own mad flight from his care.

She did not mention Sir Alexander's person, the slate eyes with their hidden spark that she couldn't quite look away from, the deep voice that made her skin taut, the hands that made her think of dancing naked.

Charlie's mouth had opened to protest, but he closed it and concentrated on his plate. He so seldom had enough to satisfy his appetite, and he had so thoroughly enjoyed eating his fill for once. She hated to see him regret it.

After a moment he looked up again, his gaze serious. "Cleopatra." He used her full name. "I'm your only male relative, the only one who cares about you at any rate. I should meet this man, question him about his character and intentions."

"His intention is to restore the East London Gas Company to operation and light St. Giles while I spend my fortune on you, or us, dearest. Sounds like a good plan to me."

"Sounds maggot-brained to me. Have you told Evershot?" He didn't ask her about March.

"He doesn't need to know until after the wedding."

Charlie looked at her. "You're serious."

"Completely." She only wished that Sir Alexander

had not smiled in just that way as they parted. His face
had a charm then that quite took her breath away.

"March will be madder than Hades."

Cleo smiled. She allowed herself that, a wide satisfied smile. "Won't he though."

ONE Sunday later Cleo observed that cold stone
under one's slippered feet, like that of the vestibule of a small church, was perfectly conducive to facing hard truths. Her wedding, the one she was about to
have, would not be the one she dreamed of as a girl.

She had once thought to make a grand catch, a duke
or an earl's son, and to marry with a great deal of show
and notices in the morning papers. She had squandered
dozens of daydreams trying to choose a fitting nuptial
celebration, imagining first a breakfast party of cham-
pagne and strawberries and next an evening ball with
fireworks. The groom in these spun-sugar daydreams
had been a charming young man with a fondness for
dogs and horses and a grand house in the country. And
he danced well.

Yet here she was in the tiny church of her childhood
about to marry a hard-eyed stranger who wanted her
money, with her reluctant brother as her only attendant
and her groom's hostile, disreputable brother as the
chief witness. They would be married and on their way
before regular services began.

"Cleo, you can back out, you know." Charlie had
made the same comment a dozen times or more since
the brothers had arrived to take them to church.

"I won't, however." If she was shaking, it was the

cold air. The turn of the year had come. She could see her breath in the little vestibule. She had left off her shabby cloak for a lavender spotted muslin gown purchased with her bridegroom's money.

"You don't know him. He looks like a statue."

"He does, doesn't he?" He had been generous in his provisions for them, however. She had read the contract a dozen times and was a little giddy with the thought of the pin money she would have.

"He looks at you like a lion looking at a lamb."

"I don't want to quarrel with your metaphor, dearest, but surely he looks at me more in the way a banker looks at a vault of gold."

Charlie shook his head. "Don't tease. Just because I'm young, don't think I don't know my duty by a sister." He fell silent, his thin shoulders hunched, his hands thrust in his pockets, bony wrists exposed by his outgrown coat sleeves. She could almost see his thoughts, his brow furrowed, his brown hair untamed.

"I should talk to him, man to man. I should make him understand that if anything happens to you, if you are made unhappy, he will have to answer to me."

"You are sweet, dearest, but he's not Bluebeard."

"How do we know? We don't know his people or his friends."

"We've met his brother."

Charlie snorted. "His brother looks like a pirate and smells like a brewery."

"What do you know of breweries?"

"I'm not totally green. What if this Jones is a fraud who just takes your money?"

"I'll hunt him down and kill him, most likely." She

thought to shock Charlie into a grin, but he only shook his head at her. "You can help me if you like."

"I'll be locked up with Uncle March." He hung his head.

She punched him on the shoulder. "No, you won't. That's why we're doing this."

"*You're* doing this. Cleo, have you thought, I mean, married people . . ." Charlie swallowed and squared his shoulders. ". . . Married people sleep together. What if you don't like sleeping with him?"

Oh, so that was the worry. She had no idea what he knew about sexual congress. Dear Miss Hester Britt had given Cleo a thorough and pointed explanation. But there was no telling what Charlie might have heard or seen on Davies's farm. She thrust Mrs. Lawful's proffered bouquet into his hands, took him by the shoulders, and looked straight into his troubled hazel eyes. She could hardly tell him she was marrying an iceman who thought of her as a gasworks. "Married people do sleep together, of course, but every couple comes to it in their own way. I expect that Jones and I will likely wait awhile."

I N the ancient sacristy of Woford Abbey, Will addressed Xander. "You're out of your mind, you know."

"Thanks for the hearty endorsement. Have you got the ring?"

Will dipped into his waistcoat pocket and pulled out the simple gold band Xander had purchased for his bride. "If you want to shackle yourself for life, do it, but that girl has no idea what she's getting into."

"I haven't lied to her." Xander checked his neckcloth in a small mirror next to a hanging surplice that had seen better days.

"Well, you haven't told her bleeding everything."

"She wants access to her fortune, and she'll have it." His neckcloth looked fine.

"You want access to her fortune."

"We both benefit then."

"Why don't you just loan her the blunt to settle her brother in school? You're good for it."

"I'm not a charity organization." Xander checked his watch. A wizened old bell ringer, hoping for a coin, had shown them to the sacristy, where the curate, Mr. Tucker, was to meet them at eight. At the last moment Xander's solicitor had been unable to act as witness, so Xander had dragged Will along.

He leaned insolently against the doorjamb. A blackened eye and unshaven chin did nothing for his appearance, but he was sober and had a decent coat on. So far the ancient church was still standing.

"You told her about your rules? She knows that you've sworn off bedding toffs? She's not expecting to mother any fine little Joneses?"

"She has her brother to care for. Stick your head out the door and see if they're coming."

Will shrugged away from the doorjamb and looked out. "No sign of bride or curate. Maybe she changed her mind." He shut the door. "You do have a way out of this, don't you, Brother?"

"Your touching concern. Yes, there's a way. It's a gamble."

Will yawned. "Do you think she's mad?"

"You mean do I believe a story that March spread about her?"

"Then you're taking advantage of an innocent. She's thin as a sapling and shakes like a leaf."

"It's a frosty morning for muslin." Cleo Spencer might be thin, but Xander had a vision of her standing up to him and thwacking her rug with furious energy. She was no simpering miss to be cowed by him, and he was sure she would hold him to every line of their agreement.

"And then there's March. You'll have to watch your back every minute, even if you do get access to her money. Especially if you get access to her money."

"If March murders me, you'll have the satisfaction of being right and the chance to arrest him." The sound of footsteps interrupted him. "Ah, here's the curate, if I'm not mistaken. Time for me to take a wife."

A T the altar Cleo studied the expression in her groom's proud face. His intensity set him apart from his mocking brother and the shrinking curate. She tried to tell herself that he looked like a man buying a gasworks, but his scrutiny unsettled her. His physical presence made her stomach fluttery, and her skin seemed alive to his gaze. She handed Mrs. Lawful's bouquet to Charlie, lifted her veil, and gave her husband-to-be as direct a gaze as he was giving her. He surprised her by laughing, his face relaxing into that unsettling smile Cleo remembered from the garden.

"Ready to become Lady Jones, Miss Spencer?"

"Are you hoping I will back out?"

Mr. Tucker cleared his throat. He looked as if he would bolt if either of the brothers said a word to him. "Is there any question about proceeding?"

"None," said the bored brother. "Get on with it, man."

Mr. Tucker opened his book and began to work his way through the marriage service. The words seemed to echo off the stones in the empty church, utterly shocking words that Cleo realized she had never attended to before. *What was the church thinking?* Every sentence mentioned carnal embrace. Charlie was probably frightened out of his wits. Mr. Tucker certainly was.

Next to her the man with the unreadable slate eyes and deep, skin-caressing voice was promising to worship her with his body, his tall, lean body that radiated heat in the cold nave. A startling wave of warmth flashed along her skin. By the time he took her hand in his lean, brown one and slipped a gold band on her finger, she felt dizzy with heat.

She steadied herself and repeated her part. Really, intimacies between them were unlikely. They hardly knew each other. Their marriage was all about money. They had aims that would keep them occupied and going in quite different directions. With the rustle of a thin page, Mr. Tucker ran out of text and pronounced them man and wife.

Her groom's glaring brother slapped him on the back. "All over but the paperwork. Kiss the bride, man," he muttered.

Cleo's new husband turned to her, his face closed and proud. The moment lengthened, and she had time to notice threads of silver in his dark hair and the pale groove of a scar that sliced across his right ear. The sensuous jut of his lower lip caught her gaze. His hesitation stretched to the point of awkwardness.

He did not want to kiss her. He would not kiss her. Whatever warmth she felt in his voice was of her own imagining. His spine was stiff, his expression frozen, all but the eyes. His heated pewter gaze was alive and fixed on her mouth. She felt embarrassment sting her cheeks.

Four years of poverty had not entirely cured her of vanity. His reluctance to kiss her wounded her pride. "What an exhausting service," she said. "Somehow the church manages to squeeze a lifetime into a brief service in language more appropriate to the lowest bawdy house than the holy altar." She shrugged and turned to Charlie for her bouquet. He seemed frozen, too. If she just kept talking, the moment would pass.

"What a shocking service, Mr. Tucker, with all that talk of *fornication*, *man's carnal lusts and appetites*, and *the poor brute beasts*. I wonder it doesn't put you to the blush. The Church of England should be ashamed— such warnings about the dreadful day of judgment and not *enterprising unadvisedly, lightly, or wantonly into the married state*. The worst sort of scare tactics."

With a quick move her new husband took control, pressing a warm, firm thumb to her lips. They tingled instantly.

"I promise not to strangle you," he said, his gaze locked with hers. His thumb brushed her lips and released them. But the sensation lingered.

Cleo looked up into gray eyes that seemed molten with heat. "I promise to hold my tongue." She swallowed. "Occasionally."

His gaze questioned, and Cleo tried to hide the something hot and alive that leapt up inside her, eager to answer that look.

He swore, a single sharp oath, and took her face in his palms, the palms that had curved around the teacup. She felt her breath catch in her chest while her heart beat a deep, heavy thump against the thin fabric of her gown. He leaned down and pressed his mouth to hers, forcing her lips open and stealing her breath with a ruthless, knowing kiss that went on and on, crumbling undefended walls of permission and participation.

Cleo's sleeping senses awoke everywhere, uncurled in her breasts and stretched in her belly and lower. Rational thought drowned in eddies of surging energy and helpless languor, until she clutched his fine wool sleeve to keep from melting into the abbey stones.

The kiss ended, and the shock of his abrupt withdrawal left her suspended, intensely alive, sensation still coursing through her. With only a quick steadying touch under her elbow, he led her to sign the register. There she put her hand to the book, marveling that her ordinary faculties functioned effortlessly, while inside some elusive sense she had not known she possessed struggled to fix the impression of his kiss in her body. The formalities accomplished, Mr. Tucker escaped into his sacristy, and the wedding party left the church.

Outside, a weak Michaelmas sun made a faint effort to warm the day. A fine rig with a matching pair of black horses stood waiting, a gawking boy at the horses' heads. Sir Alexander Jones pulled on his gloves and set his hat on his head. "I'll put an announcement in the papers."

He turned to his brother. "Ready, Will?"

Her groom's piratical brother raised the brow of his good eye and tipped his hat to Cleo. "So much for the treacle moon," he muttered, and they mounted the rig.

With a glance over his shoulder, her husband said, "I've ordered you a breakfast at the inn if you like. Whenever you're ready to come to town, let Mrs. Lawful know. Arrangements have been made for your transport. If you need funds, you can apply to Mr. Taylor, my man of business."

He drove off.

Cleo and Charlie stood in the arched stone doorway of the church and watched the brothers disappear down the empty road. The sky looked threatening, and they had a long walk home. Cleo's slippers would never survive a rain.

"I thought he might kiss you again." Charlie sighed.

"I suspect he's off to buy his gasworks." She would do well to hold on to that thought. Whatever her husband's kiss had done to her, it had left no mark on him.

"The banks aren't open."

"But the inn is, dearest. Shall we enjoy a very large breakfast?"

Chapter Five

❧

ARCHIBALD March's fondness for his London club was undeniable. The loftiness of its rooms and the civilized comforts of its service had sustained him through the long years of living in cramped bachelor quarters before his brother's passing.

It was his habit to be seen in the subscription room most evenings, where his fellow members left his chair undisturbed. There he read the papers and drank a glass of wine to fortify himself for the demands of a London evening. From his usual corner he greeted supporters of his various charities, MPs who could be counted on to vote as directed, and indeed the Home Secretary himself, a fellow member.

In his chair he could forget that he was a mere footnote in the pages of the peerage devoted to the Spencers. He was his mother's son not by the Right Honorable

Lord Woford, whom she'd married when Archibald was two, but by John March, an obscure country squire with a few good freehold acres. Archibald never forgot that though a baron had encouraged Archibald to call him *father*, though he had shown Archibald every sign of affection and favor in his lifetime, in death that baron had with a most unfatherly lack of feeling left Archibald no title and no property, and a mere thousand pounds a year. It was left to Archibald himself to correct the accident of his birth by any means available to him.

London, with its endless supply of beggars and thieves, had shown him the first way; the second he had discovered on his own.

This October evening, the slap of the *Morning Chronicle* hitting his chair and then dropping folded open into his lap caused him to jostle the glass at his lips and spill a faint drop of wine in the artful folds of his cravat.

"I assume you have a plan, March." The voice coming from above his chair spoke in the glacial privileged accents of an ancient title.

Since he'd first heard it, Archibald had studied to understand why the icy voice both thrilled and terrified him. By birth, by wealth, by power, the possessor of that voice should never speak to Archibald March, stepson of a mere baron. That he, Archibald, had so fashioned his own position of power, which brought this man to his side—that was the thrill. Archibald had done His Exaltedness a favor, put His Exaltedness in Archibald's debt.

However, it was a voice fundamentally indifferent to Archibald March, willing to destroy him if he proved inconvenient. That was the hazard in doing favors for the very powerful. Archibald was careful. He protected his escape routes thoroughly. He simply did not relish testing whether the voice could find him if he chose to disappear.

He put down his glass and picked up the paper. He had seen the announcement of his niece's marriage to the one man in London who would overlook her tainted reputation, the one man in London who would use her money in a most inconvenient way for the powerful man at Archibald's side. Now with the unfortunate event proclaimed to world, he tried not to let the oh-so-polite voice unsettle him.

Long habit prompted him to offer reassurance. "Of course I have a plan. The marriage is an obvious fraud. My niece has been practiced on by an unscrupulous man of low birth, thinking to rob her of her fortune. I have engaged Lushington to bring action in the London Consistory Court."

Nothing changed. No response. The quiet hum of club life continued around a cone of silence that held March and the man at his side in place. Waiters busied themselves as the room filled with more members, but no one caught Archibald's eye. An annoying prickle made him conscious of heat pooling under his arms. Really, his niece was proving more inconvenient than anticipated.

"Shall we say a fortnight, then," the voice resumed, "to resolve this matter?"

"A month would be better." If his niece became any more troublesome, an accident would have to be arranged.

"No, March, a sennight would be better."

It was some time before Archibald felt steady enough to again lift his glass. He thought it best to make a complete change of linen before his evening engagements.

I hope Bluebeard doesn't murder you directly." Charlie had his face pressed to the glass of Sir Alexander Jones's elegant hired chaise as they rumbled up Park Lane in the October dusk, passing a long row of grand bow-fronted houses. Cleo remembered dining and dancing in several.

"You'd like some time to see the sights before you're forced to flee town again?"

Charlie drew back from the window. "I've never been to the Menagerie."

"I'll put it at the top of our list, dearest, but I do think Jones will want to be sure of my fortune before he does away with me."

Charlie frowned and fidgeted with his jacket. Cleo suspected that his banter about Bluebeard was a thin cover for genuine uneasiness, and the truth was she didn't know what to make of her husband's character or motives. He said he wanted a gasworks, but Cleo had had a long week to think about that. No man just wanted a gasworks. Still he had sent for them, and she thought the first generous installment of her allowance a good sign that he meant to honor their bargain.

The coach turned a sharp right corner forcing them both into a lean. Charlie frowned.

"What?"

"Cleo, I want you to know that I am prepared to defend you." They came upright, and he reached into his boot and drew forth a lethal-looking blade that was all point with a heavy iron ring at its base.

"Charlie Spencer, what on earth is that?"

"It's a pig-sticking knife. Davies gave it to me. Said I ought to have something to protect you with."

"Give it to me." Cleo held out her hand. "This is Mayfair, not the East India Company docks. The only weapons you need here are a raised brow, a sharp wit, and a quizzing glass. Lethal enough, but hardly bloody."

Charlie shook his head, holding on to the thing. "Promise me, Cleo, that you'll use it if you have to." He looked solemn and brave in spite of his unruly hair and thin face. The coach began to slow.

"I promise," she said.

He handed the blade over with apparent relief. "The thing is, girls don't have good hiding places for blades."

"I'll put it under my pillow."

He brightened at once. "Good thought. Just the spot for it."

The coach pulled up, and they alighted on Hill Street in London's smoky dusk, a half dozen blocks from where Uncle March kept their father's house. Their bags were handed down, and a tall servant with ginger hair, narrow shoulders, and a long, solemn face emerged from the house to pay the coachman and postilions. The coach rattled off down the street with Cleo and Charlie still standing on the pavement under gray skies. A chill wind pressed their thin clothes to their bodies as they gaped at Sir Alexander Jones's house.

From the basement to the attic its windows blazed, long rectangles of light like gold bars. Scores of candles burned at a staggering cost. Charlie turned to Cleo with a sheepish look. She still had the knife in her hand. "It's lighted up like a stage," he whispered.

"No wonder he needs to buy a gasworks," Cleo replied.

The silent servant with the thin, horselike face bowed and picked up their bags. "In here."

Then her husband stepped out of his own door, his features shadowed by the light behind him. She really needed to get used to his austere good looks so that she didn't gawk at him every time. His expression under the dark brows was unreadable.

The quick ceremony, his hasty departure, and a week of activity had erased that unsettling moment in the church when his lips had lingered on hers. Now his dark gaze found Cleo's and instantly revived the memory of that burning kiss in the church. She tried to pinpoint the elusive sensation. Her stomach did a little flip, which could be no more than her body's response to the end of a long carriage ride. To go from the swaying, jouncing motion of coach travel to firm contact with unmoving stone explained it. She tucked the knife-holding hand into the folds of her cloak.

An awkward moment passed until Jones came forward and shook Charlie's hand. "I must borrow your sister for a meeting with our solicitor."

"Now?" Cleo protested. "I can't desert Charlie before he's even in the door."

"Norwood is waiting."

"Don't worry, Cleo." Charlie followed the servant. "A witness is good," he whispered as he passed.

Cleo's husband led her through a hall so dazzling it made her blink, past a marble nymph at the base of a soaring iron staircase, and into a book-lined library where the light was only somewhat subdued.

A stout, square-faced gentleman, his substantial girth straining a bottle green waistcoat, lifted a writing desk from his ample lap and rose. He had a wide face and kind features with brows like cotton tufts, but his blue eyes sparked with keen intelligence.

"Lady Jones, I'm Norwood, at your service. It's good to meet you at last, ma'am."

Cleo shook his hand and took the seat he indicated near a welcome fire. Norwood remained standing and cast a prompting look at her husband.

"May I take your cloak, wife?" came the baritone Cleo could feel in the pit of her stomach.

"Of course," she said, rising, and loosening the tie, "husband." She felt the brief touch of his hands on her shoulders as the cloak slipped away. Just enough to set a little flutter going in her. She settled back in her chair, facing the lawyer, whose gaze had fixed on Charlie's knife.

Cleo put it on the pretty cherrywood table next to her chair. "It's a pig-sticking knife. My brother recommends that I be prepared to defend myself in London."

She caught a quick gleam of amusement in Norwood's eyes before a more businesslike expression took over. "Let's hope, Lady Jones, that the laws of England remain strong enough to protect a woman in your circumstances." He settled himself on the sofa and rested his hands on his broad knees. "Xander asked me to explain how the case stands at the moment. We want everything aboveboard, an open book, so to speak. Shouldn't want you going about town blind to your situation."

"Is there a situation?" *Xander*. The nickname distracted her, imperious, but out of the ordinary. It suited him. He stood with one elbow on his marble mantel looking on with cool detachment. It was the third personal detail she knew of him. He didn't like peppermints, he kissed like a man who knew what he was about, and most surprising of all, there were people in his life who called him by an affectionate nickname.

"Well, yes and no," Norwood was saying. "All the documents are in order. Been examined by the bank's own barrister. No fault to find with the paperwork."

Cleo braced herself. There was a something else, a difficulty that required a barrister's involvement, and that could not be good.

"One of your trustees . . ."

"My Uncle March?" She could feel Xander watching her. She hadn't been entirely open with him. He didn't know March, and Cleo hadn't confided her opinion of her uncle. He probably thought he could marry a discarded heiress without anyone's raising the least objection. After all, even her uncle had found only one taker when he had sought to arrange a marriage for her.

"Has Uncle March made trouble about our papers?" She believed she had escaped March's reach by marrying.

"As I advised Xander when he first came to me about your marriage, it would not be surprising for your trustees to question a man's intentions." Sharp blue eyes focused on Cleo. Norwood might be genial, but he would catch any hesitation or concealment. "So I must ask you some awkward questions."

"Certainly. We would not want my uncle to doubt

the sanctity of our union." She looked to Xander, who wasn't exactly playing the doting bridegroom.

Norwood settled a pair of glasses on his nose and pulled the small writing desk into his wide lap. "Now, when Mr. Tucker married you, did he omit from absent-mindedness or uneasiness any of the necessary elements of the rite?"

"Not to my knowledge. I've not been married before, but I assume he read all the necessary parts."

Norwood's pen scratched away. "Is it your wish to be married to Sir Alexander Jones? And do you consider yourself married to him?"

"It is, and I do." She was aware of him as always. Unmoving, unspeaking, he managed to distract her by holding up the blasted mantel. The turn of his body and the cock of one hip exposed his flat belly and the muscled line of one leg.

"And who was present at your nuptials?"

Cleo pulled her gaze and her thoughts back to Norwood. "Just family."

Norwood gave her a quick, sharp glance, his snowy brows contracted in a worried peak above his glasses.

"My brother, and my . . . husband's brother. And Mr. Tucker."

"And your brother is how old?"

"Thirteen."

"A minor." Norwood made a note. Cleo was sensitive now to his scratchings.

"Is that a problem?"

"And is Mr. Tucker a legitimate minister of the Church of England?"

"He's been the curate in Woford for many years. I know of no reason to suppose him to be otherwise."

"Very good."

"Mr. Norwood, excuse me, may I know the reason for these questions?"

"Of course." He put down his pen and leaned back. "How shall I put it? Your uncle strongly objects to the circumstances of your marriage. He suspects that there may be fraud involved, a deliberate conspiracy to deceive the bank. He's going to lob some shots across our bows, legally, so to speak, and we want to be ready for him."

"Mr. Norwood, as I am of age, and the money in question is my money, by marrying I have done all that's required to gain access to it, have I not?"

"To be sure, Lady Jones. However, if the London Consistory Court determines that the marriage is a mere stratagem, a ruse for obtaining money, you could be liable to serious criminal charges, even prison or transportation."

Cleo found she could not breathe. She could not go to jail. What would happen to Charlie? Xander Jones had hinted at such consequences. He had realized, even if she had not, how serious a risk a mere imposture would be. But they had made their vows in a church. Their marriage was legal. What happened between them was private, was it not? She turned to Xander, trying to penetrate his cool mask. Whatever his true motives were, he wanted that money, wanted his gasworks. She could count on him to push forward with their bargain.

"Lady Jones?" Norwood called her back to attention. "May we proceed?"

Cleo nodded. She needed to keep her wits about her.

"Has there been consummation, penetration, and ejaculation?"

"You can ask that?"

"The court will," Norwood assured her. "Consistory Court is a panel of lay and clerical judges who can determine the validity of a marriage."

Cleo glanced at her husband again. His slate-colored eyes were at their stoniest. He had known the question was coming. "You may take my word for it, Norwood," he said.

Norwood did not look up. "I will need the lady's word as well."

"You have it, then," said Cleo. She hoped the lie sounded convincing.

"Good, good." Norwood stopped writing and put aside his pen.

"Now what?" Cleo needed to know.

"Now we make sure the world sees you as Xander's wife while we wait for the hearing." Norwood sanded his notes, shook the paper dry, and tucked his glasses into his waistcoat pocket.

"When is the hearing to be?"

"We'll delay as much as we can, but likely within the month if March has his way. He has retained Dr. Lushington, and the man's no fool. He's trying the church court first to see whether he can block Xander from exercising his conjugal rights. And he'll try the King's Bench if he suspects perjury. I must warn you that he's likely to go after your curate." Norwood looked to Xander. "How susceptible is this Tucker to the lure of money?"

"His coats are threadbare."

"Well, it might be wise to warn him that he could be suspended and fined for solemnizing a clandestine wedding."

"Surely, *clandestine* is not the proper term," Cleo pointed out. "We didn't have a large celebration, but it was hardly a secret in Woford."

"Nevertheless, with few witnesses and one of them a minor, March can contest the validity."

"But other people knew of the event," Cleo insisted.

Norwood paused in putting away his notes. "Other witnesses would be good. Did you have someone bake the cake? Can you name the fellows who rang the bells?"

"No cake. No bells." Xander shoved away from the mantel and came to stand beside Cleo.

"I purchased a gown. A wedding breakfast was ordered." Cleo realized she was showing every bit of the dismay she felt. The thought of Mr. Tucker facing Uncle March was not encouraging.

"There's one last worry, Lady Jones." Norwood reached out and patted her hand. "Your uncle has made statements about your mental state. Nothing of record, of course, just rumors. We don't want to land in Chancery Court, however."

The court that settled the affairs of lunatics. It was a warning, politely made, but it told Cleo that both her husband and his barrister had heard Uncle March's mad-girl story. She would be watched for any sign of instability.

Norwood stuffed his notes into the case, pulled the straps closed, and tucked it under his arm. He rose to leave.

"Is my money available to me at present?" Cleo asked him.

"It is, unless and until the Consistory Court investigators rule against the validity of your marriage."

"Norwood, you've hardly consoled Lady Jones. She needs a strategy."

"Well then." Norwood's blue eyes twinkled. "Here it is. Be a good wife. Present a picture of wedded bliss to the world. Give a few dinners, go about town, leave your cards, have your at-home days, that sort of thing." Norwood shook Xander's hand, bowed over Cleo's, and turned for the door. There he paused and turned back to them, tapping his broad chin. "I forgot. There is one sure way to gain the advantage over March," he said, looking at Cleo. "Is there any chance that you are already in a family way, Lady Jones?"

Cleo noted that the question caught Xander off guard for once. He flashed her a dark, warning look, but she could see that he didn't know how to answer. She did. She would do anything to break March's hold on her life and Charlie's. She lowered her gaze to her hands folded demurely in her lap and managed the needed syllable. "Yes."

Norwood broke into a broad grin. "Excellent. That'll do it. The Consistory Court will regard a child as a sign of a valid marriage. Have you had a physician conduct an examination?"

Xander stepped behind Cleo, and his hands settled on her shoulders. She felt the tension in them, a clear signal to remain silent. "Norwood, Lady Jones and I must ask you to keep our happy news in confidence for the present."

Norwood looked puzzled, but he nodded. "Yes, well, until our court date, perhaps. Congratulations, then, on your marriage. Time enough to get a good sawbones on our side, and then we'll drink to your other news."

The door closed behind him, and Cleo felt the weight of those hard hands on her shoulders. Her husband was seriously displeased. "You promised not to strangle me."

"I did," came the deep voice from above her, "but that still leaves shooting, drowning, beheading, or dismemberment, all of which seem reasonable at the moment, unless you are, in fact, pregnant." He released her shoulders and came around to stand in front of her.

"Of course not." *He would prefer that she had a lover?*

"You lied."

Cleo stood. She did not like the way he towered over her. "You lied first. I merely followed your lead. Consummation? Penetration? Ejaculation? On the church steps perhaps?" She threw up her hands. "Besides, how hard can it be to make the lie true? I rather thought the difficulty was to avoid getting in a family way."

"You did not seem eager for carnal embraces when we made our bargain." He was not looking at her.

"That was before your own legal advisor mentioned criminal prosecution. Apparently, if we want to avoid jail, we must indulge. Surely, whatever our inclinations, the act itself need be no more disagreeable than an application of leeches or a session of blistering."

A faint smile touched his mouth. "I will keep that in mind." He moved to the door, walking out on her.

"You were willing to get Miss Finsbury with child."

He paused and turned that flat, impenetrable gaze on her. "Miss Finsbury's father is a grazier."

"My father was a peer? That's your objection to sexual congress with me?" She did not understand him. How could *he* object to her birth? More likely he believed the mad-girl story her uncle had told about her. She wanted it out in the open, whatever it was.

He went still, as still as he had in the bank when Miss Finsbury had called him a bastard. He was definitely keeping something from her.

His face had its stone look. The man who had kissed her in the church was somewhere behind that flat, fixed gaze. "You have access to your money and a chance to do all you wanted for your brother. That was our bargain. Norwood will keep March tied up in court for months if need be."

She had not understood him in time, and now he thought she would tamely accept the risk he was taking, a man arranging her fate, like her uncle, like the lawyers. He would use banks and courts to his advantage. Before them she was the beggar. A cold rage took hold of her. "I will not leave my brother alone in the world."

He stiffened, but he did not turn. "My man Amos will show you which rooms are yours. His brother Isaiah tends the horses, and their cousin Alice will be your maid. Cook has a supper ready. I'll be out this evening."

The door closed, and Cleo began to shiver. In a minute she was shaking hard. On wobbly legs she sought the fire, standing as close as she could, feeling the burn of it through her thin skirts. She had returned to a London she thought she knew, but it was as if she had taken a wrong turn down an unfamiliar street and couldn't get her bearings.

Charlie. She had to think about him. He would be her compass. He was the reason she had made this mad marriage. She looked at his pig-sticking knife, and a painful laugh escaped her tight throat. She reached down and scooped it up. Apparently, she would not need it to hold off an over-amorous spouse, but maybe she could use it to drive her reluctant groom into bed.

Chapter Six

⁂

XANDER Jones's silent man Amos led Cleo up more stairs to the back of the house, where dozens of candles illuminated a room so pretty it made her breath catch. She never imagined his house could possess such a room. It was another contradiction about him.

Pale yellow walls like butter in winter, a pair of honeysuckle chintz chairs by a glowing fire, and a bed like a wedding gown, all creamy crocheted lace, piled high with plump pillows. French doors with gauzy drapery led to a small balcony overlooking the dark garden. Miss Finsbury with her quivering bows would have been right at home.

The room had not been made pretty for Cleo. It had existed long before Xander Jones found her at Fernhill Farm and made his proposal. She need not be pleased that he had put her here. He meant to keep her out of his way; no adjoining bedrooms for them.

"And your master's room?" she asked the servant as he bowed his way out the door.

"Front west, ma'am." *As far from her as the architecture of a London town house permitted.*

Cleo told herself not to feel wounded by Xander Jones's reluctance to bed her. She had no more pretensions to beauty or dancing eyes, and he certainly had heard the mad-girl story. But, she discovered, a tiny ember of vanity still smoldered in her heart. Her husband's willingness to bed Miss Finsbury stirred the hot coal to envious life, and it burned. She wanted him to want her. How satisfying it would be to the turn the tables on him.

She put Charlie's pig-sticking knife on the table by the bed. At least there were no restraints attached to the bedstead. Her husband might believe the rumors her uncle March spread about her, but he hadn't consigned her to an attic or tied her up. Yet.

Cleo opened the doors of the narrow balcony and stepped out into the night. The restless hum of London sounded in her ears, familiar and yet strange after the country. Below her in the garden the bare branches of two plane trees tossed fretfully in the October wind, shaking loose their last leaves, making a dry rattle like scurrying footsteps. Light pouring from every window of Xander Jones's house made a flickering pattern of shadows on the ground below.

She tried to think what her reluctant bridegroom might have heard about her. March had claimed that her father's sudden death had deranged her. He had accused her of starving herself and finally of turning on him with a fireplace poker. There was some truth in the story. She had been bone-thin with grief in those days, but Uncle March never mentioned that she picked up the poker when he wakened her in her bed in the midst of spreading her hair upon her pillows. He claimed she was susceptible to delusions.

Her case had been less sensational than Caro Lamb's, but society's tolerance for Caro's outbursts years earlier worked against Cleo. Her cousins cut her off immediately. Lady Jersey did not hesitate to remove her name from the list at Almack's, a laughable attack, as if Cleo could have danced in those days of grief. The only advantage to Uncle March's story had been that it made her flight easy. She had left town in the company of Miss Hester Britt without arousing anyone's suspicions, and the farm had swallowed them up for four years. Only Miss Hester Britt's passing had brought Uncle March down on them again. She blinked hard against a sudden pang of loss for her old friend and for the farm.

At that moment a sharp gust exposed a patch of white brighter than the flagstone path. Wind tore the white patch from the pattern and blew it away in the shadows at the back of the garden. Cleo began shivering again. Her balcony seemed exposed, a stage, on which she stood in the light while in the dark an unseen audience watched.

Well, that was vanity or madness for you, imagining yourself on stage! Cleo bowed to the indifferent darkness and took herself off to find Charlie.

THE Tooth and Nail listed on its ancient foundation up a court in a warren of streets an easy distance from Covent Garden. Its doors swung open to all comers. In the mix of patrons, Xander and even Will represented the celestial end of prosperity while their guest Dick Cullen, a lean fellow of about twenty-five with a checkered waistcoat and a bitten ear, represented those presently out of luck. As Xander and Will were buying, Dick Cullen drank steadily. The man could put away ale.

A woman's warm laugh triggered an image in Xander's mind of his ragged bride, but he banished the thought. "So you're out of work."

Resentment had soured Cullen's thin features. "Had a good situation at Truman's Brewery until that night. A year ago 'twas."

"Hell," Will muttered. "A bleeding year ago."

Xander quelled his brother with a look. Cullen spat on the straw-covered floor. "Took a cursed room. That's my luck, you see, always rum."

Cullen's insistence before the magistrate that only his cursed room had led him afoul of the law had first alerted Xander and Will to his story. "Where is this cursed room?"

"Bread Street, where Mother Greenslade collects rents."

Xander did not meet Will's gaze. Bread Street ran northwest past Bredsell's school toward the heart of the St. Giles rookery. "Why cursed?"

"Bloke died there. I had the lower. 'E and 'is boy had the upper. Something not right about the man." Cullen shook his head.

"Tell me about the boy," Xander invited, careful not to signal his deep interest in a seemingly random detail.

"'Ad nothin' to do with *'im*." More ale washed down Cullen's scrawny throat.

"But you knew he was there," Will prodded.

Cullen shrugged. He was not interested in boys, only in his own grievance. Will filled Cullen's pint pot from a pitcher.

"Small, fair, almost pretty. Fellow never let 'im out. Boy like that should be good for some'at."

"How old would you say he was?" Xander asked.

Cullen raised the pint pot. "It was Mother Greenslade 'at knew 'im. She'd sneak the boy a bit o' cake on the sly, found 'im chained to the bed more 'an once."

Chained. Xander did not look at Will. A bitter taste filled his mouth, like ashes. He felt oddly cold, but he wanted to strike something. He could see himself swinging a pick, the pick biting into Bread Street, the pavement cracking and crumbling under blow after blow, the houses trembling and collapsing.

After three years of searching, he knew those ruined houses with their grimy rooms and broken furnishings, empty cupboards, foul smells, and dabs of greasy candles. He expected hunger and beatings would be part of Kit's story, but *chained*. With effort he kept his hand steady as he produced a sketch of Kit made by their mother. "Did the boy look anything like this?"

Cullen glanced at the sketch and took another long pull at his drink. Kit had been eight when the sketch was made. He would have been near fifteen when Cullen encountered him. Maddening to have only this scrap of an image from long ago.

"Could be 'im. That's the look of 'im. 'Ard to say."

"You said the boy was fair?"

"Not so fair. Not so dark as yerself, mind."

"You never spoke to the boy?" Xander continued, trying to keep a rein on his galloping impatience.

Cullen gave a vigorous shake of his head. "Wouldn't do to cross that fellow. Fists like hams. 'Eard 'im knockin' the boy about regular."

"Never tried to stop him, did you?" Will did not hide his contempt for Cullen.

Cullen's thin, sour features registered only indifference. He was the sufferer in his story.

"So, how did you get the room?"

"The big man died. You could 'ear 'im smashing about, crashin' into walls. Wrenched the door clean off the jambs, came out on the stairs, just wild, waving his arms, 'is face blue like an 'anging, only no noose. Staggered back in the room and croaked."

"What happened to the boy?" Xander asked as lightly as he could.

"Gone before the death cart come. Mother Greenslade give me the room. That's when my luck turned. Lost my situation inside of a week. Now no one will give me a place. Cursed is wot I am." He hung his head over his drink.

"Maybe your curse is being too fond of Truman's product," Will said. "You'd best take care not to drown in it."

Cullen glared at Will. "Wot's a gentleman like you know about curses? They should pay is wot I say. Truman's should pay. No one should take a man's work from 'im."

Xander put a hand on Will's shoulder. To Cullen he said, "If you want another situation, I've got a need for men. Can you remember anything more about the boy?"

Cullen tugged his ragged ear and looked about at the other patrons hunched over their pewter pots or shouting beery oaths at one another. He clearly didn't like to be seen talking to toffs. "I'll come about. I know who's on my side. Truman's should look out for Dick Cullen."

He fell silent and took another long pull of ale. Apparently he remembered the prime rule of the rookery—*don't nark.*

Only the injustice of the curse had made Cullen reveal so much of his history before the magistrate. He had been threatened with six months in the stir, which he had taken ill, being a man, he claimed, who didn't follow the usual larcenous practices of his neighborhood. He never dipped, never did a click. The constables had swept him up from the crowd around a fire in Gerrard Street, where he'd been an innocent bystander.

After a minute Cullen's dull gaze swung back to Xander. "Mother Greenslade said one more thing. Said the boy was mute. Never 'eard 'im say nowt."

"Hell," Will muttered. "What are we doing here?" He shoved back the bench he sat on.

Xander stood. They had a lead. A look at the weekly Bills of Mortality would tell him exactly when and where such a man had died. There would be a name and a street number to start from. With his wife's money he could hire men in the neighborhood and get them talking.

Xander tossed Cullen another coin. "If you want a situation, the East London Gas Company is hiring."

Cullen fingered the coin with a dexterous move that put the lie to his ignorance of the pickpocket trade.

Honest employment wasn't the first means of eking out a living in his neighborhood.

Will laughed. "Watch out, Cullen, this fellow's going to light your bleeding street. You and your kind will have to do an honest day's work."

"'Ey, I told you I was no prig." Cullen was still protesting as Xander walked away. The smoky air of the dark street was welcome after the noise and stink of the Tooth and Nail.

"Cover up, man," Will advised, "unless you want to end up lying on the cobbles with a bloody head and no boots."

Xander closed his greatcoat over the snowy linen at his throat. "Kit's alive." He breathed biting air with the hint of an early hard frost.

"Not bloody likely. Cullen's the worst kind of snitch. He'll say anything to wet his throat. Maybe the boy was fair, or maybe dark-haired."

"Cullen lacks the wit to invent such a story. Injustice makes him accurate."

Will swore. "Cullen lacks the wit to see anything beyond his nose."

"Kit was alive a year ago."

"Dream on. Cullen's boy was mute. Or did you miss that fact?"

It was an old argument, not worth pursuing, and they walked on in silence. In Will's mind, it was plain that Kit was dead. They were searching for bones to bury and an end to hope.

Xander didn't accept that. Maybe because he was to blame for Kit's disappearance. "You've said all along that every drab, every bullyboy is tied to someone in power, someone who knows something. Cullen's just the first step."

Will grabbed Xander's coat and spun him to a halt. "If Kit's alive and free, why hasn't he come home? If he is, or *was*, Cullen's mute boy, why didn't he come home a year ago? You burn enough bleeding candles he could find the way from France."

Xander shook off his brother's rough hold. It was a hard question, but there would be an answer. Xander had read the Bills of Mortality for nearly three years and investigated the deaths of countless children. In all that time, in all those losses, he was sure no child, no matter how nameless, had been Kit. But, as Will demanded, if Kit was not dead, where was he? Was the man with fists the one who had taken him? Had the man acted alone? Was there some threat or some harm that kept Kit from coming back to them? If he had escaped his captor or captors, how did he live and where, and what had he endured?

Once again the unanswered questions escaped the dark corners of Xander's mind and clamored for his notice. At the next turning Isaiah waited with the carriage.

"Cullen's story doesn't mean that Kit's in London, you know." Will stood at the curb. "He could have been sold to some damned sodomite ship captain for a cabin boy and be halfway around the world."

Xander paused, staring into the darkness. He stood not a mile from where Kit disappeared. No lamps illuminated the way. Only a faint glow came from behind grimy windows. It was a dark place to experience sudden clarity of mind. In a space smaller than one of his father's grand estates lived thousands of Londoners like Cullen, dogged, soured by life, scrambling to survive, men and women down on their luck. Two of them had seen Kit *alive* within the last year.

Maybe it wasn't a clear mind after all, maybe it was just an untwisting of his gut, released from gnawing uncertainty, but Xander felt the rightness of it. Of all the fates they had feared for Kit, he could only have one fate after all, and this was it.

When Xander had first brought the news of Kit's disappearance to their mother, she had cried out, "They've taken him," and swooned. Her reaction had fixed in Xander's mind the idea of a conspiracy, of a plot to sell boys for profit. Cullen's story refuted that theory. Kit's fate was this. In a crime of opportunity, a stranger, an odd man, almost a goblin of the night, had snatched the boy.

Xander swung himself up into the coach. Tomorrow he knew where to begin. The East London Gas Company would pry open Bread Street, with money, with ale, with picks and axes, with whatever it took to unearth the secret of Kit's disappearance. Maybe he would have to offer an army of Cullens free beer to loosen their tongues.

CLEO found Charlie flopped on a low bed in a room under the attic ceiling, his nose in a book. It was a boy's room, furnished with worn wood and wool, plain and homey. Nothing like the room her husband had assigned to her.

Candles burned in all the sconces and in a lamp on a table by the bed. A coal fire blazed extravagantly in the small hearth. A framed map of the world and a pair of hanging shelves crammed with books filled the wall above the nicked table and plain chair. A stack of faded quilts covered an old trunk next to a pine wardrobe, its door ajar. Charlie's discarded valise lay on the floor in a corner.

Cleo knocked and Charlie looked up. "What did you find?"

"Ben Franklin." He held up his book.

"Really?" Cleo came and sat on the bed. Charlie rolled over and pushed himself up against the headboard.

"Bluebeard didn't murder you, I guess."

"Not yet. Shooting, drowning, beheading, and dismemberment were mentioned, however."

Charlie's eyes widened. "I counted twenty closets on the way up here," he confided. "Oh, the house is all light and fine furnishings, but the man has secrets. Did you see how many keys his servant Amos has? I tried some of the closet doors. All locked."

"I was bamming you. I'm here, alive, and you look cozy enough."

Charlie had the grace to look sheepish. "It is a bit, like my old room."

Cleo peered at a small, framed saying over the bed, trying to make out the letters in blue stitching on plain muslin.

> *Are all the dragons fled?*
> *Are all the goblins dead?*
> *Am I quite safe in bed?*

The words made her smile. Likely her fearsome

husband had been a boy in this room once with a
no-nonsense nurse who tucked him in with a rhyme to
banish his fear of the dark. She shook her head at the
idea. She could not imagine Xander Jones ever needing anyone's comforting embrace, but he had once
been Charlie's age, and once, younger still, and there
had been no father. At least she did not know what his
relationship with his father had been. The Marquess of
Candover had a pair of daughters, the Lyndhurst girls.
Cleo had known them, had been present at Sally Lyndhurst's come-out, a grand affair. She was sure Xander
could not have escaped the knowledge that his father's
heirs danced and glittered mere blocks away. Yet, if this
had been his room, someone had cared for him and even
loved him as a child.

"Do you think we've sold our souls for clean sheets,
real candles, and someone to carry coals?"

"No." *And some of us haven't even succeeded in sell-
ing our bodies.*

Charlie yawned and slipped down against the pillows. "We aren't ever going home again, are we, Cleo?
Not really."

"What a thing to say!" She rumpled his hair, the
one gesture of affection he permitted her these days.
"You are going home as soon as you come of age, and
I will live here, not a mile distant. We will see each
other every day, and if you don't marry at once, I will
come and redecorate your whole house in the Egyptian
style." She swung her legs off the bed and headed for
the door.

"If your husband doesn't murder you and March
doesn't take me away."

"Sorry. You'll not be so lucky. Shall I predict your fate like an oracle?" Cleo held her arm before her eyes. "Wait, I see your doom—a haircut, new clothes, and hours of work with the best grinder we can find, and by January term—school."

Chapter Seven

❧

CLEO did not have her knife handy when she encountered her new husband at breakfast. He had returned to the house some time after two, while she lay sleepless in the unfamiliar bed, in the restless city. Apparently, neither her money, which he now controlled, nor her person, which he refused, had the power to move him.

In the night his footsteps had paused outside her door and passed, and the blaze of light in his house had gone dark.

Now he sat over an untouched plate, reading a pamphlet from a stack in front of him, looking sartorially splendid and entirely too rested. She, on the other hand, in an old green wool dress, looked as seductive as a dusty yew tree. And she did not have the first idea how to coax her husband to her bed. She would have to relearn the arts of allurement.

His gaze met hers briefly. "You don't have to rise for breakfast."

"Would you rather I lay abed in silks, sipping chocolate while you go to the bank?"

He returned to his reading, and Cleo stepped to the sideboard, loaded with platters of eggs and ham, toast, and pots of jam. She filled a plate and took her place at the table.

Her husband quirked one dark brow upward.

"Am I looking with too much longing on the ham?"

"I won't let you or your brother starve."

"I suppose I am so used to our lacks that it will take me a while to grow accustomed to abundance."

He handed her a week-old issue of the morning paper, folded open to a three-line announcement of their union under the heading "MARRIED." The paper listed their nuptials with singular appropriateness in a long column of commercial transactions between "PARTNERSHIP DISSOLVED" and "DIED."

Cleo put down the paper. "It's official then. I may confidently take up my wifely duties."

He did not look up. "Would you consider attending a dinner sufficiently wifely?"

"Will it stop Uncle March?"

At the mention of her uncle, his cool gaze met hers. Nothing betrayed his feelings about her question.

"It will help."

"I have nothing to wear. How is that for a wifely response?"

"I've sent for a dressmaker."

Ahead of her again. "After our trip to the bank, of course." Cleo had a long list of plans for her funds.

He put down his pamphlet. "I'm not going to the bank today."

"But we agreed. My brother needs clothes and a tutor for his entrance exams. He needs a haircut." Cleo's plate clinked as she put it down. Now that he had access to her money, her husband was going back on their bargain. She had pinned too much hope on a solicitor's papers and that kiss in the church.

Once, she had accepted kisses, as if she were collecting tributes to her desirability. Her entrance into London society had been managed by a widowed cousin of her father who had been careless at best in her approach to Cleo's debut. Cousin Lydia's advice had been—*You're greener than grass in May, and they'll all be about you for your papa's money, so mind your step*—a fair warning that Cleo herself would be of little interest to men.

But oh, how London could go to a girl's head. To Miss Cleopatra Spencer it seemed that the whole glittering city was present and took notice when she entered a ballroom. She knew better now, or thought she did. Xander Jones was teaching her still more lessons in her own insignificance. London loved money even more than beauty and would flatter and court those who had it as long as they had it, and drop them when it was gone.

The morning room door opened, and Will Jones sauntered in, unshaven and ripe-smelling. "Did you find it?" he asked his brother without any acknowledgment of Cleo's presence.

Xander Jones held up the pamphlet. "A plasterer named Harris died at Number Forty Bread Street last November."

"That confirms only one part of Cullen's story." Will turned to the sideboard.

Cleo stole a glance at the pamphlet. The Bills of Mortality. Xander Jones was reading the weekly printed record of those who died in London. He had a stack of them beside him on the table. Her breakfast congealed on the pretty plate. She put down her fork. Uncle March read them, too, a habit of his she'd discovered when he moved into their house following her father's death.

Will Jones immediately began to fill a plate. "You're not coming with me dressed like that," he said over his shoulder to Xander. He glanced at Cleo. "She'd do better on Bread Street than you. Put a greasy apron around her middle, and she'll fit right in."

"She's not going near Bread Street," Xander said.

"Good morning to you, too," Cleo said to her brother-in-law. He paused in his plate loading but offered no greeting. The two brothers seemed different because of the contrast in their dress, but now Cleo could see that both had the same hard-edged profile.

The scrape of Will Jones's serving spoon filled the ensuing pause.

"Go naked then, Xan, or come by my place. I've got proper rags for you." Will Jones sat down next to Cleo and dug into the mound of buttered eggs and ham on his plate. Cleo wondered that he could enjoy them with all the smells that emanated from his clothes. Smoke and stale spirits dominated the mix. She shifted to give him room.

He stiffened and shot her a caustic glance. Then he leaned close, one beery shoulder nudging hers, and said, "It's not polite to think ill of people." He righted himself and stabbed a piece of ham. "But"—he winked at her—"it's very smart."

Cleo turned to her husband. "We have a bargain about the bank."

"When I go, you go." He rose and withdrew his pocketbook and put a stack of bank notes on the table. "Amos gives a good haircut. I recommend Mr. Hodge as a grinder. Tomorrow Serena Perez is coming to fit you with some clothes."

"Am I restricted to the house then?"

His level gaze didn't change. "Go where you wish. Alice will accompany you. Local tradesmen are quite accustomed to calling. Even at this house."

The door closed behind him.

She stared at her plate, her appetite gone. She had intended no insult. She knew that tradesmen would call. She was just out of practice with London ways. Her shoulders slumped. It was a poor start to a campaign of seduction.

Beside her Will Jones ate steadily. The scrape of his knife and fork against the china filled her ears. After a minute he stood and leaned over her. She could see his empty plate. "Next time, love, choose your ground more carefully. The battle won't be won over eggs and a rasher of bacon."

XANDER stood at the foot of Bread Street, choking on its foulness and thinking inconvenient thoughts about his wife. He had dreamed of her naked. She had been under his roof less than a day. He had spent three-quarters of an hour with her in the company of his lawyer, had walked by her closed door, had banished knowledge of her nearness from his conscious mind in the last minutes before sleep, and still she had invaded his dreams, had stepped down the hall on light feet in a white lawn shift to stand beside his dreaming self, reproach and invitation in those green eyes. His unconscious mind had reached for her like a beggar.

He was long past unprofitable fantasies about gently bred ladies. At seventeen he had fallen in love and proposed marriage to a widow. Newly arrived at Oxford, he had broken his collarbone in a football match. When his friends carried him to the nearest house, Anne Reede had opened her back sitting room and eventually her arms to him.

In pain, and under the influence of his first and only dose of laudanum, he had been unable to leave the makeshift bed arranged in her sitting room. In that waking daze Anne had passed in and out of his sight, a gentle vision in gray silks, unhurried, unruffled, caring with sweet sternness and ready laughter to her own small boys. She handled his friends' inquiries with ease and authority, and had procured from them some necessities for his comfort.

On the third day she had shaved and bathed him, and his sleeplessness had had an entirely new cause. She came to bid him goodnight, her own sleepy boys clinging to her skirts, her hands idly ruffling their hair, and he had fallen irrevocably in love. With her unerring perceptiveness she understood his need before he did, and for all her quiet voice and calm manner, she contained a storm of passion. When she became his lover, he learned how strong a streak of sensuality his nature possessed. He offered marriage.

She refused him with gentle firmness, but when he took his suit to her family, they removed her to the south and married her to a man of standing in the world. His collarbone healed perfectly.

So Xander knew a man might dream of fairy princesses locked in their high towers, but princesses always came with nasty dragons. Even an unwanted princess, like Cleo Spencer, had March. It made no sense then that from their first meeting, he had been aware of an electric attraction, more than he had felt in years for any woman. His nerves trapped the charge of her presence, bottling up a most inconvenient desire when his plan was to end their marriage as soon as he found Kit.

Her demand that they make a babe was no part of that plan. To imagine her with his babe at her breast was like offering the dragon a piece of toast on a stick. A babe was permanent. A babe tied two people into a bargain or a contest that could last a lifetime and that did the babe very little good. A babe became an inconvenient boy, stuffed in a closet, blind and choked, ears filled with voices that deceived, accused, blamed, and parted.

He would not bed his bride, and he would banish her from his dreams.

In front of him Bread Street was real enough. It twisted up a slight hill to the west. Buildings of crumbling lath and plaster, soot-blackened brick, and rotting wood tilted against one another, their steep roofs at crazy angles. A foul trickle ran along both curbs and disappeared in black gully holes at the edge of the cobbles. Men and women slouched in and out of the public house on the lower east side and in and out of the fish shop where the curve of Upper Bread Street began. Strings of crisp-fried, shiny brown bloaters hung in the window, six for a penny. Below the fish shop the street opened to the east on a wide, rubbish-filled court.

A group of idlers, as filthy and oddly sorted as the buildings around them, slumped on a low set of steps opposite the court. A stranger who tried pass to them, even in rags, faced a reckoning. They knew their own. A man from a rival street or a lost soul would be set upon, stripped of his possessions, and left to come to consciousness on the foul stones with only the lint in his pockets. According to Will even the police rarely ventured to enter the neighborhood and always came in sufficient numbers for self-defense.

The idlers roused themselves to jeer as a woman at an upper window tossed out the contents of a night soil pot, narrowly missing a donkey cart driver. A grimy urchin with an empty beer can seized the moment to dart from one of the basement dwellings past the loafers, headed for the pub.

Not a chance. A large, leather-faced fellow snagged the boy with one long arm and dangled him by his scrawny legs, shaking loose a few coppers from his pocket. The child slunk back toward his hole with a tear-streaked face.

"Welcome to Bread Street," Will mumbled at Xander's side. "Ready?"

Xander nodded. The loose, outlandish clothes felt freeing. He'd have no trouble swinging a fist in the purple velvet jacket Will had insisted he wear over a checkered waistcoat and baggy breeches. They were supposed to be pugs, prizefighters who had made it out of the rookery by the smashing skill of their fists, coming back to lord it over those whose grand escapes remained mere daydreams. Their movement drew all eyes.

"We'd do better to come with a detachment of the Ninety-fifth," Will said. "That lot won't talk to us. We got lucky with Cullen because he wanted to complain about being sacked."

Xander kept moving, a deliberate challenge to the idlers, violating their territory. They exchanged sly glances, though not so much as a finger moved.

Even in full day, the narrow street was a place of shadows. Xander could see where his gas line would have to go and where to mount the lamps to cast the most illumination on the street. His mind began calculating. "I could hire forty men, women, too. Put a hoarding up on that building there. Offer decent wages."

Will laughed. "Hire that lot? They don't know what work is. They think doing a click is work. You put tools in their hands, they'll break each other's heads with them."

"They need money."

"But pour it down their throats. Cullen's not the only thirsty sot in the neighborhood. Drink and gaming take any extra blunt that comes their way."

"Some will jump at the chance to earn a wage," Xander insisted. The thing in a man that was a man wanted to be recognized in spite of rags and dirt. "I'll put up hoardings there. Cash will draw them, and someone will talk."

They reached the midpoint of the street. The leather-faced fellow of button-popping girth pushed away from the building against which he leaned, and the others followed. The ends of sticks and rods, protruding from ragged sleeves, filled their lax hands.

Will took up the accent of the street. "We're lookin' for Mother Greenslade about a room."

The idlers plainly doubted. "Maybe yer lookin' for a mill."

"Just Mother Greenslade." Xander shifted on his feet at the man's blatant challenge.

The big man's glance sized them up. "Yer a pair of skirts, then, that won't come up to scratch."

An unholy grin broke on Will's face. "I don't know. My brother 'ere"—he thumped Xander on the back— "is always game for a bout. A short contest, lads?" He drew a leather purse from his coat and got their full attention. "Right hands tied in back. First man to three hits with his left wins five pounds."

The idlers could not believe their luck. Easy pickings. They shuffled into a half circle behind the big man. Xander watched as the fellow slipped the long iron rod out of his sleeve and submitted to having his right arm, now weaponless, tied back.

Xander shrugged out of his coat and let one of the crowd tie his arm back with his shirt. Narrowed eyes assessed his build. Someone drew a charcoal line on the cobbles for them to toe. The combatants stepped up to shouts of encouragement for the local champion.

"Do 'im, Bob!"

"First one to get in three hits," Will reminded them. He dropped his raised arm.

Bob flung his great fist at Xander like a boulder. Xander leaned back a fraction, turning his head and letting the blow roll past him, Bob's knuckles just grazing his cheek. In reply Xander's left shot out straight from the shoulder and cracked his opponent's nose. Blood spurted. Bob shook his head, spattering the onlookers. Falling back, he swung again wildly. Xander ducked and rose, evading the big man's long reach. The crowd howled and stirred, egging Bob on. He squared himself and pulled back a third time. The huge fist was still swinging Xander's way when he administered two more unerring jabs to the man's crumpled nose.

Will yelled, "Three!" and stepped between the combatants. The big man staggered back from the line, air gushing noisily through his flowing nostrils.

Will held the leather purse aloft. "Gents, the purse can still be yours. We're looking for Mother Greenslade."

"She's takin' an 'oliday for 'er 'ealth." The bleeding man's second pressed a filthy cloth to his gushing nose.

"Sometimes people talk that ought not to talk," said another.

"It's a fact." Will shrugged. "You can tell 'er we want rooms at Number Forty. Gentlemen, thanks for the sport." He tossed the leather purse high into the air and nudged Xander into motion as a scramble started behind them.

Xander freed his right arm and shrugged back into his shirt and purple coat. "Were you trying to get me killed?"

"Good thing you've still got that left."

"I haven't thrown a punch in three years."

Will shrugged. "I'd say you were overdue, and don't tell me this place doesn't make you want to smash something."

Xander kept moving until he came abreast of Number Forty at the edge of the open court. The building had no door, just a gaping hole where a door had been, long since burned for fuel, or broken up and used in battle with neighboring streets. At street level, two dark, mine-like openings with multiple numbers tacked to the jambs led to basement rooms. Rows of empty pint pots marked each entrance.

Above him in the room Cullen now had, Kit had been chained. Will was right. Xander wanted to smash something. Up the street he could see Cullen's view of the backyard of Truman's Brewery. Above the crumbling brick wall that surrounded the brewery were three wooden vats, dark with age, each over twenty feet high.

"Now there's a sight for a thirsty man," Will said. "No wonder Cullen's throat is bone-dry. He looks at ten thousand gallons of ale every day and knows he lost his free wet."

Opposite the brewery the brick corner of a plain, dark building poked a sharp edge onto Bread Street.

"Bredsell's school?" Xander asked.

Will nodded. Both the brewery and the school stood with their backs to Bread Street, as if the place offended.

"Does Bredsell get all his boys from the court?" Xander asked.

"He offers them cake."

"Cake?" Cullen had mentioned Mother Greenslade bringing cake to the chained boy.

"I'm serious. He offers the boys cake. Never underestimate the power of wanting something you can't have."

Xander glanced back down Bread Street to the knot of idlers. Change Bread Street and change London. "I'll put up signs tomorrow."

S HEPHERD Market was the last stop in Cleo and Charlie's outing, a tangle of streets with shops favored by the servants of Mayfair. In the maze of narrow streets, where their father had taken them both as children, they gawked at shop wares hanging from the awnings and exclaimed over the season's last apples piled high in hawkers' carts. The Flying Pieman went by, all in white, with his powdered wig and tray of hot puddings. They had milk at the dairy on Queen Street, stopped to watch a puppet show, and Cleo gave alms for the first time in four years to the old soldier sweeping the crossing at Charles Street. She thought for a moment that he knew her, but the recognition faded from his glance almost instantly.

She had not enjoyed spending her advance from Xander Jones rather than her own money, but it was only practical to order calling cards for herself and shirts and breeches for Charlie. With her last coins they bought gingerbread men to sustain them on the walk home.

Cleo had forgotten that unspeaking Alice was with them until her voice made them both turn.

"That boy is following us, ma'am."

"What boy?"

"A boy with white teeth and a dark blue cap." Alice's gaze was fixed on the crowd outside the gingerbread shop.

Cleo swept a glance back at the market. Dozens of

people maneuvered in the narrow street, errand boys among them, bustling about their business. An empty doorway caught Cleo's eye. A jackdaw in a wicker cage squawked. Hadn't there been a shop boy leaning there where doormats and birdcages hung, cap pulled over his eyes and grimy apron about his waist? The boy had been so still Cleo could not be sure whether she had seen him or imagined him. Now the doorway was empty.

Chapter Eight

❧

CHARLIE woke late in the unfamiliar room. Bright morning light startled him upright. He threw off the covers and swung his feet to a warm carpeted floor before he remembered he was on Hill Street, not in his room at Fernhill Farm. He had neither chores to do nor Bess to thump her tail and hurry him along, and Cleo had not sent for him, either.

He curled his toes in the carpet and ran a hand through his hair, trying to recall Cleo's plans for the day. He was sure she had plans. He had a feeling he was neglecting important duties. It was as if he had returned to an earlier time in his life. The room around him seemed to belong to his younger self, filled with possessions like those he had prized before they fled London to live on the farm.

His Greek and Latin books looked out of place on

the boy's desk. In this room he could not believe that he had already memorized his Greek vocables and made his way through Aesop and the *Anabasis*. This morning he could not remember any Greek at all. So how could he be ready for Herodotus? He knew he wasn't ready for Latin.

His stomach knotted as much with uncertainty as hunger. He was supposed to prepare for his entrance examinations, but he had no idea what passages the school examiners would set him for the tests. And really, his schooling depended on whether Cleo's marriage freed them from Uncle March.

It felt strange to be so near their old home and not in it. He knew Cleo had avoided taking them too close yesterday, but he wondered if Uncle March knew where they were and what he would do. Cleo believed Sir Alexander Jones would protect them from March, but why would Bluebeard protect them from anyone?

He stood and stretched and squared his shoulders and told himself he was older now; he was supposed to protect her. He was taller than Cleo, even though she had ruffled his hair last night as if he were still the boy he had been when they'd left London. He tried to summon a feeling of courage and strength, but felt instead a twinge in his stomach. He'd had a moment of weakness in the coach when he gave her the pig-sticking knife. The lowering thought that he had no courage at all made his shoulders slump.

In the market when Alice had said they were being followed, he had felt a red-faced consciousness of his mistake with the knife. He'd seen no danger, but he'd had no weapon. At least this morning Cleo was safe. He remembered that she was meeting with the dressmaker at the house. He was free to study after breakfast. That was the plan.

Once again his stomach complained. A man needed to eat to have strength. The kitchen was three floors away. He'd been there last night, and he would have to pass by Jones's silent servants to get there. They reminded him of old Hades' three-headed dog, Cerberus.

The good thing about hunger, he thought, was that it made a fellow brave enough to face a dog.

A FTER breakfast on the morning of her second day back in London, Cleo found Serena Perez, olive-skinned, raven-haired, and disapproving, waiting for her in the well-furnished back parlor of Xander Jones's house. La Perez drew two elegant curving black brows together in a serious frown as Cleo entered. Gowns hung in linen bags on a rod stretched between two tall cases. A cheval glass stood in the far corner, a sturdy deal box before it.

Cleo had to admit that she offered a challenge to even the most clever of modistes. In her four years at Fernhill Farm she had abandoned one by one the rituals of fashionable dress that had once been second nature to her. Alice offered a thin, reassuring smile.

"To begin madam is to have three gowns," the Spanish woman announced. With a shrug of her shoulders and a snap of imperious fingers at her sharp-featured assistant, she ordered Cleo up onto the box and set to work stripping her of her worn green wool. At least a good coal fire burned in the grate.

Still there was a moment of shocked silence when Cleo stood in her mended shift, loose corset, and thin drawers. Cleo faced three pairs of dismayed eyes. She knew that hopeless look. Plainly, they thought her personal charms utterly unequal to the task of making a presentable wife for Xander Jones. No one moved.

"He does not expect miracles, does he?" The Spanish woman plainly spoke to herself. No one answered.

Cleo regarded herself in the glass. She could not remember the girl she had been. She rather liked the sturdy, unadorned person in the mirror, but she knew that person would be invisible to London eyes, and Xander Jones was a Londoner to the core.

"With such a man, one has little time and many rivals. We must make no mistakes." The Spanish woman's doubt was palpable. She looked at the gowns hanging in their linen cocoons and back at Cleo.

Cleo squared her shoulders. She had Charlie's pig-sticking knife. Perhaps she could get the señora to devise a special pocket in each gown so that she could have the knife handy for persuading her reluctant husband to bed her in spite of her lack of feminine charms.

The señora recovered first. She clapped her hands, and her assistant sprang into action, opening a case. The señora flung forth shifts and stockings and garters and corsets, while the assistant spread them like lolling tarts over the blue damask sofa. For endless minutes La Perez looked from that display of soft, floating femininity to Cleo as if she were trying to solve an impossible puzzle. At last the dressmaker plucked up a set of beautiful undergarments with lace edges and deep pink ribbons.

"These. At once." She waved her elegant, long-fingered hands at Cleo and Alice and stepped out of the room.

Cleo had a moment to digest the obvious. Her new husband had a world of intimate knowledge about women. None of which he had gained by having a sister. He claimed to have no mistress, but he had not used Senora Perez's talents to make drapery for his drawing room.

When Alice had helped Cleo into the new underclothes, Serena Perez sent the girl away to burn the offending rags. "Now we begin."

The Spanish woman circled Cleo, appraising her with sharp black eyes. In English with only a hint of her native Spain she talked about Cleo as if she weren't there. "Good shoulders. Arms like sticks." She took a pinch of Cleo's left arm between strong fingers and shook her head. "Skin brown, but clear." She shrugged her shoulders. "There is nothing to be done about such a plain nose, but with a new corset we can give the breasts more emphasis." She nodded. "Two breasts pull more than four horses."

Again Cleo stood gazing at herself in the glass undergoing the dressmaker's dismayed scrutiny. She looked as straight and brown as a beech tree in winter with a dusting of snow.

With a deep sigh Serena Perez at last nodded to her assistant, who opened the hanging bags, gently laying out three gowns of jewellike radiance, copper, garnet, and emerald.

CHARLIE's luck held, and he encountered no servants on the way to the kitchen. There he found a woman who, in spite of layers of skirts and aprons, was a bony stick. She vigorously stirred batter in a large crockery bowl.

"You, boy," she growled at him. "What do you want?"

Charlie didn't even start at the gruff voice. Taking in the bubbling pots, a ham as big as a pumpkin, a large round of blue-veined cheese, and the warm smell of baking that filled the room, he instinctively understood the woman in the puffy white cap. She was a woman whose very nature required her to put food in front of other people, the more the better. Her greatest pleasure would be to watch a hungry boy consume her offerings. Charlie knew exactly how to compose his features in a look that would make this gruff woman happy. Bess could not have done it better.

Thus he was sitting at a long, plain table, spreading raspberry preserves on a biscuit, helping Cook fulfill her purpose on the planet, and having a rather pleasant daydream in which he told Uncle March that he and Cleo were taking back their own home, when his mysterious brother-in-law entered the kitchen from the garden.

The daydream evaporated like steam from a pot when Cook lifted the lid, and Charlie knew himself for a boy again. He stood at once.

"Sir." His brother-in-law carried his elegant coat and cravat over one arm, making his breadth of shoulder more striking.

"Good morning. Mrs. Wardlow's taking good care of you, I see."

"She is, sir."

"May I join you?"

Charlie nodded, unable to speak. He tried to find some reference to place the man's way of moving.

Farmer Davies did not move in the same easy, contained way. Mr. Tucker's shuffle had none of the power in it that Charlie sensed in his sister's husband.

"You can sit, Charlie."

Mrs. Wardlow put a plate of cold chicken in front of her employer and set a foaming pint pot on the table. When his left hand took up the knife, Charlie spotted the scraped knuckles.

Mrs. Wardlow saw them, too, and put a jar of salve on the table.

Inexplicably, while Cook fussed over them, bringing sliced apples and plum cake, Charlie found himself explaining the Latin problem to the man sitting across from him. Not the knife problem. He would have to figure out how to recover the knife and get some courage on his own. He knew enough about courage to know that.

"I can get you a Latin lexicon from the study," his brother-in-law offered.

C LEO's arms ached, and she seemed to be wearing a nettle shirt. Pins pricked her back and breasts and under her arms. All three gowns had been adjusted to her figure, and still La Perez was not satisfied.

"Take down your hair," she ordered Cleo.

Cleo dutifully pulled the pins, and her curls tumbled down around her shoulders.

La Perez nodded, studying Cleo with the same intensity she had shown through the morning. At that moment the parlor door opened, and the dressmaker, turning to frown at the intrusion, froze. Xander Jones's gaze, hot and startled, met Cleo's in the mirror and held.

He had evidently not expected to find his bride standing on a box in dishabille. Cleo tried vainly to read the intent flickering there.

Here in his luxurious house where a curving marble nymph displayed her lush charms at the base of the stairs, Cleo stood like a brown crockery jug on the kitchen shelf. His naked gaze made her conscious of her bare feet and loose hair and the way her breasts swelled against their constraint. She lifted her chin.

"Blame my parents if you will for the folly of naming an infant after a great Egyptian seductress and then bequeathing on her a plain English nose, square jaw, and scant charms."

Her husband did not seem to hear her.

"Is it there, sir?" Charlie's voice came from behind her husband's shoulder.

At the sound, her husband's lashes came down over his burning gaze. Cleo's last glimpse of him was that lean, brown hand taut on the doorknob. She heard him speaking with Charlie about Latin, the easy rumble of his voice sending a shiver through her.

"Ah," said the Spanish woman, "now it is decided. First, the copper gown, for courage. A dinner with the partners, yes? They will snap like dogs." For the first time in a long day, the Spanish woman smiled, an ally's conspiratorial smile.

"I will bring the copper gown in three days."

I T took Cleo three days to spend her way to her husband's notice. Each morning she interviewed potential grinders for Charlie from the notices in the paper.

Superior Classical Education, 3s 6d per hour. In the afternoons, she shopped. At night her invisible husband escaped her company, but she heard him pause outside her door before the blaze of light in his house went dark. She heard no word from her uncle or her husband's lawyer. It was possible, she supposed, that Uncle March thought her marriage suitable after all, but in case he did not, she had to get Charlie into school.

On Friday evening she stood on her balcony, a new shawl wrapped around her oldest brown cambric muslin, staring at the flickering shadows in the garden below when Alice knocked to tell her she'd been summoned to the master's library.

Xander looked up as his wife halted inside the library door and caught a fleeting smile on her lips. She had buried his desk in receipts, like white leaves raked up in a pile.

When she lifted her head, their gazes locked. Her faint smile faded at once, and a tremor shook her. She was right to distrust him.

He took one of the thin sheets in his hand and let it drop again without reading it. "I take it you wanted to see me."

She kept that green gaze level. "I merely insist on keeping our bargain, a weekly exchange of receipts."

Oh, their bargain. He, of course, had been thinking other thoughts when he'd summoned her. "I admire your energy. Did you patronize every establishment in Mayfair?"

"All those that cater to ladies."

He glanced at another of the receipts, for seven yards of brown cambric from Hodgekinson, the linen draper.

In spite of the sheer volume of paper, her bills could easily be settled with a trip to Evershot's bank. Or he could have had Amos deal with them. Instead he had summoned her to his library.

"Apparently, you have a fondness for brown cambric and potatoes. Mrs. Wardlow tells me forty pounds of potatoes, at ten pence a twenty-weight no less, arrived for her larder. Are you afraid I'll starve you?"

"I promised Charlie we'd eat them every day." She took a stand in front of the mantel, facing him, her arms crossed in the folds of a fine patterned shawl.

"Mrs. Wardlow has no good opinion of potatoes, food for the lower orders, so she says." He watched the little stiffening of her spine and the interesting way the move lifted her bosom.

"I'm sorry to offend Mrs. Wardlow's sensibilities, but with butter and cream, potatoes are truly . . . comforting."

He had scrupulously avoided her from the moment he'd opened the back parlor door to see her clad in thin lawn and white lace. Now even in faded brown cambric, a color as vivid as potato sacks, she was fully alive. Her presence in the room occupied all his senses, made him unseeing, unthinking.

Blindly he picked up another receipt. "Apparently you're spreading all these guineas about for Charlie. Gunter's for ices in October?"

"You think I spoil him, I'm sure."

"He's your brother."

"I know you have a brother, but it's not the same, is it? Your brother is not young and vulnerable. You don't fear to lose him."

He rose. Again she managed in her frank way to spear him with a careless remark. Warily, she watched his approach. For a woman who claimed to want a babe, she looked remarkably uneasy in her husband's presence. He stopped in front of her.

"You know I can't compete with you in extravagance," she said.

"You try, however."

"I'm not the one who burns candles at a rate to outdo the royal household."

"No point in a meager glow." He lifted her drooping shawl around her shoulders and did not miss the quick catch in her breath at his touch. It was only a brief hesitation. She plunged into speech in a strategy he was coming to recognize. Whenever he made her uneasy, words tumbled out of her.

"This household burns a week's worth of candles per room per night. Amos and Alice spend hours cutting wicks, removing wax, and filling and cleaning lamps. It's a wonder they find time for any other household duties."

"You like potatoes. I like light." He said it lightly, easily. He did not think he gave away anything, but the green eyes watched him intently, and he caught a dangerous glint of sympathy in their depths.

Coals shifted in the grate. A warm current of air stirred her skirts. He steeled himself to ignore the faint brush of them against his leg. He didn't want her sympathy. Sympathy and desire made a bad mix, and he knew better than to confuse the two.

"Blindman's bluff is not your game, is it? One would think you had been cast into the outer darkness as a child, brought up in a cave, raised like a mole, and now you crave light . . ."

With a quick press of his fingers against her mouth, he cut her off. He shook his head at her. "My turn."

She closed her lips under his touch, and he released her. He could stop that mouth with his own, but then they would both be lost.

She recovered first. "You have receipts?"

"You buried them." He took her by the arm and led her to the door. "But here's a rough accounting of my spending. This week the East London Gas Company bought two hundred shovels, a thousand wash box scrubbers, fifty gauges, two tons of coal, and ten thousand feet of thirty-six-inch pipe."

"I can't compete with that."

He opened the library door. "The first of your gowns has arrived. When Amos is through lighting candles, I'll have him bring it to your room."

A FTER dinner, the great room of Arthur Fuller's Conduit Street house held all the partners of the Metropolitan Works Group and their ladies quite comfortably. While the cardplayers staked a place for themselves around a pair of tables, and Mrs. Dimsdale claimed the pianoforte and began to play, six gentlemen found Xander's wife in her copper brocade dress.

With the perfect clarity of hindsight, he realized that asking his mother's good friend Serena Perez to dress his bride had been an error. He hardly recognized her as the ragamuffin from the bank. Tonight as she turned from one man to another, or as she laughed, her burnished curls caught the light and glowed.

He accepted a cup of coffee from his hostess and attached himself to the group listening to the earnest piano player. Except for their brief meeting in the library, he had avoided her. He had already learned more about her than he'd planned. She wore no scent, and yet a presence that was *her* lingered in his senses. Unexpected encounters with her were particularly hazardous to his plan, and until he rid his dreams of her, it made sense to keep his distance. He simply had to endure the public scenes necessary to his plan.

Tonight's dinner among his staid and respectable partners had seemed safe in theory, a far cry from the company of his youthful evenings. Proper ladies in yards of silk and trimmings surrounded him, but Xander could think only of clinging lawn and fluttering pink ribbons, a narrow waist, flaring hips, and long legs. A clock chimed, and he shifted his gaze away from his wife, aware of the war of contradictory desires inside him—to dismiss her from his mind and to release her hair from its pins and lay her down under him.

Cleo counted the little clock's chimes. She had allowed her husband to ignore her through the interminable dinner. She understood his situation better now. He was the lone wolf in this particular pack of dogs. They might all chase a hare with baying enthusiasm, but only he would hunt his prey.

Something she'd said in the library had touched a sorrow in him. She had seen its shadow in his face and held her breath, waiting for him to speak, and when he had not, she had been unable to contain her exasperation. Now she extricated herself from the gentlemen around her and went to his side.

If he sensed her presence, he did not turn until the piano player finished her piece. Other women slanted him admiring glances from a safe distance.

"You know some women might prefer a carved stone husband, a piece of statuary to stand in the garden, or a bust to put in a niche."

"Would that suit you?"

"As long as the statue came with a bank account."

He laughed, a pleasant, easy sound, and looked at her fully.

Cleo tried to take the measure of that reluctant gaze—admiring or critical. "You misled me grossly with the term 'dinner party.' This is like no party I ever attended."

"What makes it so different in your experience?"

"No flirting."

He watched her still. It was a perfectly public moment, but his gaze felt intimate as if the guests around them had turned to indifferent shrubbery.

"Do you know there is a young man here seriously concerned about the number of flushes per each new water closet in London? He fears that the Thames will be an open sewer in ten years."

"You met Tom Ruxley, I take it?"

She nodded.

"The state of the sewers didn't provoke your wit?"

She shook her head. The low gravel of his voice seemed to waken her skin. Cleo could hardly name the thing that he stirred in her, a need to be naked that fluttered with helpless wings against the cage of her stays and silks.

"Did you meet Miss Finsbury at such an event? If you did, it would explain much."

"I didn't. You aren't expecting me to flirt with you?"

"If you do not, I must suppose it's my matronly appearance that quells your ardor. Do I look wifely enough, do you think?"

"I hardly recognize you without the straw."

"Thank you for the gown." It was all wrong for their staid company. She had known it from the moment they'd entered, a gown for a mistress perhaps, but her hostess, a woman of great tact, had set an accepting tone. The gossip would start later.

"It suits you." His glance shifted away, and Cleo felt the loss of it.

"And the undergarments, the shoes, the cloak, the jewels. Did I leave anything out?"

"The stockings." His coffee cup now seemed to have his undivided attention.

"You're remarkably thorough and knowledgeable in the matter of women's apparel. To think I accused you of not knowing the female mind. Have you dressed many women?"

He swung back to her, pressing his warm, strong thumb to her lips, just as he had done in the church, in the library, a response so swift, Cleo could only blink.

"Am I making you uneasy?" His thumb slid away, leaving her lips tingling and hungry.

"Why?"

"Because you generally say something outrageous when you're nervous."

The pianist took up a new, livelier tune. They stood shoulder to shoulder in silence while the sound of the party grew loud around them. There was talk of dancing. She wanted him to touch her again. Which was all backward. She was supposed to seduce, to make him do the wanting.

He seemed not to hear and turned to her with a sober look. "Alice says a boy followed you through Shepherd Market the other day."

"So she claims, but Charlie and I did not see anyone."

"You might be on your guard."

"Against my uncle? Shepherd Market is the last place he'd ever go. I assure you he has no interest in gingerbread and birdcages."

"Do you trust him?"

"No, but your lawyer said my uncle would act against us in the courts, not in the streets."

"In court your uncle will want to offer a spy's report on the state of our marriage. His scrutiny is likely to be most thorough."

All the magic of the copper gown left Cleo in a rush, a spell turned to ashes. She had counted on its glowing power to seduce her husband and had barely held his notice for an hour. Her feet hurt, and her new stays pinched. Wine and rich food churned in her stomach. Of course her uncle would spy. It made perfect sense. He had lied and deceived and ruined her, and now when she sought to escape his control, he would block her. And then Charlie would be at his mercy. Powerlessness coalesced in her. She wanted to seize Xander Jones by his elegant lapels and shake him.

"You could stop my uncle's plan by behaving like a husband and taking your wife to bed and getting her with child, which even the regent managed with his most disagreeable wife."

His gaze turned cold. "I don't think you want to cite the prince as a model of husbandly behavior." He left her, and in less time than any hostess could ever consider polite, they took their leave.

Cleo heard Tom Ruxley wrongly asserting, "Let them go, let them go. Jones is eager to get his new bride alone."

On the pavement outside, Xander was a shadowy figure except for the white of his linen and the silver glint of his eyes. Isaiah brought their carriage to stop in front of them, and Xander opened the door, taking Cleo's hand to assist her. "Can you give a dinner in two nights' time?" he asked.

She looked down at him from the carriage step. "A dinner?"

"I've arranged to hire extra servants." He handed her into the vehicle.

"Another wifely act to stop my uncle?"

"That's two today. What could be more wifely than laying your bills before your husband and attending a dinner party?"

"Lying naked in bed with my nightrail around my neck?"

He laughed. "Believe me, when desperate measures are called for, I will act." He closed the door firmly and nodded to Isaiah to drive on. The coach lurched into motion.

Cleo fell back against the seat alone. *Desperate*

measures—that's what he considered bedding her. No danger of being flattered by her husband.

I N the magistrate's room at Bow Street Will had bad news for Xander. "Your curate's been arrested. A writ of *qui tam*, for perjury."

"March works fast. Where've they taken him?"

"Newgate."

"How long has he been in?"

"Two days. Long enough for March to cross-question him in his own sweet way. I'm sure he has bullyboys on the inside. Do you have a hearing date set?"

"Not yet."

"Count on Mr. Tucker to deny he ever married you."

"That would be unhelpful at this point. Can we get in to see him?"

"Of course." Will grinned. "Always easy to get in. It's getting out that's the devil."

Chapter Nine

✀

On a drizzling morning Cleo finally abandoned her quest to find a grinder on her own and sent for the man Xander Jones recommended. As much as she hated to give her husband credit for being right, Anthony Hodge immediately impressed her as the perfect tutor for Charlie. He had a shining, round countenance, twinkling blue eyes, and a laugh that made his shoulders shake.

She left Charlie to show off his Greek and Latin, while she planned dinner for her husband's guests. The approaching party had thrown off the rhythms of Xander Jones's strange household with its silent help, so unlike ordinary gossiping London servants. Charlie called them Hades' three-headed dog, a joke they'd shared over dinner alone in the pretty dining room. Now aloof Amos, who guarded the door, was overseeing

extra footmen and kitchen help hired for the occasion.
Gruff Isaiah, who talked more to horses than to any
human person, had additional stable hands to manage.
Even steady Alice, who handled dozens of daily tasks,
seemed harried.

Cleo wasn't fooled by her husband's tactics. Two more
days had passed without a trip to the bank. Xander Jones
was off managing his gasworks, reinventing London,
spending her money. She was setting his table, overseeing
his dinner menu, and waiting for her uncle to unmask
their facade. She left Xander Jones's efficient servants
to their work and took time to sew a concealed pocket
on the inside of the bordered hem of La Perez's garnet
gown. From now on she wanted her knife at hand.

She imagined drawing it in their carriage and holding it under his iron jaw between all that fine linen and
his throat and demanding he ravish her. Several problematic details intruded at once in her vision of the
plan. From years of caring for Charlie as a little boy, she
knew something of the layers and fastenings of men's
clothing and had a perfectly clear idea of the youthful
version of what lay beneath wool and lawn. She certainly could not undo those fastenings while holding the
knife. The knife itself would have to persuade him to
unfasten the fall of those dark gray trousers of his and to
release . . . Here she ran into further mental difficulties
because she knew that the male parts her husband possessed would exceed her experience and thinking about
the probabilities made her stomach do odd flips.

A further difficulty was simply imagining a credible
threat she could offer him. She had no experience

threatening anyone but her brother's dog, and Bess was hardly a test of one's intimidation talents. What could she say that could possibly scare such a man? Should she threaten to cut off an ear? He would never believe her. And she liked his ears too well and wanted to know how he came by that scar. Well, she would have the knife with her and trust to the inspiration of the moment.

When she returned to the great room, Hodge commended Charlie on his progress with Greek.

"The Latin will come," he said. "Practice will see you through the entrance tests."

They agreed upon terms and meeting times, and Hodge looked about the room and commented, "Does me good to be back here, Lady Jones. I've spent many hours in this house. Good lads, the Jones boys. Good scholars all." He shook his head solemnly. "I've not been here anytime these three years now." He smiled a little sadly. "It all looks just as I recall. Good to be back."

Cleo dismissed the scholarly lapse in counting the years since Xander and Will Jones had been boys. Even if Hodge wandered a bit in his mind, his encouraging manner was sure to do Charlie good.

He turned and shook Charlie's hand. "We'll have you ready for your entrance exams in no time." He clapped the boy on the shoulder. "Now get that copy of Virgil by Monday next."

The door closed behind Hodge, and Cleo realized Amos had not appeared to see the tutor out. "Quick," she told Charlie. "Grab a coat. Let's go."

"Where?"

"Out."

"But your dinner party?"

"Not till nine. Go."

They spent the chill, wet afternoon outfitting Charlie in fine style. Only the proprietor of a shoe shop questioned Cleo's right to patronize his establishment. When a haughty accent and ready money failed to persuade, Charlie mentioned Sir Alexander Jones by name. To Cleo's chagrin, the mere name rendered the shopkeeper humbly apologetic. He promised to deliver Charlie's new boots as soon as they were ready.

At every turn Charlie and Cleo made a game of counting errand boys with caps—brown caps, tweed caps, checkered caps—none of whom seemed inclined to follow them. Cleo made one last stop at a chemist's shop in South Audley Street. A stiffening wind sent them home.

XANDER turned from the table gleaming with silver and plate to stare at the street below, willing his bride to appear, his patience fading as night took over Hill Street. She and her brother had vanished without a word to anyone in the house. On a whim or as an act of willfulness she had put herself at risk. He knew she had gone about London on her own in the past, but that was before they crossed Archibald March, before she'd been followed, before George Tucker had been arrested and bullied out of his integrity.

In Newgate he had been cross-questioned as Will suspected, until he no longer knew what was true. Fear ruled his thinking. He would be turned out of his curacy.

Prosecution would ruin him. His wife and children would starve. His immortal soul was damned. Xander had counted on March's legal moves. Now that he knew March's underhanded style, he would shift his own tactics. All he needed was time. If Norwood could keep delaying their hearing, Xander would have it.

Today, he had answered March's tactics by setting up signs on Bread Street, offering prime wages to any man willing to bust up the street with picks and haul off the stones and filth of London. A pair of former pugilists of formidable size had put the signs in place on the old building facing the open court. In a week Xander would employ the same giants to hold interviews and sign up workers. At the other end of town, he had reopened the failed gasworks, and the engineers had begun to assess what needed to be done.

He stared into the dark from his lighted window, a reasonable, civilized man, a forward-thinking man, a man in control of his passions and appetites. He, of all men, knew that a woman valued her independence, and that Cleo Spencer had long fought for hers, but in this she had to let him rule. Their bargain would work to the advantage of both, if she would let him manage things and not fight so to take charge of the plan. The game Xander played with March was not meant to put her at risk, but he found he had an unexpected savage streak when he thought of March spying on her.

Reasonableness vanished when he saw them come round the corner. He turned for the stairs, checked his stride, and looked back, scanning the street behind them. Early evening traffic passed unconcerned below his window. Cabs, carters, servants, a pair of gentle-men—no one sinister, no one who seemed to follow the two heading for his door. He went to welcome his wife home with some heat.

She came in laughing, looking much as she had the first moment he'd seen her, green eyes wide and fringed with dark lashes, bedraggled cloak, cheeks pinkened by the cold. Her hair, loosened from its pins, caught fire in the lights of the entry, as it had two nights before every time his gaze had turned toward her down the Fullers' long dinner table.

Her gaze met his, and she sobered at once. He made a note to buy her a new cloak.

"Charlie," he said.

"Sir?"

"I want a word with your sister. Mrs. Wardlow has sup-per for you in the kitchen. You and I will speak later."

Charlie cast his sibling an imploring glance.

"Dearest, I'm sure you're hungry," she said, and he took himself off.

Xander didn't shift his gaze from her. "Were you followed?"

"No." The green eyes sparked with interesting fire.

"Did you look?"

"At every shop and errand boy. Believe me, we were beneath the notice of your common pickpocket."

"Let me remind you that dozens of reputable trades-men are quite willing to come to this house. If you must go out, let Amos or Alice know where you are going."

"Just as you let your wife know where you go at night in this wicked old city."

"I can take care of myself."

She looked away. It would be a mistake to think he saw something wounded in her eyes. She thought he sought another woman's bed. Any wound he offered was to her vanity, not her heart.

He watched her gather some resolve, shaking off whatever momentary injury he'd dealt her pride. She opened a bag, so old and shapeless he had not seen it hanging from her arm against the folds of her cloak, and offered him an apothecary's jar filled with black curls of lazy movement.

"I bought you a gift. To remind you of me." This time there was a wicked glint in those eyes.

He took the thing. Living black coils wriggled in a murky, watery mass. "Did you cut off the tails of all the blind mice with your carving knife?" He held the jar to the light. *Leeches*. He couldn't help the laugh that escaped him. "You persist in thinking our coming together will be a medical procedure."

She brushed by him, heading for the stairs. "Would you prefer a commercial transaction?"

Xander caught her arm, arresting her easy escape. She had no idea of the temptation she offered. He leaned close to whisper against her ear, "If we ever come together, I guarantee you your twenty thousand pounds' worth. Remember we have dinner guests tonight."

C LEO strode across her room, feeling a rush of satisfaction. She searched her memory for some sensation to match this wild elation. She flung off her gloves.

She was an indifferent rider, but she supposed she might have felt such exhilaration once or twice when she managed a good jump. She loosed her cloak. Or perhaps it was more like the feeling she had when she faced down a snarling dog at the edge of the village. Perhaps it was nothing more than pleasure in the startled look on her husband's face when he realized she'd given him leeches.

Her dress for the evening, the garnet silk, hanging on the outside of the wardrobe, checked her jaunty stride, a reminder that her goal was seduction. This time Perez had said the dress would show off her sweetness. That, Cleo thought, would be a miracle. She doubted her husband could be induced to think her sweet even if she offered him treacle instead of leeches. Certainly, he was learning that she was not biddable.

The dress glowed in the candlelight, and she tried to believe in its magic. Dressed in its soft folds she would dazzle him, and he would come to her bed. She took her knife from beneath her pillow and tucked it into the sheath she had devised in the elaborate border of the gown. The hem dipped under the weight, but not noticeably. Tonight she would be ready.

In plain terms she needed a babe in her belly to keep Charlie safe, to defeat Uncle March, to keep courts and papers and lawyers from taking control of her life again. Xander Jones could give her that babe in the time-honored way of husbands whatever their feelings or lack of feelings for their wives. Later, once they defeated March, they could be friends or whatever people became in such marriages.

She threw open the balcony doors, and the breeze

blew them back with bang. A cool rush of night air met her, and a dark shadow uncurled in one of the plane trees. She caught a glimpse of a white, upturned face, young and male. In a blink it was gone, a fleeting phantom vanishing in the dark beyond the lights' glow. Cleo doubted for a moment that she'd seen anything. Then her heart began to pound until it shook her body.

Chapter Ten

❧

A little after midnight Xander stood with his arm around his wife as their guests departed, reflecting that for a man who wanted to impress his partners as a host, such a dinner was a disaster. For a man who meant to resist his wife's charms, it was nothing short of catastrophic.

Her silk dress glowed like candlelight gleaming through port. It gave to her skin a sweet, creamy luster that was driving him mad. All evening whenever he looked at her, he was caught by some tantalizing bit of flesh that made him want what he saw in his dreams. Now he stood with the curve of her waist warm in his palm, and her hip brushing his as she waved their guests into carriages.

It was the first time he'd observed the bustle of leave-taking from his own door. He had an odd sensation of watching himself play host and husband, not knowing exactly who he was. Tonight his partners had seemed like friends. They had come to his mother's house, curious perhaps about its scandalous past, but easily settling down to their endless talk of London's future.

Ruxley and Phillips were arguing even now as they waited for Ruxley's carriage to come round, with Phillips declaring that the overcrowded city would soon be a heap of ruins, another Babylon, and Ruxley staunchly countering that the Metropolitan Works Group would change all that. Xander hoped Ruxley would win the argument. They needed Phillips's vote in Parliament for the charters to build some of their more ambitious projects.

Just at that moment Fuller's wife discovered she was missing her gloves. A servant was dispatched to recover them, and Mrs. Fuller entered into the debate asking Ruxley whether their plan would cure London of its stink, which, she claimed, was the source of all disease in the city.

Xander willed himself to patience. He had only to endure his wife in her maddening dress for a brief spell longer. In a few minutes his guests would be gone. Within an hour the hired servants would be off, among them, he had no doubt, at least one spy for March. As impromptu as the dinner had been, and as reputable an agency as he'd employed to hire the extra kitchen and serving help, Xander knew that he and Cleo were being closely watched. He didn't need Will's experience as a spy to feel the scrutiny.

Will lurked somewhere in the recesses of the house with another reeking set of clothes Xander would need for their evening search for Mother Greenslade. So far they had been unable to locate the woman, but Will's sleuthing had turned up some chilling information on March. He owned the brothel on Half Moon Street where Cleo Spencer's father had died.

Amos interrupted Xander's thoughts with his search for Mrs. Fuller's gloves by opening the main entry closet not six feet away. As a boy he'd spent long hours in that dark place, eyes seeing nothing, ears filled with muffled, distorted sounds of voices—angry, yearning, bereft.

Xander had not willingly opened that door in years, but now he tried to calculate the closet's dimensions. It could not be as small, as close, as dark and stuffy, as he remembered. After all, tonight it had held all his guests' cloaks and coats and more besides. Light probably seeped in under the door. In that closet, he could do what he could not do in the full view of departing guests and hovering servants. Images of the possibilities distracted him.

"Do you think they liked the potatoes?" His wife's voice recalled him to their present, public position.

"Let's hope so. You served them five ways."

"Best to offer guests as much as they can eat. Which did you prefer?" She looked up at him, and the little lift of her chin exposed her throat to his view and pressed one creamy breast against his ribs. He felt the slight give of soft flesh against the wall of his chest and a swift answering pulse of desire in his groin.

He pressed his mouth to her hair and tried to think rationally about the entry closet. Its interior was at least the size of a roomy carriage. He rode in carriages every day without feeling trapped. He imagined the closet walls fading away as he pushed his wife's flimsy sleeves over her white shoulders, yanked her corset down to release her breasts, and buried his face between them where the flesh was sweetest.

"You think the house is being watched in this cold weather?" she asked. She reached down and made an adjustment to the elaborate hem of her gown where it covered her evening slippers.

Apparently she was not overcome by lust as he was. Whatever else she was, she was ignorant of the full sensual surrender he could wring from her. He was a good judge of desire in a woman. He knew all the stages of interest that led to an encounter. His bride might be aware of him and alert to his presence in a room, but she had not taken even the first tottering step on the path of sensuality that would lead her willingly to his bed. She had only her single-minded concern for escaping March and protecting her brother.

He was the one so far gone in desire that he was thinking of taking her into a closet. He was staring at his wife's chest when the shift in her tone registered in his brain. She no longer doubted the existence of March's spies.

"Your uncle's spies are well paid," he said, wondering, with the working part of his brain, what had changed her mind.

"A spy must grow cold standing about watching a house from the outside."

"Better to be hired on and work from inside."

"Oh. The extra servants?"

"At least one or two."

She stiffened. "No wonder then that you've had your arm around me this quarter hour, and you just nuzzled my hair, a first. I thought perhaps the gown was having an effect."

The last of the guest carriages rattled off into the night. Xander guided his wife from the door.

"Should we take a bow for our performance?"

"Not till the hired help leave," he advised. He kept a hand on her arm above the elbow.

She halted. "Perhaps we should stage a dramatic conjugal onslaught for their notice."

He turned her in his arms so they were front to front. Her unscented sweetness rose to fill his senses. *Just what I was thinking.* "Did you want me to drag you into a closet?"

She cast a startled glance at the closet in question. He caught the hesitation, so brief it might have escaped his notice. He had just enough pride to want her to come to him out of desire for his person, as unlikely as that seemed.

He waited, letting her look at him and judge his intent. She hadn't a notion of what he'd been thinking. Even for a virgin, she had peculiarly uninformed notions of sexual congress. Behind them a door closed quietly. They were alone. He watched those green eyes alive with doubt as she wrestled with the idea of the closet.

"No?" His voice was a rasp. "Not a closet for your first time?" She wanted her babe, her guarantee that March could not touch her, but she wanted to be in charge, and she had no clear notion of how completely she would have to yield herself to him. A little push and she would back down.

Just when he thought her resistance would crumble and she'd slip from his hold, she came up on her toes, leaning into his body, her mouth inches from his, the scent of her making his head swim. "Would a simple kiss for the spies be too much to ask?"

"A simple kiss?" Not really a possibility, but Xander would let her discover that. He pulled her up full against him and held her, letting her absorb the way they fit together. "You think you know desire because some lordling politely groped you in a garden, put his tongue in your mouth, and popped your stays." He shook his head. "You don't know the first thing about desire."

He lowered his mouth to hers, just to show her how uncomprehending she was, or maybe just to nudge her onto that path where he was already leagues ahead of her.

She made a small sound in her throat as he joined their mouths. It was like the moment of joining in the church, only more intense. Without intending to, he was demanding entry, demanding that she acknowledge him wholly, fully, his real, substantial presence, his maleness, as if penetrating her with this one kiss could undo all the messages of a lifetime that he should disappear.

A mindless moment followed until the demand of his body, hard and aching, made him cup her hips to meet his. Too many layers separated him from her sweetness. He wanted her breasts, and she, he knew, would yield them. A sound from above them caught his notice, and with a faint glimmer of his fading reason, he broke the connection and lifted his mouth from hers.

And felt a sharp prick against his belly through wool, silk, and linen. His brain cleared instantly. She had drawn her pig-sticking knife. The little moment when she'd reached for her shoe came back to him. But her angle was wrong; not much sticking experience, his bride. He lifted his head and met her gaze.

"You have a bad habit of abandoning your bride at night. Not tonight," she whispered, her voice ragged, a fierce glitter in those green eyes.

He shook his head. Desire pumped furiously in his veins, but the voices of a lifetime whispered that it was not him she wanted but her own power.

"You don't really want to introduce a pound of flesh into our bargain." He leaned into the knife, deliberately pushing back, feeling the tip slice deeper into wool and silk. Her fist was against his groin, the knuckles pressing into his flesh inches above his aching erection, but the sharp bend in her wrist meant she had no leverage.

Her eyes went wide, determination and uncertainty at war in their depths.

"A charming conjugal moment." Will's dry voice interrupted.

They turned as one, and the move threw her off balance. She stumbled back, wrenching free of Xander's hold, her knife catching and splitting the fabric of shirt and waistcoat, raking a thin scratch up his skin from the band of his trousers to his breastbone. He sucked in his breath as the white edges of his eveningwear fell loose. Cool air and his wife's hot astonished gaze met his flesh, her green eyes wide with shock and discovery.

While she looked, he stood, an alabaster saint, enduring the gaze of a woman with no talent for concealing desire.

Then she fled.

Will tossed him a bundle of clothes. "Haven't bedded your bride yet?"

"There's some disagreement about how to proceed." Xander loosened his cuffs and stripped off his ruined eveningwear, conscious of his brother's amused regard.

"Apparently you've reduced her to pursuing you with a letter opener."

"It's her pig-sticking knife."

"Oh, that makes much more sense."

Xander shrugged into the loose, stinking jacket. "Where do you find this stuff?"

"My neighborhood has tailoring possibilities you've never dreamed of. Mother Greenslade will love it."

"If we find her."

"A bit testy, are you? Pity about your poor disappointed cock. If you weren't such a bleeding saint, you'd have enjoyed your bride six ways to Sunday by now." Will grinned. "And in case you think you can hold out for much longer, guess again. Once she discovers her real power over you, you're done for."

Chapter Eleven

IN the morning Xander took his wife to the bank. It seemed the best way to turn her thoughts from seduction. On the way he reminded his squawking conscience that his plan of marrying Cleo Spencer had a symmetry that was fair and just—as long as he stayed out of her bed. Their bargain meant each got the money to save a brother. She would save hers from March, and he would release Kit from whatever monstrous thing in London's darkest depths had got hold of him.

March's legal maneuvers would ultimately free them both, and meanwhile Norwood would tie March up in the courts long enough for Xander, with furious effort, to get the gasworks going, get his charters and permits, and get the support of the Metropolitan Works Group. He had no doubt he could repay any of the trust money he spent from gas company profits over the years. And

once he and Cleo Spencer parted, he believed Norwood
could help her break the clause in her trust that left her
under March's control.

Cleo had to admit that entering Evershot's bank on
Xander Jones's arm was an entirely different experience
from entering alone in her old cloak. This morning he
had given her fur-trimmed silk to wear. She could ask
for and receive her money in any amount she chose.
Meese couldn't touch her.

But the moment was not as satisfying as she had
expected it to be. It was her husband's power that inspired
Meese's deferential bow, not her own. Power in her own
person eluded her. She was the one who had contributed
piles of lovely money to their bargain, but Xander Jones
didn't feel the least bit like kneeling before her or giving
in to her idea of how to defeat her uncle.

Last night she'd endured the humiliation of fighting
for his attentions when, obviously, he was a man who
found his pleasures elsewhere. To be discovered in that
moment by her mocking brother-in-law had reduced her
to tears. Her own response puzzled her. It was no part
of her plan to desire her husband, but she had to admit
that his kiss melted her brain. She had barely retained
enough wit to press her knife against his belly when he
pulled back from their embrace. Even then she hadn't
got it right. And it hadn't helped her clarity of mind to
find herself staring at such an intriguing bit of male
flesh. There were definitely gaps in Miss Hester Britt's
explanation of sexual congress.

When he leaned into the knife, that moment, well,
the whole kiss, if she were brutally honest with herself,
said how confident he was of his power. She had not

been as forceful as she'd intended to be, and once again he'd disappeared into his other life in which she had no part.

But once she had her own money in her hands, she was sure she would not care where he went or with whom he spent his nights.

Men of business who had ignored her weeks before parted to make way for them as they strolled across the marble floor. Meese bowed and hurried to open the door of Evershot's office.

Evershot did not bow. He came forward awkwardly, smoothing the thin gray strands over his wide forehead. "Congratulations on your unexpected alliance."

"We have you to thank, Evershot, for our fortunate chance meeting in your office," Xander said.

"We could say that your bank brought us together," Cleo added.

A pained look crossed Evershot's round, bland face. He made a vigorous gesture of denial. "Oh no. We wouldn't want to say that, nothing of the kind, a sheer accident your meeting here, the bank not involved at all."

Cleo shot a quizzical glance at Xander. She wondered what he made of Evershot's unease.

"You have drafts ready for us?" He led Cleo forward.

Evershot nodded. "I took the liberty, Sir Alexander and Miss . . . Lady Jones, of preparing your advances in a smaller amount, should you wish maintain prudent habits of spending."

"Advances?" Xander Jones spoke quietly, politely even, but Evershot drew forth a large handkerchief to dab his brow.

"A mere precaution, Sir Alexander, recommended by Miss . . . Lady Jones's other trustee, you understand."

"Lady Jones no longer has trustees, Evershot."

"Nevertheless, as your banker, I must advise caution. With the validity of the marriage in question before the London Consistory Court, surely you don't want to draw down the fund beyond your power of repaying. The danger of bankruptcy from this lighting venture is quite real."

Cleo watched her husband. She was coming to know the unbending way he responded to threats.

"Evershot, your bank need not be concerned about the state of our marriage. You may disperse all funds requested."

"However, if the court—"

"Evershot, if you don't give Lady Jones her money today, your bank will bleed funds."

Evershot dabbed his brow again, plastering the thin strands to their damp, gleaming surface. He looked trapped.

Cleo felt sorry for him. "Mr. Evershot, while I might agree with you on the questionable profit to be gained from lighting London's poorest streets, I do insist upon the full amount requested, for Charlie's sake."

"As you wish, Lady Jones."

For the next half hour clerks scurried in and out of Evershot's office, laying documents before Xander Jones. At last he nodded his satisfaction.

Cleo requested that they stop in Rose Street at Stanford's so she could buy Charlie a gift with her own money.

The clerk was writing a receipt for a fine leather-bound

copy of Franklin's papers when her husband spoke. "You can't stop buying him gifts, can you?"

Cleo felt the pricking accusation in his tone. It robbed the moment of pleasure. "You object? You think I spoil him?"

He seemed to consider what to say, his hand resting idly on the glass case next to hers. "Buy him all the gifts you like. But you should not call him 'dearest' any longer."

"Why ever not? He is dear to me, and we have only each other." She thanked the clerk and collected her package. They turned to leave.

"It makes him feel like a little boy, and he wants to be a man."

"You presume to know him well after mere days."

He held the shop door for her. "No, just to know boys. If you want him to do well in school, you'd do better to call him Charlie than to buy him fine leather-bound books."

"I decide what is right for my brother and me."

Her husband nodded and handed her into their carriage without a backward glance. She had a long journey home through London traffic to rail to herself that she knew Charlie best and to smart under the mortifying sting that her husband was probably right.

Mother Greenslade's absence from Bread Street was not a topic a stranger could broach with the regulars at the public house, no matter how convincing a disguise he wore. Bread Streeters were a suspicious lot, but today the doors of the public house, propped open by broken paving stones, allowed customers to wander freely in and out. A stranger with no worries about the contents of his pockets could mingle at will among them to pick up any rumor going about, and Xander had nothing in the old brown corduroy jacket he wore.

Reverend Bredsell was preaching from a donkey cart with *Truman's Brewery* painted in red and gold lettering on the side, leveled and anchored in place by a bale of hay under the wagon's tongue. This makeshift stump stood directly in front of the signs Xander's men had put up earlier in the week. Indeed, Bredsell was preaching against them.

"Bread Street belongs to itself. Around her an indifferent London gets rich, a London that pays no heed and offers no help to Bread Street. Look around you. No, Bread Street must take care of its own. Outsiders who know not Bread Street come here only for profit. But what they offer is bondage, bondage to commercial interests, bondage to the police. Bread Street, do you want bondage?"

"We want free beer," came a jeering answer.

Xander listened with intermittent attention to Bredsell and scanned the crowd, his eyes drawn to boys as well as to women of Mother Greenslade's age. There were dozens of women in the street, dirty aprons over mud-splattered skirts, grimy shawls around thin shoulders, pint pots in work-worn hands. A young mother holding a dull-eyed infant in her arms passed a brimming pot back and forth with a neighbor. The true Bread Street genius, Xander supposed, was for dying. Babes who knew nothing else knew how to catch every disease in London.

Bredsell warmed to his subject. "A Bread Street man

must be strong against the outsider. He must not betray Bread Street. Sadly, we've been betrayed, my brothers and sisters, and the man who has betrayed us must atone. He must act alone to turn away the outsider."

Several people muttered the word *nark*, and a tall man in a rusty top hat with a beggar's message tacked to the crown called out, "We'll break his 'ead for 'im if there's a nark."

Bredsell shook his head.

"Bread Street has friends in high places. Bread Street can call on the Almighty himself to send fire and flood on those wicked commercial interests who would profit from the poor."

Will, in a ragged seaman's coat, a pot of dark beer in hand, slipped through the crowd to stand beside Xander. "I suppose he means March."

"I don't like the reference to fire and flood. I think Bredsell wants someone far less exalted than the Almighty to take a hand here."

Will's gaze made a lazy sweep of the street over the rim of his drink. "Fire would be a nightmare here."

"You don't see Cullen anywhere, do you?"

Will shook his head. A faint scoring, as of fingernails, marked the stubble on his jaw. "I do see our friend whose nose you rearranged. Let's move. Keep your head down." He passed his drink to Xander, and they shifted position in the restless crowd.

Will spoke again from the other side of the street. "You know Mother Greenslade doesn't own Number Forty. I think we should find out who does."

Chapter Twelve

᪥

A letter from Uncle March arrived by private mes-
senger as Cleo was dressing for the evening in the
third of the Spaniard's gowns, an emerald green so deep
it was nearly black. She sent Alice off and tore open the
letter.

My dear niece,

*Do not be alarmed. Deepest concern moves me
to use all means to reach you. Know that you and
your brother are most welcome to return to your
father's house and my protection. Say the word,
and I will arrange it.*

*In the meantime I fear for your reputation and
indeed for your health of body and mind. You have
evidently been taken in by a most unscrupulous*

fortune hunter and led by him into an unsancti-
fied union, a dangerous position for a woman of
your uncertain frame of mind. No less a witness
to your fall than Reverend George Tucker assures
me of the falseness of your position.

We must do all we can to free you from this
entanglement and restore you to your rightful
place in society. As to the harm such an arrange-
ment does your brother's character—to reside in
the home of an infamous whore—no other word
can describe her—it is incalculable.

A message at any hour of the day or night
brings me to your side.

March

Cleo felt the color drain from her cheeks. *Any hour*
of the day or night. Her knees buckled, and she sank
heavy-limbed into the nearest chair. This was where her
husband's strategy led them. The court would declare
them not truly married. They could be arrested for
fraud. Her smooth, unscrupulous uncle would win. She
wrenched herself into motion, took up her knife and her
uncle's letter, and headed for her husband's room.

Unlike the other rooms in his house, it had been
stripped of luxuries. It was spare and plain, with
blue-papered walls above the white wainscot and a
serious dark expanse of bed covered with a woven rug
of Oriental design. Beyond the open clothespress and
a desk piled with papers, Cleo saw what she supposed
must be his dressing room door. Her knife and letter in
hand, she pushed her way into his private space.

He lay back in a large footed cast-iron tub, his eyes

closed, dark head resting against the porcelain lip. Her gaze went to the strong column of his neck exposed to her view, and his shoulders and arms, more powerful in repose than she had imagined. Beads of water sparkled in the dark hair on his chest, and fragrant steam rose around him.

His eyes opened and his arrested gaze locked with hers. "Nice ribbons."

Cleo looked down at her shift, corset, and drawers. A dizzying scent enfolded her. "Thank you again."

"You have a complaint, I take it."

"Only the usual. Your strategy isn't working. My uncle has sent a politely poisonous letter."

"You want me to read it?"

"Oh, I insist." Cleo waved her knife at him. "Particularly if it might motivate you to take desperate measures."

"Towel?" He pushed himself upright with a shift of muscle under the smooth skin of his shoulders. Rivulets of water trickled down his chest, and Cleo realized the heady scent was warm, wet male flesh.

"Towel?" She found one hanging at the edge of a heavy dark chest on which stood her jar of leeches. He dried his hands, tossed the towel aside, and reached for her letter.

As he read, Cleo studied his head, his shoulders, the damp curls at his nape, his hands, anything but the pale limbs under the water. His chest she had seen briefly two nights before, but strangely what she remembered was not the taut symmetry of it, the line of dark, curling hair, the red scratch left by her knife, as if she had scored his flesh. What she remembered, with her body's memory, a memory that was in her limbs, was the sensation of being crushed against that chest in a long embrace. She wanted to use the strength she sensed in him against Uncle March, but she had not imagined that it would be seductive, that she would want it for its own sake, for the pleasure of feeling that strength surround her.

He looked up, handing the letter back to her. "I don't think you mad."

"Yes, well, I am grateful that you did not house me in the attic or attach restraints to my bed. So we must assume you've simply no taste for the most expedient procedure to defeat my uncle. I imagine you put off visiting the tooth-drawer as well, but sometimes there's no avoiding it." She brandished her knife again.

"Is the knife meant to encourage my amorous attentions?"

Cleo began to pace. She couldn't just stand there looking at him so at ease in his . . . nothing. "In truth, Charlie gave it to me to keep you *from* my bed. He was worried, you see, but of course, the problem appears to be not to discourage your attentions but to provoke them."

"Desire on your part might be more provoking than cutlery." He said it quietly, matter-of-factly, an unexpected revelation.

"You want provoking? I am here in my shift in your dressing room. Provoking?" Cleo stepped into the tub. Water sloshed up around her legs, plastering her stockings to her calves, and her thin drawers to her knees. Xander shifted his feet. "Stand." Cleo jabbed her knife at him.

He flashed that rare grin of his. "Oh, I'm standing."

"Up." She gestured with the knife.

"Done." His hands gripped the edge of the tub, and he pushed himself smoothly to his full height. The water shifted again, lapping against her legs.

Cleo swallowed, eye level with his lean throat, and the pulse that beat there. She felt the insistent beating of her own pulse in the most intimate of places. A rush of sensation like a swollen stream overspilling its banks flooded her limbs. Unsteadily, she brought her knife up to his ribs.

"Are you sure you mean to encourage me?" His voice stirred all her nerve endings.

She nodded. "I don't want my uncle to win."

"You make things very difficult." His voice was low and hoarse and sent a shiver all over her.

"What things?" Her own voice had dropped into a timbre she did not recognize.

He took her chin in his hand and tilted her face to his. "Honor." His lips touched hers.

"Patience." A slow brush of his mouth against hers made their lips catch and cling.

"Sense." He kissed her fully.

Cleo tried to keep the knife steady, to hold him to this joining of mouths, but as the kiss deepened, her free hand came up and pressed against solid, warm flesh, while the knife hand dropped to her side.

In a flash he caught and twisted her wrist, and the knife fell into the tub at their feet. His other arm came around her, and he lifted her up and out of the tub and carried her to the door. Cleo twisted and squirmed against his iron hold until he set her on her feet at the door, turning her face to it and pinning her there.

"Let's put that wounded vanity of yours to rest." Cleo was pressed to the door, her breasts flattened against its smooth wood panels, behind her, her husband, lean, hard, urgent, pressed his male fullness against her backside, his breath a rasp against her ear. The pressure against her breasts sent aching messages to the place between her legs that beat with an answering pulse. She squeezed her eyes shut against the sensation.

Behind her he was unmoving. She had pushed him farther than before and sensed that he was a man on the edge. Only his chest rose and fell against her back. His arms and weight trapped her in a warm cage of male strength. Held helpless, soaking up the imprint of his male body on her female flesh, her skin hungry for the heat of him, she waited for him to yield. He kissed her shoulder, just that, and the kiss floated down into the deep aching well between her thighs.

"If we do come together," he said in a low voice at her ear, "it won't be like any tooth drawing you've ever experienced."

With a quick flex of his arms, he pushed back, turning her, yanking open the door, and propelling her through it. She heard the lock click into place behind her.

Cleo dripped back to her room and stood by the fire, making puddles on the hearth stones. A realization, shocking in its frank carnal interest, held her standing absently. She wanted to see her husband naked.

Sometime later Alice appeared with a pot of tea and scolded Cleo out of her wet clothes.

When Cleo was dry, changed, dressed, and ready for her evening, she stood at her window and stared into the London dusk of a clear, cold night in which smoke from hundreds of chimney pots rose ghostly and straight toward the distant heavens. No leaves hung on the trees.

The longing he stirred so easily in her receded, leaving her hollow. She stared unseeing into the dark.

The trunk of the nearest tree seemed to shake in the cold. Cleo's senses came alert. Without moving she fixed her gaze on the quaking tree. A pinched white face glanced up and met her gaze for an instant with a look of potent longing. Then the shadow shivered, turned, and bolted for the back of the garden. Cleo could not describe the face of her uncle's spy, but she knew the strange, haunted look in the boy's eyes—hunger.

Chapter Thirteen

❦

Xander's grip on her arm stopped Cleo in the shadowy rear of the theater box. Around and below them in the tiers of gilded boxes the crowd twittered and stirred, a restless flock of birds with gorgeous nodding plumage.

"How badly do you want your money?" he asked, the low vibration in his voice starting its usual answering quiver in her. She noted the white scar across his ear, realizing for the first time that he didn't hear perfectly on that side. He smelled of soap from his bath, but she was most aware of how his manner changed in public.

Here, they were not among his friends, prosperous, civic-minded Londoners, men of enterprise and science, who invited him to their homes or came to his. Here, people she knew or had known, people she had once counted as friends, looked on. When they stepped forward in the little box, all the blue-blooded misses and all the Miss Finsburys of London would gasp at the baron's daughter become the bastard's bride. Any friend Cleo thought she might reclaim would turn away. She might as well toss her newly printed calling cards on November's Guy Fawkes bonfire. Appearing with Xander Jones in this most public way would proclaim them married.

His studied indifference to the crowd below told her he knew what her choice meant. And more, it told her, she could wound him somehow with her choice. An unexpected surge of power swept her, almost dizzying in its intensity. The same reckless impulse she'd felt from the first moment of their acquaintance prompted her again.

She slipped her arm from his grip and faced him, undoing, with trembling fingers, the ties that held her cloak in place. The black silk slid from her shoulders, and he caught it, a gentlemanly reflex. His gaze claimed her throat and the daring décolletage of the last of her Perez gowns. She was conscious of a warm pulse beating where his glance burned. *In flint is fire.*

She smiled up at him, offering her gloved hand and naked arm. "Oh, I want my money."

She turned, stepped into the light, and leaned her hand on the edge of the box, a black fan dangling from her wrist. He stepped to her side, his hand came around her to cup her shoulder, and she tilted her face up to his.

The crowd paused in its seeing and being seen as Cleo's husband leaned intimately toward her, reporting on the hiring he planned to do. He had the gasworks going now, and he had chosen a route for the first pipes to light the dark heart of London.

She knew what he was doing, putting on a show for the gossips below. She realized she should most distrust those moments when he seemed open to her. She really knew nothing of him and his intentions. Still she grew edgy under the effect of that gaze and the low, intimate voice. "If you are going to look at me like that and talk of pipe feet and gas capacity, I won't be responsible for my actions, in public though we are."

"You object to my besotted husband look?"

"Deeply. Since it's all a hum and you don't mean to act. Very wounding to a woman's vanity." At least that was the part she wanted him to believe he wounded.

"I thought we had resolved the issue of your wounded vanity this afternoon."

She tried to read his expression, but the besotted look had vanished, and she saw only cool detachment. "That moment was meant to be a compliment? When in spite of your evident readiness for the most carnal of embraces, you shoved me through a door and locked it? My vanity might never recover."

"You just don't recognize male sincerity."

"Maybe I need practice."

He actually laughed then, and heaven help her, she liked the sound of it. She looked out over the crowd and caught the startled glance of a tall, silver-haired gentleman entering a box opposite theirs and offered him her most dazzling smile. The Marquess of Candover, with the same brow and carriage as his son, turned back to his party at once.

"Your father's here. Did you know he would be?" She

risked a glance at him and caught a fierce look, instantly
quelled.

"Our paths sometimes cross. I don't plan my life to
avoid him." He looked away, and Cleo found she had an
excellent opportunity to study his profile and that ear
with its white scar and the place above his collar where
his dark hair curled, and which she suddenly wanted to
explore with her fingers.

"Did he do nothing for you?"

"He made me. He was young, however, and careless,
and it certainly was not his intention."

"You, on the other hand, are careful."

He turned back to her, his expression closed. "I've
learned to be careful."

The buzz in the theater began to subside. He offered
his hand and led her through the formalities of a gentleman seating a lady at the theater in full view of London.
His warm palms slid down her arms briefly and slipped
away, leaving her skin slighted. Cleo had no other word
for it. Her skin craved his attention, his notice, and the
withdrawal of his touch felt like that moment when a
friend turned away.

A thought occurred to her then that his reason for
refusing to get her with child had less to do with a dis-
taste for her than with all the slights and difficulties of
his own past. But she looked at the vast, dazzling crowd
and knew that their fickle interest in scandal would not
save her from her uncle.

She stared at the stage. "My Uncle March has done
something to Mr. Tucker, hasn't he? That's why Evershot was so cagey about our funds, isn't it?"

"Tucker is in Newgate on a charge of perjury." Her

husband leaned back and reached into his coat, offering her the pig-sticking knife. "Keep it for your real enemy."

Cleo took it from him with unsteady hands and returned it to the sheath inside her gown in the border of black jet beads.

"Has the hearing been set?"

"No. Norwood has won us another delay."

Below them the manager came to the stage front to announce a change in the program. One of the dancers, Miss Becky Lynch, was to be replaced by an understudy, Miss Eliza Hunt. The change seemed to cause considerable consternation among a group of fashionable gentlemen standing quite near the stage. A smattering of boos greeted the announcement, and a pair of young men had to be restrained by companions from coming to blows. Then the gold-tasseled curtains parted, and everyone turned to the play.

"I won't lose to my uncle, you know." Cleo leaned and whispered in his ear over the orchestra's rousing opening.

He turned, and his breath stirred her hair. "Trust me, and we both win. Tonight all London thinks that we are well and truly married."

At the interval a message arrived, and her husband left her alone in their box. Cleo assumed her haughtiest look and kept an unfixed gaze over the heads of the crowd. From the back of the box came a knock, and the door opened to admit one of her former friends. Cleo summoned the name, Millie Eldon, not a close friend, but someone with whom she had shared the delights of many a ball. She felt her spirits lift.

Millie had a bobbing feather headdress and diamonds strung like lanterns across her chest. "Cleo, how lovely, you're back in London!"

Cleo's spurt of gladness died. Millie greeted her from well back in the shadows at the rear of the box. A wise precaution, Cleo had to admit, as she moved to join her visitor. No sense in involving anyone else in her ruin. "Yes, I married Sir Alexander Jones. You may have seen the announcement in the *Chronicle*."

Millie's perfect oval face expressed a kind of greedy horror at the idea. "You are safe, then? You've not been abducted or sold to this man?"

"Quite safe, just getting settled, is all. I shall make some calls on old friends soon." Cleo let Millie take that as she would.

Her delicate nose twitched, and Cleo had a perfect recollection of talking with her in the past. "He's handsome as sin, of course, but the stories. I heard he went on a debauch and lost his brother in London, or the boy was murdered or something." Her gloved hand covered her mouth.

Cleo almost laughed. "Oh, if only he were the violent sort. I'm afraid he's more likely to bore me to death with the details of his gaslight project than to cut my throat with a knife."

Again Millie's little nose wiggled. It was plain she wouldn't let Cleo's remark interrupt the flow of lurid tales. "Oh. Well, he did bed who knows how many ladies of quality. His knighthood made such a scandal. The prince only went through with it, you know, to embarrass Candover. There's no good feeling there. But no one dared call him out, your husband, I mean. No *gentleman* could meet him on the field of honor."

Cleo had her own idea of why no man wanted to meet Xander Jones on the field of honor, but she did not speak it. "What about you, Millie?" she asked.

"I married Trentham, naturally. You remember how he always doted on me. We live with his mother, but she could go any day now, so it's really quite all right."

The tide of visitors heading back to their own boxes sent Millie on her way with a cheery farewell, but not so much as a squeeze of Cleo's hand. Cleo saw her appear three boxes down and immediately fall into conversation with her neighbors.

The red curtains parted for the second half of the performance as Xander Jones stepped back into the box.

Cleo had no cause to object to his husbandly behavior again until their carriage stopped a short block beyond the Opera House. She was thinking that with a postponement of their hearing, she could wage a slow campaign of seduction. Maybe she would start by leaning against her husband's shoulder on their way home.

A man rapped sharply on the coach window. When Xander opened the door, the stranger muttered a single terse sentence. Cleo's husband descended and vanished into the night. *Trust me*, he had said, but how could she when he disappeared before she could even remove the pig-sticking knife from her skirt to stab him in his false heart?

Chapter Fourteen

෴

WHILE Cleo sat stunned, Opera House traffic brought the carriage to a halt. She slipped her knife from her hem, pulled her cloak over her hair, and pushed open the door. Isaiah protested as she slipped into the dark, but she knew he would not leave his horses.

She moved down the line of stopped carriages, scanning the moving shadows, and cut back to the pavement behind a monstrous coach. Xander Jones's wide shoulders and purposeful stride made him easy to spot, and she set herself to follow, heart beating high, between determination and uncertainty. He was likely going to some low pleasure palace in Covent Garden. That would not violate the strict terms of their agreement. A whore was not a mistress, after all, but she didn't want her fears confirmed. And she wasn't sure she had the nerve to follow him into an actual brothel, to find him in another woman's arms.

At the lower end of the street, he entered a stark, squat building of brown stone. Cleo had never had a cause to go there, but she knew the place, the Bow Street police office. She entered with a rough crowd in all states of drunkenness and violent annoyance, keeping her gaze on Xander as he worked his way into the packed, high-ceilinged room where the magistrate held sway. Her rich evening clothes drew stares and comments from those around her. Hands tugged at her cloak, holding her back.

A redheaded behemoth with an unshaven jaw blocked her way. "Here now, missy, wot's a fine dove like you doing in this lot?"

"Mebbe she's lost, Joe," said another male voice.

"Then I'm the one to help 'er," said big Joe, putting a heavy arm around Cleo's shoulders.

Cleo touched her pig-sticking knife to Joe's wide ribs. "Thank you, sir, for your kindness, but I have all the assistance I need."

Joe backed off, lifting his arm from her shoulders. "Pardon me, ma'am."

Cleo pushed and squeezed her way through ragged women with squalid babes in their arms. It was past midnight. Constables led London's wrongdoers before the magistrate to determine whether they would stand trial in the morning when the court opened. Xander Jones was near the front, his gaze fixed on the proceedings.

Cleo felt silly and confused. It made sense for him to seek a bawdy house of some sort, but what message made her husband leave his wife's side to come here for a low spectacle?

The crowd was laughing at the interrogation of an old woman with a pox-pitted face under a large black bonnet.

"Now, Mother Greenslade, explain yourself," the magistrate demanded.

The woman drew her russet shawl about her thin shoulders. "Why, Yer Worship, I collect my rents same as always and takes the money straight to the bank."

"What's the complaint then, Constable?"

"She tried to pass a five-pound note from the Bank of Scotland, sir."

The crowd roared with laughter. A man called out, "Collecting rent with a tap on the bloke's head, was ye, Mother Greenslade?"

The crowd hooted its derision again. In their midst, Xander Jones was a still point, neither amused nor distracted by the show. Cleo had managed to squirm her way a foot closer when she stopped. Her uncle entered the court, said a word to the magistrate with obvious familiarity, took a seat, and cast his bland gaze right at Xander Jones. Cleo shrank back behind a beefy man in a leather apron. She felt numb with betrayal. All along her husband had a connection to her uncle. It made no sense.

A fist of iron closed around her arm and a rough voice hissed in her ear, "Lady Jones, what the devil are you doing here?"

Cleo turned and found her brother-in-law beside her. "He left me at the Opera House. I had to see where he . . ."

"You thought he had a ladybird tucked somewhere?"

Realization struck her. "This is where he goes at night? To meet my uncle?"

"Don't be daft. Did your uncle see you?"

"No. Why is my uncle here?"

"Because he's a maw worm that preys on London. Let's get you out of here." He stepped between her and the front of the crowd.

"What about Xander?"

"He needs to talk to Mother Greenslade."

"That old woman? Who is she?"

There was no answer. Will Jones split a path through the crowd like Cook slit a fish. Outside he still gripped her arm, jerking her after him up the dark street. He whistled, and Isaiah pulled up, apologizing for letting Cleo go, more words than she had ever heard him speak.

Will silenced the apologies. "Home, Isaiah."

In the carriage, he told Cleo, "You scared the vinegar out of Isaiah."

"I didn't mean to."

"Just so you know, Isaiah would pay first if you disappeared."

"Disappeared? I went armed into a police station full of officers of the law. Surely, there was some safety in that."

Will hauled her roughly from her seat. Her knees collided painfully with his. His dark eyes blazed into hers. "I'm a blasted officer of the law. Do you think you're safe with me?"

She could smell the usual spirits on his breath and see a dark scratch on his stubble-covered right cheek. For a moment she thought he meant to kiss her. She refused to flinch. He wouldn't. He might not respect her, but he respected his brother. He shoved her back onto her bench. Cleo bounced and righted herself.

"My brother's a bleeding saint. You think you have a rival? London's your rival, a pox-ridden old tart of a city that lifts her skirts when a man presses a coin in her filthy hand and kicks him in the teeth when he has nothing."

Cleo held herself perfectly still, waiting for the anger in him to subside. Dangerous as it was, it had nothing to do with her. After a moment he spoke in a calmer voice.

"A stupid dream is your rival."

"What dream?"

"Ask him, and get him to bed you if you want to beat your uncle."

"Do I have to dance naked for him?"

"That might do it."

At Hill Street, Will Jones hustled her out of the carriage. Amos, unruffled as ever, led her inside, and the vehicle was gone before the door closed behind them.

Cleo studied her husband's butler. He seemed like a man under a wicked spell, compelled to serve in silence in an enchanted castle where doors were locked and secrets kept. Cleo wondered what would break the enchantment.

"You would not be surprised if a dragon knocked, would you, Amos?" He took her cloak without a word, just a jingle of his keys as he moved.

"I'll take those keys, thank you."

He looked just the least bit uncertain then, but Cleo did not back down. "If I'm to be Lady Jones, I need those keys."

Amos would not do anything so open as to plead. A fierce battle seemed to rage behind his unchanging face before, his reluctance plain, he handed over the ring of keys. Cleo watched him go. She would start with her husband's study and uncover his secrets, one by one.

His desk was orderly, her scraps of receipts cleared away. A ledger of gasworks accounts lay atop plans, drawings, and maps. She stopped at a large pile of weekly Bills of Mortality for London. There were years of them. She lifted the most recent number. Here one could read the names, ages, and addresses of the deceased of every parish in London. Her uncle's macabre practice of reading them had shocked her when he came to live with them after her father's death. How could anyone read about dozens of deaths every week? One death had undone her world. One death was an inescapable fact in her life.

She held the pamphlet, trying to understand the facts in front of her. It made no sense that her uncle and Xander Jones had the same odd habits. Was Xander her partner in the fight against her uncle, or was he her uncle's ally?

She took a calming breath. Archibald March and Xander Jones weren't the same sort of man at all. If she looked, she would find an explanation for the odd coincidence. She made herself open the pamphlet in her hand, for the second week of November 1818, and thumbed through it, finding an item marked *Timothy Harris, plasterer, aged thirty-five years, 40 Bread Street, an apoplexy.*

She paused for a moment, sitting in Xander's chair. This man's death could have nothing to do with her or with their partnership. But he had mentioned just this entry to his brother at breakfast days ago, and the death happened where Xander meant to put his gaslights. She took up others and flipped the pages, looking for entries he had marked. A chilling pattern emerged. He marked children's deaths, the deaths of boys.

An odd shiver shook her. He was searching for someone, a child, in all the graves of London. And her uncle was somehow involved. She couldn't sit any longer with such a pile of losses.

She started up through the house, unlocking all the closet doors as she went. She had to laugh at herself. It turned out that her husband possessed a remarkable collection of dainty dressing tables and damask-covered chairs and gilt looking glasses. One closet was stuffed with perfumed silk gowns in dazzling colors. But there were no beheaded brides. He was hardly Bluebeard.

ORDINARILY, Xander supposed, a man would be delighted to find his wife kneeling on the floor of his bedroom in silks with her hair down. Unless, of course, she was examining the contents of his private drawers, a knife on the carpet beside her.

She looked up at him, a sober curiosity in those remarkably frank green eyes of hers. Amos's ring of keys lay like a fan of iron at the edge of her emerald skirts.

"You have stacks of Bills of Mortality that you do read and a drawer full of perfumed letters that you don't. They are all unopened." She let them fall from her hands into her lap.

"There you go, finding all my secrets."

"Even those locked in the closets, though why you are concealing a warehouse of over-dainty furniture from me remains a mystery."

"You have been thorough."

"You've been out most of the night." Her gaze held his.

He leaned against the doorframe. "At the Bow Street police office, as you discovered."

"Well, you could have told me. A wife wonders when her husband leaves her every evening at bedtime."

"True, but your idea of going to bed is more suited to an afternoon appointment at the offices of a tooth-drawer than a night of unbridled passion."

She looked at letters in her lap. "You know I have no objections to conventional wifely acts even with spies peering in at our windows."

"You've seen one of March's boys?" He had reason to press her. Tonight Mother Greenslade had confirmed Will's suspicion that March owned the property on Bread Street where Harris had died. Apparently he owned Number Forty, a neighboring tenement, and the brothel on Half Moon Street, hardly the investments of a noble benefactor of the poor. That was the only information they had wrung from the wily old woman before she made her escape into the night. Not even ready coin had made her willing to say more.

"I can't be sure. I may have imagined. Why do you say March's boys?" She looked up again.

"Will thinks March uses boys from a school on Bread Street to spy on prominent people."

"My uncle? Why?"

"To find their weaknesses, vices, sins—whatever high-placed men don't want exposed to the world. March lets them know he can expose them. The threat of exposure gives him influence over them."

An arrested look came into her eyes, as if she had

just made sense of a puzzle that had teased her mind for some time. "He knew about my father's gaming debts."

"Were they bad?" Xander kept the question light, but a disturbing notion crossed his mind at this second conversation of the evening about Archibald March.

"I never suspected my father owed such sums until he died. It was naïve of me not to suspect that he would gamble or seek a brothel. He was a single man. My mother was long dead, and he loved company, loved play of all sorts. He took part in our games. He used to ride Charlie on his shoulders around the house."

"Not the same thing as faro." Xander came into the room and lowered himself to the floor across from her, leaning back against the wall. He stretched his legs out, one booted foot over the other. He never shared confidences with anyone, but this sharing with her felt comfortable.

"Uncle March helped me see that all my father's debts of honor were paid at once."

"Did he force you out of your father's house?" His feelings for Archibald March shifted again from mild contempt to savage hostility.

"You heard the story of my deranged actions, turning on him with a poker?"

"Yes. I suspected that your uncle inspired your reliance on weapons in dealing with men."

"I woke to find him arranging my hair against the pillows. It gave me a shock. I could have done a dozen more sensible things, I suppose, but I picked up the poker and threatened him with it."

He was definitely coming to share Will's opinion of March. The thought of March's hands on her woke something violent in him, but he had to hide a grin. What else would she do but pick up a poker? "And left your home?"

"As soon as I could arrange it. Our old nurse, Miss Hester Britt, inherited Fernhill Farm from her brother. By the time I left, the mad-girl-with-the-poker story was in wide circulation. Everyone who knew me was relieved, I think, that I was gone. No one tried to find us. Even Uncle left us alone for three years."

She scooped the letters from her lap and let them slip through her fingers back into the drawer. As she came to her knees, Xander came to his, too, and helped her up from the floor.

She offered him a rueful half smile, slipping her hand from his. He felt instantly deprived. He gathered up Amos's keys and handed her the knife.

"Tonight I set out to find out about you, to unlock your secrets, and here I am telling you my sad history." She squared her shoulders and lifted her head. "You mustn't pity me for it. Really, Charlie and I were quite happy, just a little hard-pressed for coin, for his schooling, more than anything. I'm grateful for our bargain. It gives me a way to fight Uncle March. I must not lose Charlie to him, you understand?"

Xander understood. He took her by the shoulders, sure he could offer a bit of comfort without losing control. "The letters are from my mother in Paris. This is her house. The Bills of Mortality tell me about the health of London. I suspect your uncle has a different motive for reading them."

"We always come back to him, don't we? Tonight at the police office, I thought somehow you were . . ."

Xander swore, his intentions no match for the look in those eyes, and pulled her hard against him, his warm, bedraggled wife. She was insubstantial in his arms, pluck and kindness and sauce. She had no idea of the danger of provoking him. He could crush her if he wanted. He could kiss her until she melted and yielded and lost herself to him, until there was no escape for her. The puzzle of it was how someone so slight could stir a hunger in him that threatened his rational plan, his desperate search, and even his grand ambitions.

He brought her face up to his. Tonight he wanted her, just her, just this moment. When he kissed her, the heat of it made of his resistance a burning vapor. She arched up to his kiss, the pair of them lurching down the path of sensual surrender until he lifted his head, trying to judge the distance to the bed, and saw instead the open drawer of letters, pleading, accusing, demanding he stay the course and take nothing for himself until he found his brother.

He groaned and pressed her close against his beating heart, holding her by the back of her burnished curls, letting the raging need cool in his veins. She was everything he taught himself not to be—reckless and demanding and headlong—and, he laughed at himself, everything he wanted. But that was not the plan.

"Let's get you to your bed." He led the way.

At the door to her room, she looked up at him again, a puzzled frown on her brow. "I have no more magic dresses to wear."

He laughed. *As if those dresses mattered.* "I don't dream of you in clothes."

Chapter Fifteen

৯৫

C LEO's next three at-home days produced no callers.
Their appearance in the box at the Opera House
had insured that. No doubt Millie Trentham was spreading her version of Cleo's marriage around the gilt-edged
drawing rooms of Mayfair. Each morning Cleo watched
Cook's tray of tea and cakes for as long as she could,
trying not to think about perfumed letters in a drawer
and broken embraces and her husband's last words to
her. He dreamed of her. Naked.

But he did not seek her out. He had some other
dream, too, something consuming, against which her
knife and her person were no match. She did not think it
was gaslights. She was absurd, wanting their next bank
appointment so that she could take his arm and hear his
voice.

She took the tray of cakes and tea and headed for

the kitchen. She had taken to making bundles of them for the boy who came to spy. He was, after all, her only caller. He might be her uncle's tool, but he was alone in the cold.

Coming back to the kitchen from the garden, she stopped, hearing the voice of her husband in conversation with her brother. She and her husband had not talked since the night of the theater, and she settled on the kitchen step just to hear the low rumble of his voice.

"Hodge says I'm ready for the entrance tests anytime. Next week even," Charlie declared.

"You're not getting cold feet, are you?"

"No. Hodge says they'll take me at your old school. He says they liked all the Jones boys there." She could hear the shyness in her brother's voice. She had a hard time imagining teachers that found Will Jones a likable student, but maybe as a boy he'd had some good qualities.

"And Amos says—"

"You've got Amos speaking, have you?"

"Not volumes." She could almost see the grin on Charlie's face. "But sentences, sometimes. Amos says, 'Master Will was the difficult one of the lot.'"

The lot. Cleo thought it overstated their numbers, but maybe to Amos, two such boys as they must have been in one household would seem a lot. There was a slight pause before her husband answered Charlie.

"That's Amos, always exaggerating."

Charlie laughed. "So, are you going to tell me how things are going at the gasworks?"

"I promised, didn't I?"

Cleo stiffened. Her brother and her husband had a

secret friendship, which neither had bothered to share with her. She felt suddenly adrift. She heard Xander rise, move about the kitchen, and return to the table.

"You can make light from it?" Charlie asked.

She pulled herself back to attention, trying to make sense of the turn the conversation had taken.

Xander's voice again. "Seems against nature, doesn't it? To take a lump of darkness that's lain in the deepest earth for centuries, heat it hotter than hell, and turn it into a thing of airy lightness that burns like six candles with a constant flame."

Oh, coal.

"How does it work?"

"Men shovel coal into dozens of iron cylinders, called retorts, and heat it until the coal breaks into gas and tar and coke. There's a use for every bit of it, but our main interest is the gas. We draw if off, cool it, purify it, and store it in great holders."

Charlie asked another question and another until Xander Jones laughed, an easy, relaxed sound Cleo had rarely heard. He went on explaining about the heat and noise and smoldering chimneys of the gasworks and how they would pump the gas through miles of pipe until the streets of London made a vast network of light.

"So you have to dig up all the streets then? Won't people complain?"

"Loudly. But it must be done to light cities all over the world."

"In Africa? In India?" Charlie's voice was full of the wonder of it all.

"Yes, but London, first, which takes charters, and acts of Parliament, and money."

"Cleo's money." Charlie's voice was sober again. "That's why you married her, isn't it?"

Cleo found herself clutching the ends of her shawl in her fists, waiting for an answer she already knew. She could count on her husband to be honest.

Instead there was the scrape of chair being pushed back. "Would you rather your uncle had that money?"

"No, sir, but maybe you could use my money."

"Thank you, Charlie. I think you should save your money for the next invention. Maybe you'll figure out how to use lightning itself or catch sunlight in a box and make a second fortune."

Cleo prepared to be discovered as she heard them move, but instead her husband and brother went up the stairs into the house. She had no trouble sneaking past Cook a few minutes later.

Later Charlie found her in her room, staring at the fire. He brought a plate of new-baked cakes from Cook. "Cook thinks you eat all the tea cakes yourself, but you don't, do you?"

Cleo shook her head. "How did you guess?"

"You look low, Cleo."

"Not at all. Not with you doing so well. I've things on my mind is all." She put the plate of cakes on the table between them.

Charlie looked stricken. "Maybe we were better off on the farm."

"I thought you were happy here?"

"I am, but we were happy before, weren't we? When we were just us?" He dropped into the chair opposite Cleo.

"It couldn't last. Uncle March would have taken you from me."

"But maybe now we could go back. I don't have to go to school."

"Of course you do. That's why I . . ."

Charlie chose a little yellow-frosted cake from the plate and held it in his hands. He had gained weight in just the short time they had been in town. "I know, Cleo. You made this marriage for me, so I could go to school, but if you're not happy, how can I be happy at school? I mean how can a fellow enjoy his happiness when someone he . . . loves . . ."—he broke the little cake in half and in half again—"is unhappy?"

Looking at Charlie's woeful face, Cleo wanted to hug him, but the thought of her husband's advice stopped her. "It's a problem, I agree. But denying ourselves cake won't feed our friends. Maybe the best we can do is to share the happiness we have with those around us. Maybe when you enjoy your happiness, you contribute to mine."

"I do like living here, Cleo. The bed's too small, but the food's good. Really good," he said. He popped the broken cake into his mouth.

In the end Charlie suggested a walk in the park to cheer her. The cold was bracing, punishing, good for driving low spirits away. She and Xander had no evening plans, which meant she did not know when she would see him again. She didn't think of leaving the park until she caught Charlie shivering.

"Oh dear, why didn't you say something?"

"Couldn't. My teeth would rattle."

They crossed the heavy traffic of Park Lane as lamplighters went from post to post, igniting a feeble glow against a coffee-colored pall of mist. People rushed to finish errands in the fading light. Maybe it was the earnest traffic in the lane at dusk that made Cleo feel so lonely. She was back in London, back on a dear and familiar street, but no one had called. London was merely dark brick and uneven stone, chilling air and choking soot. The noise of vendors and vehicles filled her ears, but no one spoke to her or to Charlie. London no longer knew her.

A donkey cart, its load covered by rough sacks, edged along the sidewalk beside them. The donkey plodded along no faster than Cleo and Charlie. Coming toward them, a boy with a dark blue cap pulled low over his ears cried, "Who'll buy? Get yer penny's worth." He shook a pan of hot chestnuts at them.

Cleo stopped. "Let's get some to warm you on the way home," she suggested to Charlie.

The chestnut boy grinned, stepping up in front of them. He had to be colder than Charlie, his rough jacket patched and open and a long red scarf wound round his neck. "Penny's worth, miss?"

Cleo stepped back to the pavement's edge to keep away from the hot chestnut pan. As she reached for her reticule, the wheels of the donkey cart brushed her skirt.

The next instant a foul sack covered her head and thick arms circled her, pinning her arms to her side. She shouted, and her throat filled with chaff and dust that set her coughing. She felt herself lifted off her feet and kicked out at her unseen attacker.

Charlie shouted her name, and her attacker lurched and swayed. Abruptly he let her go. Her back smacked against the cart, her breath left her in a whoosh, and her feet hit the pavement. She tumbled sideways, her shoulder slamming the stones with a jolt. Desperate for breath, she writhed and squirmed in the foul sack. She fought her way out of the rough cloth and pressed her fists to her aching chest, trying to gasp the cold night air.

She was covered in bits of chaff, and pinpoints of light danced before her eyes. In the circle of dancing pricks, she could see Charlie fastened to the back of a large man who staggered in a strange dance, clawing at Charlie and trying to butt Charlie's head with his own. The man swung violently around to smash Charlie against a lamppost.

"Run, Cleo," Charlie yelled.

They seemed invisible, cut off by the fog from any notice of passersby. The donkey brayed displeasure as the cart blocked them from the traffic.

Cleo pushed herself up on her knees, trapped in an airless place, swaying dizzily. She reached for the knife in her hem, but her fist would not close around it.

The big man scraped Charlie off his back against a lamppost and smashed him to the ground. He lifted an enormous foot as Charlie raised his head. Cleo tried to find the breath to yell.

Out of the dark came Xander Jones. He launched himself at the big man with a shoulder to the man's gut that sent him reeling against the cart. The brute's bellow died as Xander's fist smashed his mouth. The giant toppled back into the cart, his legs flying up. Xander reached to grab the man's shirt, but the cart driver cracked his whip, and the cart rumbled away.

They stood in the gloom, harsh breaths steaming in

the cold air. Cleo simply looked at Xander Jones. He looked back at her. Anger vibrated off him, but something else that she knew was in her, too. She needed to touch him. She dropped her gaze from his. As if she had spoken the need, he answered, pulling her up into a fierce hold.

"You had the wind knocked out of you." His voice was rough, his breath warm against her ear, his body's strength solid. He took the pig-sticking knife from her shaking hand and dropped it in his pocket.

He reached for Charlie, pulling the boy to his feet. Charlie shook, and his wild hair stuck out every which way. "It . . . happened . . . so f-f-f-ast."

"You acted fast." Xander Jones clapped a hand on the boy's shoulder. "You saved your sister."

Charlie looked around at the street. There were no signs of the brief attack except the chestnut pan, its coals and chestnuts spilled. "That giant was trying to put her in the cart."

For a moment they stood, Xander Jones holding them together. Cleo felt her lungs contract painfully, her heartbeat slow its frantic tempo. The image of Charlie on the ground with the brute's boot aimed at his head flashed in her mind, a moment of utter powerlessness. She began to shake.

"Got your breath now?"

She didn't yet. He held her while she coughed violently, covered in bits of dry, fragrant leaves.

When her lungs and throat felt clear, she nodded. "Thank you," she said to Xander. "You saved him."

"He saved *you*, Cleo." Charlie turned to Xander. "There were three of them, weren't there, sir—the chestnut boy, the brute with the sack, and the donkey driver was in on it, too?" His eyes relived the attack.

"Could you say what any of them looked like?"

Charlie shook his head. "Who were they? Not thieves."

Xander Jones caught Cleo's eye, a question in his glance. She shook her head. They both knew March was behind this. One minute the world was an ordinary and familiar place of donkey carts and street vendors. The next, it was violent, alien.

"You were following us."

"You never saw me."

XANDER heard the tentative knock on his door as he knotted his cravat. Not his wife then, unless she was feeling subdued by the aftereffects of the attack. "Come in."

Charlie poked his head in. "Sir, could I have a word with you?"

"Xander," he corrected, motioning the boy in. "Brothers-in-law can call each other by name, I think."

Charlie swallowed. "Xander, then, thank you. Again. You knocked that fellow to Jericho, and . . ." Charlie looked at the fire.

"And?"

He met Xander's gaze with apparent effort. "And, well, we, *I*, haven't been as grateful as I should be for your hospitality, for having us both here. You see I thought you just wanted Cleo's money. But you've been decent to us both. Well, more than decent. My room. Mr. Hodge. Telling me about the gasworks. And . . ."

"And?"

"You protected Cleo. I'm supposed to protect her because I'm her only male relative, but she's always been older. She always protects me even though I'm taller and grown, and I should protect her, but she just takes charge and goes and does what she wants, and she calls me *dearest*, and I gave her the knife when I should have . . ."

"Charlie, sit." Xander pointed to a chair by the hearth.

"Yes, sir, Xander, sir."

Xander took the chair opposite. "You are not to blame for the attack on your sister. And you will always be an important man in her life, but she does have me. I should have been closer instead of following to prove a point to your stubborn sister. She and I have to sort that out between us."

He expected the boy to look comforted and relieved, but Charlie squirmed in the chair.

"Got more to confess?"

"Yes," he blurted.

Xander controlled his expression. "Go on."

"You're being decent as Jupiter." Charlie gave a sigh. "And we've been calling you Bluebeard."

"Bluebeard?"

"You know, the fellow in the story who murders his wives."

Xander raised a brow.

"You have the house and the secrets and you seem not to like Cleo very much, but then you did protect her, so you can't mean to murder her for her fortune and stuff her in a closet."

"I see those closets trouble you both."

Charlie nodded.

"This is my mother's house, you know. She lives in Paris now, and the closets hold her things."

"Oh, makes perfect sense."

"I'm glad to relieve your mind."

"I won't call you Bluebeard again. I started it, not Cleo."

"Good to know I've come up a bit in your estimation."

The boy lapsed into silence.

"Is that it?"

"Yes, sir, Xander."

Xander stood. "Thanks for your frankness."

"You're going out?" Charlie stood up, too, looking sheepish again. "I've held you up."

Xander shook his head. He was not about to tell his young brother-in-law that he had to distance himself from Cleo or bed her. Their marriage would end soon. He and Will were close to finding Kit, closer than they had ever been. He could use his wife's money and repay her twice over, but he would be the bastard Miss Finsbury named him if he took her body and her affections.

He had never been more tempted to do both. She had walked away after the attack when he thought he could not let her out of his sight. Only the blaze of light in his house had kept him standing in one spot as she disappeared up the stairs.

March had tried to take her from him. Of that he had no doubt, which meant that even with Tucker's willingness to perjure himself, March didn't expect to win their legal battle, or he didn't want the matter to reach the court. What did March fear to have exposed in that court? That was a problem Xander would take up with Norwood in the morning.

"Yes, well, I wanted to be honest." Charlie's words reminded Xander that the boy was still standing there.

"Pass your entrance test, and I'll show you the gasworks."

The boy's eyes widened. "Yes, sir, Xander."

"Charlie, if you remember anything more about your attackers, you'll tell me?"

The boy nodded.

There was something, a detail that nagged at Xander, but it was another wagon he saw. He was walking up a fog-shrouded street with Kit, the rumble of cart wheels fading in the darkness before them.

CLEO clutched the rail of her little balcony, already too numb to feel the cold. She wanted her husband. He had a power over her quite different from her uncle's power. Little tremors still shook her, and impressions flashed in her mind like the countryside seen from a runaway gig. *The chestnut boy's face concealed by the cap and scarf. Falling. Gasping for air. Seeing the boot raised above Charlie's head. Will Jones warning her that she could disappear. The shadow with the white face in her garden.* She tried to picture the chestnut boy's face. Nothing came. She saw his oversized cap and heard his accent, pure London street. She did not want to think she had been a fool, leaving food for him in her garden only to be so wholly betrayed, but the boy in the cap had been part of the attack. He must have been watching her from the first to know her face and her habits.

Voices drifted up from the kitchen. She took a steadying breath, scanning the darkness below. The kitchen door opened, spilling a stream of light into the dark. Instantly, a shadow shifted at the base of the tree on the far side of the garden. Cleo swung her gaze to the place and kept it there while Isaiah passed unknowing through the gate.

Nothing moved below her for a long frozen moment. Cleo studied the thick trunk of the tree where she had seen movement. Her bundle was gone. She heard Isaiah putting the horses to the carriage. Alice called from behind her, and in a flash, a shadow tore itself loose from the tree and sped toward the back of the garden. It scrambled nimbly up the wall.

"Wait," she cried.

A pale face turned her way for an arrested second, then the shadow dropped out of sight, and she heard light footsteps fade in the lane. And she knew her spy was not the chestnut seller. The chestnut seller had strong, white teeth.

Chapter Sixteen

❧

XANDER returned at two and found his wife in his bed. He tossed his jacket on a chair by the hearth. "Did you come to express your gratitude?" he asked, though the answer did not matter. He had delayed this reckoning as long as he could.

"No." The green eyes flashed, startling him with their certainty.

She sat propped against his pillows, her coppery hair loose about her shoulders, a heap of discarded silk, her wrapper, on the floor. Candlelight made the white ridge of her collarbone soft as pearls. Other women had invited him to shadowy beds in dim rooms to exchange guilty pleasure. Only this woman met him in the light, wholly and frankly herself.

His hand closed mindlessly on the end of his cravat, a fragment of intention caught in a rushing Thames of desire. He jerked the linen loose and tossed it after the jacket.

Deliberately crossing away from the bed, he repeated the litany of resistance he had been saying to himself since her arrival on Hill Street. She was here because her uncle attacked her. She was here to free herself from March whatever the cost. She was here to get a babe. She had not come for him.

It was no use. He felt himself yield to her, to the dream released from his sleeping mind. At the door to his dressing room he tried one last tactic.

"Is this an attack? Do you have your knife?"

"I believe you have it." Cleo could not be sure he really saw her, understood her presence in his bed. He spared her the briefest glance, a look that was not cold steel, but a volatile quicksilver flash, the leap of something alive.

Xander's feet, less bedazzled than the rest of him, carried him into the dressing room, away from her. But such was his weakness for her that he had already filled the room with her presence. Her knife lay on the chest of drawers next to the straw and the jar of leeches—a brief history of their marriage. He worked the buttons of his waistcoat, finding his fingers unexpectedly clumsy with the silk. He was a man who had undressed before frankly appreciative ladies whose accomplishments went far beyond piano playing and embroidery. Already his cock pressed insistently against linen and wool.

Cleo's gaze followed her husband's back as he passed into his dressing room. The sight of him stripped away the layers of reasons in which she had clothed this one action of waiting naked for Xander Jones in his bed. Really she had no other reason than wanting him.

She understood now the import of that first moment in the bank. It had led inevitably to this one. His back, straight, broad-shouldered, clothed in fine wool, had revealed him to her as clearly as any volume of the history of his life. That back, that stance invited the world to do its worst. He would shake off whatever blow fell on those broad shoulders. He would not bend or bow if the world called him bastard or laughed at his dreams or blocked his path. He had risen above his birth and the world's taunts to become himself.

Her knife had always been useless, a puny thing against his will. She hadn't seen that until now, but desire, this longing that consumed her, filled her up, and shook her, made her body a force against him that would overwhelm his will.

"It's only me," she called. "The only weapon I have is myself."

Then I am in trouble, he thought. He freed himself of gentlemanly trappings, except for his trousers, a moment of sanity taking hold before he presented himself to her in all his evident need. In the bedroom he stopped a few feet from the bed.

"You've put yourself in an interesting spot." His voice sounded rusty in his ears.

"You said you dreamed of me naked." She caught the flash of his gaze before his dark lashes swept down. His plain room revealed him, too, its drawers firmly closed on perfumed letters with overflowing script. He had closed himself off against emotion and sensuality, her saint.

"I understand that I have been cast as Bluebeard in your story."

"Oh dear. Charlie told you?"

"He confessed."

"Well, I've unlocked all the closets, so I know the truth."

"I wasn't going to do this." Xander stared down at the princess who had landed in his bed while a nasty dragon napped. He'd made off with her, he who was no king's son.

Marrying her for her money had seemed a reasonable plan, no riskier than dozens of ventures he'd gambled on before. They would have months to use her money, and once he found Kit and she got Charlie in school, March would obligingly take them to court to undo their marriage that was no true marriage with no harm to either. A baron's daughter, a baron's sister, she would find a gentleman to marry, and somewhere there would be another Miss Finsbury for him.

But he realized his plan had been in peril from the first because he wanted his pauper princess, had wanted her even when he pocketed a piece of straw from her muddied hem. And neither his plan nor his conscience was a match for the desire that gripped him now. He inhaled a shuddering breath, gathered the bed coverings in his fist, and stripped them back.

Cleo gasped at the sudden exposure. A good blaze crackled in the fireplace, but her skin pebbled in the air, the tips of her breasts beaded. She held herself still for his gaze. It was her dream from the first day in the bank. But now, experiencing it, she understood her own impulse. She had wanted to be herself with him. She had thought nakedness vulnerability, but it was power.

He dropped the covers, and his palm, warm and

slightly rough, came to rest on her knee. Slowly he drew his hand up her thigh, fingers spread, the faintest raking touch, stirring her body to pulsing life. He paused briefly at the juncture of her hip, brushing with his thumb the crease. She closed her fist against the shocking desire to arch into his touch, opening to him.

His hand continued its journey up over her abdomen and ribs, parts of Cleo she had not given a thought to, awakened by his touch, to want more. Then his hand caught her breast, lifted it, molded its curve to his palm, a possession that sent currents of feeling jolting along her veins. And she knew he had wanted this, too.

"I want to taste you everywhere," he said. Unhurried, he mounted the bed, kneeling above her on hands and knees, his legs straddling hers.

He looked down at her. "You think you've won."

She swallowed. She had won. He would give in to the demand of her female body that his male strength yield to her and join with her in one strength.

"Think again. My bed, my way, and it won't be the least bit medicinal." He smiled then, and the stony saint vanished in that sure and wicked smile.

He dipped his head and took the breast he had touched into his mouth, his eyes closed, his face intense. Cleo slid her arms around his shoulders and pushed her fingers into his hair and clung as he rubbed lips and teeth and tongue and face against her breasts. The slight dragging scrape of his jaw sent shivers through her, and her body flared like a candle around a burning wick of desire.

He lowered his body to hers, his chest against her breasts, an urgent pressure that she had to answer by arching upward. Sensation overpowered her—the fine wool of his trousers against her legs, his weight a pleasure to take. He distracted her with openmouthed kisses and deep penetrations while his hands stole her secrets, opened her body, touched her everywhere. His hand at last found the secret she had never told anyone, the secret that she spoke the language of desire, a language of soft cries and throaty exhalations. His touch made her sing in that new tongue, her body straining, reaching for a note so high, so right, it would swell to fill her whole person. And when she hit that perfect note of pleasure, the joyful vibration lingered, hung in the hushed air, and faded in long echoes down all the pathways of her body.

He shifted to lie beside her, his gaze on her, his hand at rest with satisfied possession on her red-touched curls.

"Poor Miss Finsbury, never to have had this."

"Miss Finsbury never would have had this."

Xander saw his mistake when she turned and drew her hand down his chest over the band of his trousers, finding the heat and pulse of him through the fine wool, pressing her hand there. Her fingers stroked the length of him, exploring. His mind went away in the pleasure of it until he caught a glimpse of her face wearing a small, satisfied smile.

"You still think you're in charge here." He worked the buttons of his trouser fall.

Cleo nodded.

He shoved wool and linen over his hips in a single motion and kicked them away.

Cleo sucked in a little breath. He was quite handsome there, too, in an unexpected way, like a ridged and helmeted column. He accused her of thinking, but really, she hadn't been. She had merely been enjoying the way he pressed himself into her touch and the way his face grew taut as her fingers slid over him.

He came on top of her in a swift move, pressing his length to hers, his sex, heavy and full, settling against her aching center. And then thinking wasn't possible, because she was skin to skin with a wholly naked male. He took possession of the back of one knee and lifted her leg over his hip, opening her body to his.

His body rocked upward, unerringly stroking hers, parts meant to fit together. Her body, hot, slick, and aching, opened and lifted.

They were joined, barely, his fullness pressing into the place that felt hollow and empty. Their gazes locked, his teeth clenched, he held himself still on trembling arms.

Cleo could touch him anywhere. She slid her hands over his shoulders and down the long slope of his back. She cupped his hips in her hands. She pressed her thumb to the furrow above his nose and drew her fingers over the strong ridge of his brow to graze the white groove of the scar at his ear.

"No, you don't." Her body he would take, but not her sympathy. He drove himself deep, surrendering to her body's demand of him, erasing the sweet, knowing look in her eyes.

She went still from the pinch and burn of it, but her arms clung to him, and he began to move inside her.

Only at the last, looking into those guileless green eyes, did Xander swear an unsaintly oath and wrench himself free of her body's exquisite hold to spill his seed in the tangled sheets. She would have one small reason not to hate him when the day of reckoning came.

Cleo lay under his arm, feeling his pulse subside, her senses and spirits leveled. She had been lost in the moment as he had intended. The startling connection not just of bodies had seemed all powerful, all consuming. But only for her, not for him. He offered heat but denied her shining looks of love, sweet expressions. She could want him, she could take her pleasure from him, but he would not let her love him. Some part of him had remained stone, detached, locked in a drawer, like his unopened letters.

The candles burned on. The fire popped and cracked. Her heart might ache, but her body floated in an odd, paradoxical languor. She felt supremely, stunningly alive, whole, all her parts joined. She stretched, flexing her feet, feeling the friction of the sheets against her skin everywhere at once. She felt like a general with an army at her command, every muscle and nerve ready to salute and serve. Oh, she could admit that he excelled in this art, while she was a novice, but she had paid close attention, close, close attention. She had already learned a thing or two. He had opened himself to her more than he realized, and she would now use the lessons he taught against him. She turned on her side and pressed her body against his, the contact of skin against skin immediately rousing her body again. She slid the flat of her palm across his collarbone and down the hard plane of his chest.

Chapter Seventeen

∾

E VERSHOT was not there to greet them at the appointed hour. Meese ushered them into the richly appointed office with perfect fawning civility, but Cleo caught the smirk on his thin lips. It made him seem sure of his power over her, like her tormentor of old. She meant to consider the meaning of that smirk, but the warm point of connection where her elbow rested in Xander's palm had her full attention. Later she would set Meese in his place.

The door closed behind them, and Cleo stopped. The silver teapot gleamed on the table with its pale white cups that fit so roundly in Xander's hands that first day. She had thought herself recovered from the mindlessness of the night before, but she could not halt a rush of images of his hands on her body.

It was just desire. But she had been wrong about

desire. She had not guessed how completely consuming it could be. How it could burn away all pretensions and leave one humbled before it. And how it could spark again even in the most spent moment. They had turned to each other again and again in the night and even by day with the candles out and the gray light of morning filling the room. Cleo had been naked for nearly eight hours by her count.

But now they were in the bank, for heaven's sake. They had business to conduct. Today they had agreed to withdraw substantial sums, Xander for the hiring he was ready to do, and Cleo for Charlie's school fees. She took a shaky breath and a firm step forward. *Gaslights and school fees first.* But Xander's warm hold on her elbow checked her movement. She glanced over her shoulder and found her husband's shuttered gaze on her. Oh well, then, she thought, turning into the pull of him. He had not given her a babe yet, but he had barely left her side since their joining in the night.

"It was a long carriage ride," he said, drawing her into a press of bodies. Leaning back against the door, he fit her to him, her breasts yielding to the hard plane of his chest. "You were too far from me."

"Yes, and then there's that tea set."

"The tea set?" He sounded lost. With one hand he held her waist, with the other he brushed her fur-trimmed cloak off her shoulder, his fingers grazing her collarbone.

"That first day. You put your hands around a teacup, and I thought . . ." She could not say what she thought. His thumb had found her breast and coaxed her nipple to a sensitive peak.

"What's behind that screen?" His voice rasped in her ear.

She looked up at him, the plain sense of his question eluding her.

"Is there a bench or a chair? Behind that screen?"

Her mind caught up to his. "We couldn't."

"We could."

"Evershot could walk in any minute."

"Consider it a medicinal procedure." Her wicked husband grinned at her. He looked young and almost happy, and Cleo had never seen that particular light in his eyes.

He gave her a little push, a cock of his hips against hers. Cleo backed up a step. He followed, his silver gaze intent.

She glanced over her shoulder at the distance to the standing screen. "It *was* a long carriage ride. We just need a moment to refresh ourselves, put ourselves to rights."

The door opened, admitting Evershot followed by Meese with an armload of account books and papers. "Ah, Sir Alexander, Miss Spencer, sorry to keep you waiting. Demands of business, you know."

"Lady Jones," Xander corrected, shifting to stand behind Cleo, his hands drawing the loose cloak from her shoulders.

"Well, of course, so used to our former Miss Spencer, don't you know? Did you have some tea?" Evershot waved Meese over to the vast desk, where Meese dropped his ledgers and papers with a thud.

"It's money we've come for, Evershot." Xander's voice had a sudden edge.

"Well then, we'll get down to it. There's a bit of paperwork to be done, I fear." Evershot did not move.

Cleo felt Xander tense, and she stepped from his hold. "More paperwork? I thought we cleared up all the necessary questions on our last visit."

"Just a few details. We bankers always take extra care." Evershot spread his hands in a gesture of apology, which rang false.

He was stalling. Cleo crossed to the big desk where Meese was arranging papers. "What is this?" she asked, looking down at a document with the seal of the Chancery Court. "I don't see our drafts, here, Mr. Evershot?"

Evershot smoothed the thin strands clinging to his brow and cleared his throat. He looked directly at Cleo. "I'm afraid I have bad news, Lady Jones. In point of fact, legally that is, you may be Miss Spencer yet. It appears you are not married."

Cleo's stomach clenched. She waited for Xander to deny it.

It was Evershot who went on speaking. "As you know, Mr. Tucker testified before the Consistory investigators that you did not make all the necessary answers during the marriage ceremony."

"Tucker already testified against us before the investigators?" She was looking at Xander. *As you know* rang like an alarm bell in her head. "You knew?"

His gaze confessed it. His face bore the self-contained expression of that first day.

Cleo gripped the edge of the desk to steady herself. He knew the court was turning against them. From the beginning she had known that he married her for her money, but he had seemed willing to take her with it. Now it was clear he meant only to use and discard her. He had been kinder to Miss Finsbury than to her. But she had been a hundred times the fool. Her stomach clenched in a sick knot.

He had resisted consummation while she begged for it. He had never intended a real marriage. She had presented herself to him, a pigeon ripe for the plucking, in this very room. She had pursued humiliation with her knife and her nakedness. Images of their night together burned in her.

Evershot misread her distress. "Now, Miss Spencer, as the advances from your own trust have been modest, most of the trust remains intact for when you do reach thirty. Your uncle and I will resume our charge of your moneys and insist that Sir Alexander repay you, as well." He looked from her to Xander, obviously ill at ease.

Her husband's gaze did not waver. His lack of alarm at March's tactics made sense now. He was careful. He had probably calculated down to the day how long he had the use of her money.

Evershot cleared his throat. "Regrettably, as a banker, my hands are tied. I can advance no more funds." He shot a sharp glance at Meese, who scooted for the door.

Abruptly Xander moved, sidestepping Evershot, aiming for Cleo. "The devil, Evershot. You set us up."

Evershot backed away, his voice rising shrilly. "Writs have been issued, you see. One from the Chancery Court, stopping the disbursement of funds from your trust, Lady Jones, until the hearing." He paused. "And one for . . ."

Xander reached Cleo and pressed her cloak into her hands, taking her arm and tugging her toward the door, but Meese, his weasel eyes gleaming, admitted two beefy constables, who made an effective wall before them.

Cleo's heart pounded. *Jail. They were going to jail.* Her uncle knew right where she was, knew Charlie was home without her, without a clue of any danger. She had to get to Charlie. She tried to yank free of Xander's hold on her arm.

"My hands are tied," Evershot muttered.

One of the pair of ox-like constables held up a huge hand. "A writ has been issued for the arrest of Sir Alexander Jones on grounds of fraud."

Xander pulled her close. "No writ for Lady Jones?"

The man shook his head. "Our orders is to keep you here, sir, not the lady."

"Where's the arresting officer?" he asked the constable who had spoken.

"Coming, sir. Expect ye have to wait some."

Cleo pulled against Xander's hold. "Charlie." Her voice was a plea. "Let me go to my brother."

"Cleo, we are married, no matter what Evershot says. The court has not ruled against us."

"Are we? You counted on Uncle March's suit from the beginning, I think."

His look did not deny it, but he did not release her.

Cleo waited for him to say that their lovemaking had changed things. She could hardly breathe for the sharp pain in her chest, and still the pull of him, in her breasts and shamefully low in her belly, made her ache. She looked away. "I forgot Charlie. Forgot him as if he didn't exist, as if you, this . . ."—her breath caught—". . . were everything." She could barely get the words out. "He only has me, and I forgot about him, forgot my whole reason for marrying you. It was for him. I cannot abandon him for what we had . . . last night." Her voice dropped to a whisper. "Last night was only . . . desire."

He released her, his eyes as cold as she'd ever seen them. "Don't leave the house." He turned away.

Cleo had only his back to plead with. She had to see Charlie safe before she could help her husband, if he was her husband.

Chapter Eighteen

✑

"M ADAM." Amos greeted her. "You have a caller."
Cleo froze at his expression. "Police?" Cold
air blew in with her entrance, chilling the hall. She shed
her bonnet and gloves, ignoring Amos's start and trying
to think what to do if Uncle March had sent constables
after her. *Norwood. She would seek Norwood's help.*

"A gentleman." Amos was at his most inscrutable.
All her mornings at home had yielded no visitor until
today. No one had come round or written or left a card.
It was laughable that she had a caller now with Xander
arrested. Xander Jones, who had married her in haste
in the smallest of churches, with no credible witnesses,
no celebration. She had had a long carriage ride to see
the duplicity that should have been plain to her from the
beginning. Make a bargain with the devil, but read the
fine print.

"Where's Charlie?" She shivered a little in the chill, struggling with the strings of her cloak.

"In the kitchen."

"Keep him there. Keep him safe. Isaiah will tell you what's happened." She handed Amos her cloak and squared her shoulders. She could not get Xander Jones, *her betrayer*, out of her head. Where would they take him? Would he go before the magistrate in the dock to hear his crimes read like a common criminal while her uncle looked on?

Her caller stood at the drawing room windows gazing out into the street, but Cleo knew that broad-shouldered, arrogant stance. The Marquess of Candover turned at her entry.

"Lady Jones."

"My lord." Cleo made her curtsy, controlling her start at the powerful resemblance of father and son. Xander obviously got his height and bearing from his father.

"I had hoped for a word with your husband." The curl of his lip instantly altered the marquess's face, erasing the resemblance. Cleo could no longer perceive a connection to Xander, stare as she might.

Lord Candover's eyes were an icy blue, his nose thinner than Xander's. The tight-fitting cut of his coat and breeches emphasized the softer, more sensuous lines of his body. Even his eyebrows curved, where Xander's slashed straight across his face. From across the room she could tell that the marquess preferred a musk-toned cologne. His lace and jewels proclaimed the sensuality that her husband kept in check.

"My husband's business keeps him from home at the moment. Would you care to sit?" She would not tell this arrogant man Xander's true situation. She was absurd, wanting to defend her husband, who was not her husband, but her betrayer.

The marquess glanced at a gilded side chair as if it were a crude bench. "I thought you had more wit than to marry a man of no birth. Or breeding."

"I beg your pardon, Your Lordship, but you can have little knowledge of me or my motives."

"I knew your father, my girl. No doubt the irregularity of his death brought you to this." He made a languid gesture encompassing the lovely room. "It must be inconvenient being situated here, so near to former friends, yet hearing nothing from them."

Cleo recognized the attempt to discompose her. He knew her situation. His daughters were among her former friends. Really, he was little like his son. She offered him a smile dripping of treacle. "On the other hand, the house is lovely."

"My great aunt owned it at one time, did you know?" He picked up a blue Venetian-blown glass globe and put it down again. "Was there a problem with your father's will?"

He was insufferable, but he had come to his son's house, and Cleo would endure him until she found out why. Politeness was clearly wasted on him. She would try frankness. "There were gaming debts."

The marquess's brows lifted. "Gaming debts? Your father? Where did you hear that tale? Your father never owed his tradesmen a shilling. Damned scrupulous fellow, good at cards, and rich as Croesus from all that copper."

Cleo looked down at her clasped hands to conceal her

surprise at the unexpected defense of her father. *Where did you hear that tale?* From Uncle March, and *she* had never questioned it. *She* had accepted her uncle's word about her father's debts. *Oh, Papa, I betrayed you, too.* Her knees wanted to buckle. She needed to think, but the marquess stood over her, and she could not show any weakness. In that he was like his son. "Surely, my lord, you did not call today to take me to task for my marriage. Did you have a message for your son?"

Her visitor stiffened in haughty offense. His nostrils flared a little. Cleo thought for a moment he might simply stalk out of the room without another word.

"Your husband, madam, is a fool, a dreamer. He refuses to recognize the very real world in which a man in his position must live. I am surprised his mother allowed him to develop such fanciful notions."

"I don't understand you, my lord."

"Then I will be plain. Tell him to stop searching for his brother. The boy *must* be dead by now."

Cleo could not conceal her confusion. *Who were they talking about?*

"Ah. He hasn't told you. I assumed. Ah well. There is another brother, my girl, a third son of sin, if you will. The boy disappeared three years ago this November."

"How did he disappear?" Cleo saw in her mind the neat stack of Bills of Mortality on Xander's desk. Her husband was searching for his lost brother in all the graves of London.

The marquess merely lifted a brow. "Other men's by-blows are hardly my concern."

"You are cold, my lord; would you care to step closer to the fire?"

His expression did not change. "Enjoy your check, Lady Jones. The boy is gone, and your husband would be wise to stop searching for him. He has powerful enemies he does not know he has."

Cleo tried to control her tongue. She wanted to smash the brittle porcelain mask of a face. "You, sir, have forfeited any right to interfere in your son's affairs."

He drew himself up. "You misspeak, madam. I have two daughters, no son. Your husband is well served for his presumption in marrying above himself, and you are like to be a widow by Christmas."

He turned and strolled toward the door, seemingly unmoved.

Cleo could not let him simply walk away. "He's been arrested, you know."

He looked back then, and she caught a brief flash of genuine alarm in those cold eyes. "For god's sake, girl, the pair of you will waken all the dragons and goblins in London."

Then he was gone. Cleo sank into the arms of a damask-covered chair. She had been wrong, out-of-time-with-the-music wrong, going-the-wrong-way-in-the-dance wrong, treading-on-her-partner's-toes wrong. She was wrong about her husband's gaslighting scheme, his dull friends, his reason for marrying her. All wrong.

The fire burned down. She began to pace the chilled room. Oh, Xander Jones had betrayed her. He had known March would attack their marriage, had calculated on that legal attack, and played a risky game to get her money and not get stuck in marriage, but facts shifted into place with the swish of her skirts. Her husband had a third brother, missing, lost in London, for whom he searched, for whom he married a mad girl and took on March. Millie Trentham's gossip came back to her. What had Millie said—he *lost* his brother. Whatever the truth of the boy's disappearance, her husband blamed himself. He had other enemies, too, unnamed by the marquess, more dangerous than March. She stopped dead. *Dear God, and she had failed him in a moment, as she had failed her papa.*

She doubted she had wounded him, as he had her. What they had was desire. He had shown her that himself. He had not given in to it as she had. He had made that plain in his refusal to take a chance on getting her with child. Oh, he wanted her. He did not deny it. She shook with the cold now, her hands icy. Heaven help her, she wanted him, and she was all her stubborn husband had to fight his enemies and find his lost brother. She turned up the stairs.

XANDER took stock of the two mammoth constables sent to keep him at the bank. Their truncheons rested lightly in huge fists. He could take out one of them but not both. He recognized the one who had spoken as a regular in the court, so not one of March's hirelings. March was undoubtedly behind his arrest, but not entirely in control.

The arrest meant little, really. It merely corrected a mistake he had always understood—yielding to desire. His cancelled partnership with Cleo Spencer had been a step in his search for Kit. She had agreed to their union because she, too, cared for a brother. They had lost their heads briefly in a dream in his bedroom, but a bank was just the place to wake one up to reality. Reality was relying on oneself, sticking to one's purpose, going it alone. He had made sure she would not pay a long-lasting price for their night of passion. There would be no babe. She would hate him, but she was strong and resilient, and she, too, would go on.

He crossed to Evershot's desk. Meese flattened his scrawny person over the documents as if to protect them, but Xander lifted him by his threadbare collar and sent him staggering toward the two constables. Meese made a show of taking a stand beside the larger men, while Evershot subsided into one of the chairs by the tea table, muttering to himself.

Xander settled down to examine the documents. He put aside the copy of their wedding lines. For a moment he couldn't see clearly. He reminded himself that he was angry, not hurt. Hurt was a closet, a dark, musty place where your skin crawled, your breath felt trapped in your chest, and your stomach knotted. Hurt was a tight place where you curled in a ball and waited and stared with open eyes in the dark and saw nothing.

He was not locked in a closet.

He took up a copy of Cleo's trust. Three nights earlier March had tried to kidnap her in spite of the legal advantage he had gained. That made no sense. If there was a clue to March's actions, it would be in the trust.

I N Xander Jones's room, Cleo found that the bed had been restored to order as if their joining there had been erased, an impression in sand, washed away with the tide. She turned from it and went straight to the chest with its drawer of perfumed letters. Their fading scent rose up, a compound of loss and longing and regret. She sank to her knees, took up a letter of recent date, and tore it open.

My dear Xander,

Nearly three years now. I tell myself you will find him soon. You must not think my spirits languish. Paris is not so cold as London, and I do not want for companions. Though you do not answer, I think of all my sons each day.
Leave the lamps burning. He will return.

Cleo tore into the next one and the next. A dozen letters later she sat on the floor of her husband's bedroom beside the remaining unopened letters. Blame or forgiveness—she didn't know which the letters offered, but she understood why they remained unopened.

Her husband's house was not Bluebeard's house, but a house of lost dreams, of a girl who had fallen in love with a lord who betrayed her for his class. A child whose father had abandoned him. A boy who had been snatched into darkness.

Xander believed that boy was alive. Could he be? Three years later? In London where children died by the hundreds each year, their names filling the pages of the Bills of Mortality?

It was fearful how fast her mind went to the pale ghost boy in the garden. She had nothing. No proof, but her mind raced on. Did he come at dusk to peer into the lighted windows of his lost home like a phantom? If her ghost boy in the garden was not Teeth, the chestnut seller, but Xander's brother, why did he not come in out of the cold? What did he fear? Whom did he fear? Xander's father mentioned unknown enemies. Not March then, but someone else. Kneeling, Cleo scooped the letters back into the drawer.

T HE bank was closing now, the hum in the vast lobby subsiding. The two constables stood as steady as ever, but Meese fidgeted with his watch. Evershot slumped, inert in his chair. The door opened at last to admit an officer of the law in his greatcoat, holding the black, crown-imprinted staff of a Runner in one hand, his face grim.

Xander looked up and grinned. "About time."

The pair of ox-like constables parted to let Will Jones pass. He flashed a writ and an answering grin. "It's not every day that a man gets to arrest his brother."

He nodded to the two constables. "Thanks, lads, this one's all mine, but you can take away the audience." The two men seized Meese and dragged him out into the main bank chamber. Meese could be heard squeaking and protesting as he was hauled away.

Xander stood. "How did you know there was a writ for my arrest?"

"The old beak himself gave me the duty."

"You took your sweet time about it." Xander turned to Evershot. "You're coming with us, man. You've got some explaining to do. Bring those papers and ledgers along."

Evershot's gray face lost the rest of its color. He started to speak. "I can't—"

"Now, Evershot," Xander insisted.

Will pulled Evershot out of his chair. "He sold you out, you know. He told March exactly when you planned to be here."

"I gathered." Xander followed Will and a stumbling, laden Evershot to a waiting hack.

Outside the bank, Will shoved Evershot and his arm-load of papers into the vehicle. Will's confederates had apparently taken Meese elsewhere.

Xander paused to take a deep breath, letting his lungs fill with cold, sooty London air before he climbed into the closed space. He didn't know why his old discomfort should plague him now. The hack was not a closet, not the narrow space in which he had hidden while his mother raged and wept after his father left, in which she had locked him while she courted her next lover. Xander climbed into the cab.

The hack had not gone two blocks when Evershot was vilely ill. They stopped briefly to clean up the man and the carriage, Will berating him in a stream of foul language. Evershot slumped back against the side of the cab, panting, indifferent to Will's abuse.

Xander watched him. "Evershot, you're in this up to your neck. You tipped March off that we would be there today to withdraw funds."

Will prodded Evershot's shoulder with his staff. "Answer, man, why are you in bed with March?"

"The . . . bank . . . could . . . fail," Evershot managed between panting breaths.

"March doesn't have that much money in the bank, does he?" Xander knew March had controlled two large fortunes, Cleo's and her brother's, for years, but Xander's own partners had substantial sums in Evershot's bank as well.

Evershot shook his head, a weak motion. "March has files."

"What do you mean files?" Will's voice was quiet, almost deadly.

Evershot's hand fluttered weakly. "Names, dates, places, parties involved. He can ruin half of London if he chooses."

"Your half, apparently," Will put in.

"You've been letting March see clients' records, haven't you, Evershot?" Xander nudged the man's boot.

A whimper was the reply.

"Where does March keep these files?" Xander asked.

"I don't know." Evershot groaned, without looking up.

Xander lifted him by his limp, soiled linen. "Your bank is about to bleed money from a dozen gaping wounds. Think of the investors you will lose when I start talking to my friends about you."

"No, no need to withdraw money, Sir Alexander. You should thank me. Truly. I saved her. I kept her alive."

"What do you mean?" Xander's chill had nothing to do with the cold.

"There's a reversion clause in her trust. If she dies without issue, her husband must repay any funds he received into her brother's trust."

"Who put in the reversion clause?"

Evershot coughed weakly. "March."

"When?"

"When she refused his choice of suitors."

"The devil," said Will. "A bleeding recipe for murder. March is a clever worm."

The carriage stopped, and Xander opened the door. Raw wintry air washed in. "Evershot, if March hurts her, I will close your bank, and you'll rot in jail."

They put Evershot down in the Strand without his papers. Cold wind ruffled the long, thin strands of his hair.

"Bleeding coward." Will signaled the driver.

A block later the hack turned north, and Xander glanced at his brother. "Where are we going?"

"Oh, you're going to jail. It'll do you good, I think. Mix it up some with true Londoners. Take some of that stiff-necked pride down a notch or two. Hard to say how long it will take to get you there."

"I'd rather see my wife."

"Not possible at the moment."

"Does March have men at the house?" Xander wanted Cleo protected.

"No, but there's a price on your head. Cheer up, I've known Runners who've hunted their man for days, weeks even."

"Is that what you're doing, hunting me?"

"I figure it could take a week to find a dangerous suspect like yourself in our vast city."

"Could your hunt take us by Norwood's chambers?"

"After dark."

The hack stopped in a murky lane off the Strand, and after Will made arrangements with the driver, he led Xander deeper into vile byways, stopping along a twisting street between a six-shilling bawdy house and a taproom.

"All the neighborhood conveniences, I see," commented Xander.

"Especially as I own the building," Will replied. "It gets better. There's a cundum warehouse on the corner, erotic prints for the asking at the 'book' store across the way, and plenty of treasures at Beck's pawn shop."

"No milkmaids?"

"Not my style."

A crescent moon with a grinning profile of its famous man marked the lintel of an unseen door, fronting the street. A darker shadow rose snarling out of the gloom and bared its teeth, emitting a deep, rumbling snarl. Will ordered the shadow into submission, and it obeyed.

"Your dog?"

"Argos, Blind Zebediah's mastiff." Will opened a nearly hidden door and led the way up a surprisingly clean and sturdy stairway to the third story.

He unlocked the door to a large high-ceilinged room with the dark paneled walls of an earlier age. A massive canopied bed with tangerine damask hangings stood on a dais. A mound of silken pillows with chocolate-colored tassels lay against the tall, carved headboard, and tangled coverlets with swirls of indigo design threatened to slide down to the rich blue carpet below. A brass chandelier hung above, and gilded mirrors reflected the bed from every angle. Xander had to shake his head. His brother's apartment was a whore's dream.

"Did you steal some sultan's state bed?"

Will caught his expression. "A friend was going out

of business. The bed is extremely comfortable, and you have to admit that Hill Street doesn't offer anything like it."

Will headed straight for the far wall, pressed a spot at the edge of the paneling, and sprang a hidden door, which swung open on a second room, furnished with Spartan simplicity. It held an unmade bed, a wardrobe, a desk, a pair of worn wing chairs by a hearth, and a remarkable collection of maps, books, and instruments.

Again Xander couldn't contain his surprise. "What have you got here?"

"I suppose someone should know about this place. It's my own police office, essentially. Don't leave it, except by night, or with me, or you'll be standing in the dock before the magistrate."

Here the lighting was bright and efficient. The walls were lined with careful maps of the city and shelves of law books. Tables held scientific instruments.

"Drink?" Will asked.

Xander nodded.

Will lit the coals in the grate and sprawled in one of the chairs, drink in hand. "Where's your bride?"

"Isaiah took her home."

"She walked out on you, didn't she?"

"My plan to undo our marriage disappointed her some."

"Let her go. You wanted to end it. Now you're out."

"It's not that simple."

"You didn't bed her, did you?" He shot Xander a penetrating look. "You did! Not the saint, after all, are you?"

"I never claimed to be."

"Man, you bollixed up your own damned plan."

Xander gazed at his wine. It seemed to trap the candlelight, reminding him of his wife's garnet dress.

"There's no chance of a child though, is there?"

"None."

Will raised his glass in a sardonic salute. "Then it never happened. Norwood would get you out of it anyway."

But it had happened.

XANDER Jones's silent servants sat hunched with Charlie around the kitchen table. They looked up at Cleo's entrance. Isaiah cast a quick, anguished glance at the others.

"You told them?"

He nodded.

Cleo squared her shoulders. She held the framed verse from Charlie's room against her chest. "You may blame me if you like, but we're going to have to act together to help him."

The fire cracked and popped.

Charlie looked from Isaiah to Cleo. "Why was Xander arrested?"

"Uncle March is trying to prove we did not truly marry, but rather, pretended, to get the money out of my trust. That's fraud."

"But you were married in a church. It was real. I was there. They could ask me."

"You are a minor."

"Will was there. He's an officer of the law. Oh, but he is Will Jones, isn't he?" Charlie looked at Cleo's face. "Are you going to be arrested, too, Cleo?"

"Xander thinks not," she said. *And I didn't believe him.*

Five anxious faces looked at Cleo.

"So what do we do now, my lady?" Amos asked.

Cleo took a deep breath. "We look for a lost boy. What's his name?"

For a long moment no one answered. Alice choked back a sob, and Mrs. Wardlow put a comforting arm around the girl. "Kit. The boy is Kit."

Cleo took a steadying breath. "I've seen a boy in the garden at dusk."

"Teeth, the chestnut seller?" Charlie asked.

"No, not our spy, another boy altogether, fair and sweet-faced."

She felt all those eyes on her, not daring to hope. She had no proof. Three years of searching. To raise false hope would be cruel. She saw clearly now why her husband never opened or answered his mother's heartbroken letters. The only answer to that drawer full of letters was a living boy, not a name in the Bills of Mortality.

"This ghost boy comes to the garden after dark. I've been leaving him food and quilts. Tonight I want to leave him something . . . Kit . . . would know. This." She turned the framed saying to them for all to see. "I don't want to frighten him. Here's what we're going to do."

Cleo directed Isaiah to take Alice and Charlie to Hodge's lodging for safety. Her uncle would not find Charlie there, and she would get a message to Norwood to protect him. She sent Charlie off without the hug she longed to give him and told him that he and Alice were to stay with Hodge until Xander himself came for them.

Then she sent Isaiah to the court to see whether Xander had been arraigned.

She ordered Cook to prepare another food bundle and wrapped the little verse in a sturdy oilcloth wrapping with a note in her own hand. *It's safe to come home. We all want you back.*

The night sky was thick with clouds and the air arctic when she returned to the house. Snow was coming. It was not even Guy Fawkes Night. She and Amos went from room to room lighting the lamps. Alone, she climbed up through the empty brightness to Xander Jones's bedroom. Only there she could not light a lamp. In the dark she removed her clothes. Naked and shivering, she buried herself in his bed. And lay still and let what they had done come back to her. It could not be erased after all.

Chapter Nineteen

❦

In the morning Cleo's bundle in the tree notch wore a white snow hat six inches tall. Snow was falling still. She refused to think what that meant for the boy; just another cold night where he had sought shelter somewhere.

She had trusted in his return. Her plan was to follow him when he took the bundle. She did not know how else to search for him. But she understood him better this morning. She, too, had hovered outside London's bright windows after three years away, conscious of herself as someone different, someone who would not be welcomed back into her old life.

She paced the great room, and the emptiness of the house wore on her. Amos brought her coffee while they waited for Isaiah to return from his vigil at the court. He was to leave a message with Norwood whatever happened to Xander.

The street was a stark landscape of brick and snow, the usual traffic reduced to an occasional sled. A group of ragged children chucked snowballs at each other. Cleo studied them closely. Apparently her uncle used such children as spies, but she did not see Teeth among them.

By nine there was still no word from Isaiah, and the snow in the garden was nearly a foot deep. A lumbering hack wallowing through the drifts was the first sign of danger. The vehicle slowed and two large men emerged. Cleo shouted for Amos. She heard the front door bang open, heard the scrape of heavy feet against the marble and the crash of furniture and porcelain. As she came flying down the stairs, two rough men barreled up them.

Amos lay insensible on the floor, around him the wreckage of a demilune table and a vase. A broad-backed man rummaged noisily through the open closet. A second man with the broken table leg in his huge hand spotted her.

"Ma'am, officers of the law."

Cleo recognized the lie with sinking certainty.

"Do you have a writ?" she asked, kneeling to tend to Amos, hoping to buy some time. A deep gash over his temple bled freely. She heard the tramp of feet above her.

The man rummaging in the closet emerged with her cloak. "Here's yer writ, miss, yer comin' with us." He hauled Cleo up and dragged her stumbling and resisting to the door. The other man dropped the table leg and grabbed her free arm, lifting her off her feet. They swept her down the stairs and tossed her into the old coach. Only the ragged children saw her taken.

Her knees hit the floor of the coach, and she braced herself against the bench. She staggered up, caught in her skirts, and came face-to-face with her uncle as the coach lurched into motion. Cleo lunged for the door handle when his fist swung out to meet her.

Archibald's blow quelled his niece's furious resistance. She sat opposite him in her wretched old cloak, stunned, and silent for once.

"Without a poker it is more difficult to overcome a man," he told her.

She pressed her hand to her jaw. He did not think he had broken it, but he had made her look at him with quite a new appreciation, those intelligent eyes of hers wide and wary. He could almost see the rapid rush of thoughts. Why did people so underestimate him? He offered her his handkerchief.

She reached for it and let it drop to the muddied floor of the cab.

He shook his head. "Don't be tiresome, niece. You have an opportunity here. And it's the last one I'm offering, so you'd best make yourself agreeable."

In his own words he heard an unfortunate echo of that chill, polite voice speaking from behind and above his favorite chair at the club. Three years earlier, the voice had thrilled him when he first heard it speaking intimately to him; now it chafed him.

It was the voice that had prompted this next step in dealing with his wayward niece. Before his visitor had dropped by Archibald's club, things had been well in hand. Her foolish marriage to Jones, while initially inconvenient in its impact upon her trust, had proved an opportunity. Archibald's legal tactics were sufficient to discredit them both, but the voice wanted more.

After their appearance at the theater, the print shops had portrayed them as the "madly mated" pair with Jones running about lighting lamps as bank notes fell from his stuffed pockets and his wife chased him with a poker.

Archibald had found he could not share the joke with his visitor. The pale, long-fingered hand with the heavy signet ring, resting lightly on the wing of his chair, discouraged familiarities. The voice simply made it plain that Archibald must stop Jones's ridiculous search for the boy.

At the end of Hill Street the rear of the hack dipped and hung for a moment on the lip of some rut in the road before it lumbered onward through the snow. They would have slow going, but he could afford to be patient now that he had everything in motion. Archibald stared at his niece. Her scrutiny never wavered. How had the chit managed to make so much trouble?

"You're not taking me home, are you?"

"Too late for that. You had a chance to come to your senses, return to my protection, and end this charade of a marriage a fortnight ago."

"Abducting me is hardly an act in keeping with your role as benefactor to the downtrodden of London."

He didn't answer. It really didn't matter that she underestimated him again. "Where is your would-be husband, niece? You can't hide him, you know."

"You had him arrested, Uncle; you must know where he's been taken."

"I confess I did want an opportunity to speak to you without his influence. It's not too late to repudiate your most unwise marriage and take a more suitable husband."

"No, thank you, Uncle." She still held her jaw, but he thought she sat straighter on the bench.

"Like him between the sheets, do you, girl?"

"As a matter of fact I do. Very wifely of me, don't you think?"

Damn her for refusing to blush. "Do you know what his lovers say about him?"

He caught her off guard but watched her quick recovery.

"He cut quite a path through Mayfair when Prinny gave him that knighthood, you know. But he'll be tossing up a different class of skirt inside of a month if you insist on remaining married."

"We are married, Uncle, no matter what you did to poor Mr. Tucker to get him to lie for you."

"Don't be absurd, girl. You've been practiced on by a presumptuous nobody with a paper knighthood, who went after your money for an unprofitable scheme of lighting London's reeking lanes."

"All London, I think. He's more democratic in his notions than you, Uncle. The hearing will determine the validity of our marriage."

"You think Norwood can convince the investigators that you meant no fraud? Let me tell you, the law does very little for bastards, and nothing at all for those who offend the rich and powerful with their searches for dead boys."

He saw something shift in her expression. "How do you know the boy is dead, Uncle?"

"He must be. Three years." That of course was the rub. The polite voice hinted that it would be a most inconvenient and entirely unsatisfactory outcome if Xander Jones were to find his brother alive. The voice implied that Archibald would be held accountable for such an unfortunate result, for promises left unfulfilled, though how the boy could have survived, Archibald did not know.

But Archibald had found a way to stop Xander Jones's search cold. Sniveling Dick Cullen with his demand for free beer had suggested the idea, and Archibald had instantly seen a chance to purge Bread Street of the likes of Cullen and Mother Greenslade and anyone else who talked too freely about lost boys for the price of a pint. He would simply wash them away on a tide of their favorite drink. And Archibald had decided to dispense with his inconvenient niece in the same flood.

"Really, Niece, the best thing you can do for your husband is to cast him off." Archibald opened his traveling case of writing materials. "I am willing to drop prosecution of your lover, if you sign an affidavit that no marriage took place."

She gave him an untrusting look, so unlike those first days after Edward's death when she had been willing to lean against him for comfort. At one time he had thought to have her for himself, but not as another man's soiled goods.

"My signature on that paper won't change the facts of our marriage."

Damn the girl for being a stubborn fool. Archibald signaled the hack to stop. They had reached a conveniently empty stretch of road. Across the way, he could see the donkey cart driver waiting in the appointed place.

A group of ragged street urchins descended from the back of the carriage. Apparently, they had stolen a ride. Momentarily they swarmed the coach with cries for alms. The driver shouted and plied his whip, driving them off down a dark lane. Archibald put the writing case in his niece's lap.

"Do you think Jones won't cast you off to save himself? You don't know men, Niece." When she dropped her hand from her jaw, he could see swelling and a bloody cut where the lip had split.

Cleo held the pen he gave her above the paper he wanted her to sign. The words were fairly straightforward, an indication that she had been misled by Alexander Jones and that she did not wish to be married to him. She tried to think how to distract her uncle.

"What happens to Charlie?"

"Why, he remains my ward, and I'll remove him from the harmful influence of that whore's house on Hill Street."

"Will he go to school?"

"I hope your brother has the wit to appreciate his own home as you did not. Like your father, you have no proper sense of what was simply handed to you."

"You lied to me about Papa, Uncle. There were no gaming debts, were there?" She signed, hoping her uncle would not examine the signature closely.

"I'm busy, Niece. You'll have to excuse me. Others will see to your . . . comfort. A vehicle waits to take you where you can await his reply. Your new situation will encourage you to have a proper understanding of the stakes in this matter."

H ENRY Norwood brought grim news to Will and Xander at his chambers at noon. He had found Isaiah trying to revive Amos in the entry of the house and had sent for a physician to see to Amos's care. Isaiah explained where the other members of the house were, but he did not know what had become of Cleo. Under the physician's care Amos revived long enough to describe the men who had taken her.

Xander saw in his mind the man who'd attacked her in the street tumbling backward into a donkey cart.

"March has her." Even as he said the words he understood something he had denied to himself in the bank as he betrayed her. He could not let her go. He had seen her and wanted her and taken her and told himself a lie that he wanted only her money.

"He'll take her to Woford House." Henry Norwood looked relieved and then thoughtful. "He may try to force her to repudiate the marriage in front of witnesses."

Xander shook his head. He did not share Norwood's optimism. "Evershot says there's a reversion clause in Cleo's trust. If she dies without issue, her husband must repay the trust. March never counted on the courts to dissolve the marriage."

Abruptly Xander remembered the detail that had eluded him the night March attacked her. *Hops.* She'd been covered with broken bits of the fragrant plant from the sack they'd thrown over her head. He had seen no lettering on the donkey cart, but he knew well where that particular cart was likely to come from. Bredsell had preached from such a cart with *Truman's Brewery* in red lettering on the side. He saw the whole strategy unfold. "March's habits are well-known. He'll be at his ease in his club when some accident befalls his mad niece."

Will nodded. "I wouldn't put it past him to burn down a building with her in it. Do you think he's got her somewhere on Bread Street, Xan?"

"Where else? No one would come to her aid there."

Norwood was shocked. "But March's legal quest has been to discredit you, to claim that he is protecting his niece by acting against your marriage. It makes no sense to harm her."

Will watched him closely. "Xan, you can't go to Bread Street alone. Officers don't go there except in numbers. Bashing in heads is the local industry, and don't forget you're a man at large, and there's a reward."

"March doesn't leave anything to chance, does he? How much?"

"Five hundred pounds."

"Quite a sum. Divided among four Runners, it would be a good day's wage."

Will's brows lifted. "A year's more like. What are you thinking?"

Xander grinned at his brother. "That you don't deserve all the glory of my arrest."

Chapter Twenty

N ATE Wilde watched the comings and goings at
the lawyer's office, judging how he could get past
the porter at the door. Snow covered the wide square
and dusted the sooty old bricks. He was too old and too
knowing to delight in an early snow as he once might
have, and besides, the unexpected snow was keeping
folks indoors, making it hard for him to pass as an
errand boy as Bredsell boys were trained to do.

There were barriers everywhere he looked. High
iron gates with spiderwebs of scrollwork closed off one
end of an open square bounded by the stone and brick
buildings. The old buildings stood straight and starchy
and had all their doors and staring brass knockers, not
like his neighborhood. Busy Oxford Street was a much
better lay for a Bredsell boy. This place was like a regular graveyard, it was.

He tucked his hands under his arms and stomped his feet against the cold. He could not complain about being a Bredsell boy. Bredsell himself was an annoyance, but the school had more holidays and gave away more cake than any school he ever heard of. The hours with the masters were few, and boys who knew their letters and numbers got jobs and wages. Sometimes he delivered brown wrapped packets to gentlemen. Sometimes he watched their comings and goings. His current job was the best yet. He loafed around a bunch of toffs all day, watching them and reporting back on them to Bredsell or the big, swell toff behind it all. He got the job because he was smart. He saw things and remembered them, and he knew his way about London. He could get from Park Lane to Bread Street faster than a grown man, and he knew the art of invisibility in a crowd.

The job was like being a Runner in reverse. He watched them, he reported on them. He was pretty sure, too, that he was working for smart, powerful men, men who knew how to get what they wanted in life. And he didn't have to do a click to have money in his pocket. Bredsell gave him three and six a week for his reports. Three and six for loafing and watching and not doing a thing for which the law could touch him. He could see himself already a high mobsman with a purple silk waistcoat and gold rings and fellows to do his work for him.

And now he'd been trusted with a bigger job and promised five shillings for it. All he had to do was find a Mr. Henry Norwood and repeat the message he'd learned earlier in the day. And he knew, too, because he paid attention to such things that his message was trouble for the copper Will Jones and his top-lofty brother. He grinned at the thought, though the cold made his teeth ache.

His chance came when two groups of wiggy gentlemen in flowing black robes tried to enter the building at one go. Nate came up behind one group as the other group finally gave way to let them pass, and then he was in the shadowed doorway. He knew right where he had to go. He was up the stairs, knocking on number five before the wiggy gentlemen knocked the snow from their shoes.

"Message for Henry Norwood," he told the young clerk who answered the door. Nate figured he probably got paid as well as the clerk, even if the fellow's shirt points were so very high and he did have a fine gold watch chain hanging across his belly. He'd lose that fast on Bread Street, and his shoes and the contents of his pockets.

The toffy clerk made him stand in the doorway until a stout old fellow with eyebrows like white cat's tails came to peer at him closely. The old fellow made him sit in a hard chair.

"Now then, lad, let's have your message, please." The old fellow held out his hand.

Nate just shook his head and grinned. "Nothin' on paper, sir." He tapped his head and remembered to take his cap off. "It's all here."

The old gentleman signaled his clerk. "Then we'd best take it down. In case our brains are not so exact as yours."

Nate squared his shoulders. The warm room, the hard chair, and the fixed stare of the old gentleman were making him uneasy.

He had the message all clear in his head, but he had to

get it out in one burst, so to speak, and he didn't want his teeth to chatter. Some of the grand words meant nothing, though he knew, right enough, that the whole of the message was a threat. "Presumption has its price. A letter repudiating your marriage signed before a notary and delivered to Woford House by five today secures your release from further prosecution."

Nate finished, and to his surprise the clerk finished, too. He'd expected to have to repeat the message more than once, but the flashy fellow seemed to think he'd got it all down.

"Is there anything else, lad?" The old fellow with the white eyebrows looked at Nate, too closely for comfort. He looked like a fellow who might remember what he saw.

"No, Yer Worship. I've been straight with ye."

"Have you, now? Well then, Bob," the old fellow said, turning to his flashy clerk, "get this boy something hot to drink before he steps out into the cold again."

Nate was on his feet at once. He had his orders, and hot drinks weren't among them. "Nowt for me, Yer Worship. I've done my job; best be off to let 'em know ye got the message."

The old fellow nodded. "Right you are. Let's get you a cab then."

"Cab, me? You must be joking like." No one said he couldn't take a cab. It'd be a lark, wouldn't it? A cab would never go up Bread Street, but Nate could ride up High Holborn in a cab. Nate tried then to look like a decent errand boy, an honest lad, the sort folks trusted. The old fellow watched him so closely, he wasn't sure he succeeded at all. "Thank you," he said.

"A cab it is then." The old fellow turned to his clerk. "Bob, get your coat, and see this boy off."

That didn't sound quite right, but Nate could see no danger in Bob. Bob looked like he knew as much about the world as a babe in nappies. Bob went off to get his coat, and there was a good bit of moving about in other rooms that Nate couldn't see. Doors opening and closing and feet shuffling like three clerks instead of one, and then Bob was back, and Nate let old Bob slog into the slush and flag a cabman. He settled back against the squabs, thinking about when he would ride in cabs all day, anytime he liked. He didn't look back once.

WITHIN the hour Bob returned from following Nate Wilde to Bread Street, and Xander saw his path clear. He would stage his own arrest there. Will's role was to assemble a cohort of trusted men from among his fellow Runners, no one with ties to March. While Xander worked his way up the street, Will would lead the group of officers down from the school, drawing attention, and claiming to look for a notorious pickpocket, spreading the rumor of a reward. Between them they would search the street from end to end. Number Forty remained a likely place for March to conceal Cleo. Xander remembered its basement rooms. The search would end there.

Once Xander found Cleo, he could allow himself to be arrested, and their police escort would get them away from Bread Street without any interference from March's hirelings.

Will had only one word of caution. "Careful, Xan, March may have sent Wilde to lure you into a trap."

They shook hands and parted. Timing mattered. March had clearly sent Nate Wilde to make them think that he still pursued legal means against their marriage, but that reversion clause stuck in Xander's mind. He did not think March intended Cleo to survive the night.

Chapter Twenty-one

ᚨ

CLEO woke flat on her back in darkness so complete, she could not be sure her eyes functioned. She was stiff with cold. Her jaw ached, and her lip felt the size of a ripe plum. She had no idea of the time. She held herself perfectly still, willing her heart to stop its sudden pounding.

A small, unfamiliar tinkling sound had wakened her. She breathed in the smell of earth and decay. The cold, damp stillness of the place made her think she had been buried. Her ears seemed filled with a roar that was no sound, her arms felt heavy at her sides. If she lifted them and met a coffin lid, she thought her heart would burst out of her chest. Xander would never know she loved him. How inconvenient to recognize her true feelings when the chance to express them had clearly passed. She closed her eyes and told herself to behave with common sense, making her numb hands move outward from her sides.

A rough, grit-covered cloth lay under her. She spread her hands further and felt a wave of relief. She was not in a box but on some sort of bed or cot. It had an edge over which the rough cloth hung down. The ringing sound of metal against glass came again.

She opened her eyes and carefully turned her head. Above her on the right a pale slit wavered against the blackness, a trick of her light-deprived eyes. She fixed her gaze on it, and gradually, the shape became clear, a long, low arch like an oven door.

She slowed her breathing and waited for her heart to calm its pounding so she could hear. Above her, beyond the pale light, voices and footsteps came and went, children's voices. She thought she was confusing things in her head. Ragged urchins had been playing on Hill Street when her uncle took her. She concentrated on her present circumstances, staring hard at the faint light above.

Then it came to her. Her temporary tomb was a cellar with a window that opened on a street or a court where people were passing.

Slowly she sat up. Her head throbbed, and her stomach roiled with nausea. She held herself still until the sickening sensations passed, refusing to close her eyes again. With a dizzying effort she got to her hands and knees, tangling briefly in her cloak. Reaching out to brace herself against the wall, she put her hand to clammy bricks. She staggered to her feet on the sagging bed, hearing it creak and groan under her. The window was higher above her than she thought. Her corset straps limited the reach of her arms, but by standing on her toes and stretching her arm out as fully as she could, she could reach the bottom ledge. She started at one end, inching her fingers along, feeling the grimy edge and the frozen glass. Snow must be piled against the other side. She stopped suddenly where a draft of icy air rushed across her fingers. She strained further, feeling an edge of broken glass and through it, snow.

As she poked the snow, her fingers met other fingers, cool and strong. She drew her hand back and almost lost her balance on the flimsy bed, coming down hard on her heels.

"Lady Jones," said a young male voice from beyond the window. "Listen, we've got to get you out. My friends and I." Pure, sweet, educated syllables, a boy's voice newly deepened into mature tones.

Cleo caught her breath. He even sounded like Xander. "Your brother has been looking for you."

For a long moment there was no answer, just the children's voices. She feared she had frightened her ghost away. Then he spoke again.

"Lady Jones, we'll get you out, but you must help. Something's coming down through the hole. Catch it."

Cleo waited, watching the hole. A shadow crossed it, and then she heard the clink of metal hitting brick. She couldn't see anything below the window, but the clinking thing tapped the wall, moving closer to her. She reached for the sound and found a thin metal rod, a broken piece of railing, tied to a bit of string. Carefully, she released the rod from the string.

"Have you got it then?" came the voice.

"Yes. Where am I?"

"You're in the front cellar of the public house, Lady Jones. It's mostly barrels and rubbish. Men are watching the place from up the street. We can't let them catch you."

"What am I to do?"

"The door is straight opposite, not more than eight steps. Work the lock with that rod. We're going to play a game, tapping on the window. When you have the lock opened, tap back. We will signal when it's safe to leave. Then take the stairs. Go up, and keep going up, as fast as you can."

XANDER became a shadow at the foot of Bread Street dressed in Will's castoffs. Maybe chance had cast him as a shadow from the start, a nameless product of London's wicked ways, one of her baseborn sons, told by his father to disappear, by his mother to hide.

Only he hadn't. He had crossed the line set for him by his birth. He had saved a prince, married a baron's daughter, and dared to dream of lighting London's blackest darkness.

Only his mad wife wanted to be seen with him in the glare of lights. He knew that now. She had heard him named a bastard in the first moments of their acquaintance, but somehow she had always seen him, not the ugly word. Something else to appreciate about her if he could bring her alive from March's hold.

Half of Bread Street lay in early evening darkness, the last streaks of a red sunset casting a lurid light on low gray clouds. Yesterday's snow, churned up and soot-blackened, made dirty drifts along the edge of the street. The telltale donkey cart leaned against the wall of Number Forty, where Xander was certain March had Cleo.

Xander could see the street from end to end. At the top of the hill, where Will would appear, the dark corner of Bredsell's school jutted out. Opposite and below it was the back of Truman's Brewery, where three vast wood holding vats bounded by black iron bands rose above the crumbling wall of the brewery yard. Thousands of gallons of black porter fermented there, enough to quench the thirst even of Bread Street.

A crowd of workmen left the yard as Xander watched, streaming out from the gate below the vats, heading up the street or stopping at the fish shop for greasy papers of bloaters. Within minutes it struck Xander that Bread Street was unusually quiet. Of the hundreds who lived there, only a handful of ragged children playing outside the public house, and a group of idlers, standing around a bonfire, gave life to the scene. The boards advertising positions at Xander's gasworks, torn from the building, made a blazing fire. So much for the wages he offered.

The loafers were bullyboys all, thick-necked and ham-fisted. Their gathering lacked the spontaneous look of true idleness. They gave off a tense air of waiting for something to happen. No one was drinking, and no women were present.

Two loafers slogged their way up the snowy street, muffled in rags. Xander pressed deeper in the shadows to let them pass.

The first opened a fist to show his companion a coin. "I know nuffin, but a toffy bloke give me 'alf a crown to stay out of the tap. Said there'd be free beer for all."

"'Ow's there to be free beer with the tap closed?"

Xander wondered the same. Bread Street loved its liquor. Every doorway, every ledge had its row of pint pots. The smallest child knew not to come between a man or a woman and drink, yet above the stone slab that marked the public-house entrance, the heavy double doors bore a chain and padlock. Instead of the usual ebb and flow of drinkers, children played a game in the front of the tap. Xander turned his gaze on those grubby urchins tagging the basement window with sticks.

The low window barely rose above the pavement in a flattened arch partly concealed by piled snow. The opening was dark and narrow as the gully holes in the curb. At least eight children played the game, young and thin and darting swift as birds. A low rumble of a voice in the darkened doorway opposite launched the children in pairs. Each pair made a quick dash, tapped with sticks at the cellar window, paused, whirled, and sprinted back. Some were barefoot in the snow. The exercise might warm them, but Xander wondered that they had not sought shelter. They, too, watched the men around the impromptu bonfire.

WILL had less trouble than he'd expected getting into March's club. He'd never be admitted as a member, but apparently the sanctity of the place depended more on the lower orders accepting their inferior position in society than on the vigilance of the porters at the door.

But then, he'd always known rats to find their way into a palace.

His appearance did not raise an eyebrow in the long room with the vaulted ceiling when he picked up a paper and strolled across the room. Only taking an empty chair caused anxiety in a nervous waiter. Confused by Xander's borrowed tailoring, and understandably wary of Will's own brand of menace, the poor fellow shifted from foot to foot, clearly unable to decide whether to ignore Will and face the member whose chair he'd claimed, or confront Will directly. Will discouraged the waiter from any thought of the latter with a savage glance.

Other members gave him sidelong looks as they came in. One chubby fellow halted, stuttered into speech, caught Will's eye, and subsided in a deep leather chair a comfortable distance away.

The room was too well lit to suit Will. Bright light was overrated. It revealed sagging chins and bellies, spotted linen, and thinning hair. What a bleeding soft lot they were, these fat fish in their scummy pond, content to swim in each other's piss, as long as their own magnificent scales flashed before the notice of all.

As he waited for March, Will's dislike of Xander's plan grew. Four officers would tramp Bread Street and risk getting their heads broken while March sipped claret and got away with attempted murder. They had to find Cleo, but to let March escape was not Will's style. The rub was that to arrest him would be premature. The bleeding maggot would likely get off.

March should sweat. He should feel every eye in his bleeding club on him, every member doubting the sterling reputation of London's great philanthropist. There must be men in the club who, like Evershot, were uncomfortable with March's information about their doings. Will wanted to know where March kept those files that so unmanned Evershot. Will wanted to open an investigation into the death of Cleo Spencer's father. He suspected that March had murdered his half brother. It was time for March to feel exposed, scrutinized, suspected.

A chorus of clocks about the room chimed the quarter hour. Will leaned back against the wings of the chair, one polished boot crossed over the other knee. Xander had his mission, and Will had his. He just had time to make March squirm before he met his companions at the top of Bread Street. He felt the room fall silent and knew March had arrived.

"Jones, how did you—?"

As Will looked up, March threw a wild glance at the clock. There was a brief, satisfying flash of something like fear in his eyes as March corrected his thinking about which brother he had in front of him.

"*My brother* unfortunately is still at large."

"Jones, this is a members-only club." March looked around again.

"Your chair, March?" Will rubbed his palms along the armrests. March could come and go from Bow Street or Bread Street, but he never expected someone or something from that end of London to ooze its way out of the gutter and into his sanctuary.

"Sadly, March, official police business sometimes takes a man among the most depraved souls in London." Will made his voice loud and clear. He kept his gaze on March, feeling rather than seeing the rest of the room grow quietly attentive.

"I'm certain no official police business concerns this club or its members." March again looked at the clock.

"Investigations have their own timetable I find, March."

"Surely, your investigation can wait for a more appropriate time and place. I often have business at Bow Street with the magistrate."

"Best to act when information might prevent murder, I find." Will took a swallow of March's claret—insipid stuff.

"I have no such information."

"I thought it was common knowledge, March, that you had files on half the gentlemen of London, that you and the Home Secretary were bosom boys. He is a member here, is he not?" Will looked around at the faces of the sheep trying not to appear interested though every other conversation in the room had died.

March's face remained smooth except for a tightening of the mouth. "Jones, apparently you've been misled by rumor and gossip."

Will stood, conscious of the clock's steady advance. He just had time to throw another coal on the fire. "March, which of your properties is most profitable— the tenements on Bread Street or the brothel where your brother died?"

The mask slipped ever so slightly, and Will caught a gleam of pure rage in March's gaze.

At the same moment an icily polite voice spoke from behind Will. "March, your sordid interview is disturbing the members. I suggest you see this man out."

"I'm on my way," Will said. He thought he knew that voice. He started to turn when something heavy broke over his back, smashing the breath out of his lungs. Staggering forward under the blow, he hurled his glass at March.

It missed March but clipped a passing waiter, who stumbled backward, dropping his tray with a clang, and the room erupted in most ungentlemanly howls of rage as men swarmed him. Will got off a few more blows, mashed a chair to splinters, and shattered a mirror before he found himself pinned to the floor, fighting the downward flutter of his eyelids.

A clock began to chime with sour bronze notes. The last thing he heard was that smooth, chill voice. "Put the trash out, gentlemen."

Chapter Twenty-two

❧

ALL warmth rapidly drained from the day. The slushy snow would soon be a slick crust of ice. Xander did not need the ringing of distant bells to tell him the time, and still no Will, no Runners. Xander had counted on the search closing in from both ends of the street.

The children kept up their game. The men about the fire stared into its glow, an advantage to Xander, as their eyes would have to adjust when they looked away. The gloom deepened, but no lights appeared in the windows above the taproom. No one seemed to be home on the lower half of the street except the untended children. *Damn, where was Will?*

Xander had been sure March would hold Cleo in Number Forty, but as the minutes ticked away, his suspicion fell on the closed tap. To be wrong was unthinkable, to wait another minute impossible. He slipped along the edge of the street through the deepening shadows.

At closer range, he heard a new element in the children's game. In the moment of pause at the window, an answering tap came from inside the cellar, like metal against glass, like a man at a dinner party, calling his guests to order to make a toast. Someone was in the cellar of that deserted building.

As his mind narrowed on the cellar window, talk stopped around the bonfire. The bullyboys peered from its glow toward the court where Nate Wilde came into view, unmistakable in his cap and wide grin. He stopped, outlined by the glare of the fire, and looked Xander's way. He turned and waved his cap at an unseen person up the street. Then he was off at a run up the court.

In front of Xander the children froze and dropped their sticks. The small boy nearest the cellar window leaned down, pressed his face to the glass, and cried, "Now, miss. Go now."

Cleo! Xander was in motion before the thought fully formed in his mind. He burst out of the shadows and hurtled across the stone doorstep, throwing his body against the chained doors, feeling old wood give under his shoulder, but not enough.

A booming voice yelled. He'd been spotted. The street filled with the thud of heavy footsteps and curses coming his way. Xander slammed his shoulder against the door again, and rotten wood pulled away from rusty hinges, opening a wedge between the door and its jamb, but the chain and padlock held. Two of the frontrunners barreling Xander's way went down in a heap of flailing limbs on the ice, but others still came on.

Then from the top of the street came a deep clap of sound, like the bellow of a great beast. It nearly knocked Xander off his feet. For long seconds it held him and all Bread Street in a jarring vibration that pressed in on him from all sides, shaking his bones. It made a sharp pain in his bad ear as the vast roar of it rumbled off across London.

Released, the tide of men veered away from the public house in a mad stampede down the hill, and the children disappeared in the black open doorway opposite Xander as if they had been sucked up a chimney. In their place stood a lean youth in a loose, hooded black cloak, like a figure from a masquerade ball. The youth shouted a name snatched away in a roar like a cataract and raised a fist holding an iron rod. He tossed it, and Xander snatched the iron from the air, turning to pry the rotting door from its hinge.

A rumbling as if the very street were being ground in a mill filled Xander's ears and shook his limbs as he rammed through the door into the dark, the floor shaking under him. By the faint gleam of the beer handles and the darkened mirror above the bar, he made out the cellar entrance and plunged down shallow steps to the cellar with its slit of a window.

Narrow walls squeezed his shoulders; a low ceiling forced him to bend his head. He pressed forward, a roar in his ears and only blackness in his eyes until he slammed against solid wood, and a world of damp and rot closed around him, cutting off his senses. He forgot how to breathe. His mind went dark.

Then a word rose up from some deep place in him. *Cleo.* He howled it out in the blackness, pounding on the barrier. In the black cave of sound, the wall gave way, and her hand found his and took hold. In a roar of splintering wood and tumbling stone, her lips touched his ear, and he heard her urgent cry, "Up."

Blind but for memory, his feet found the steps. He hurtled up them, pulling her in his wake, into the paler gloom of the taproom and up another flight of sagging steps to the apartments above as a frothy black tide burst in the doors. *Beer, a raging torrent of beer.*

Xander would have laughed, except that wood and glass splintered below them in a churning mass, threatening to sweep away the rotting stairs and suck them into the hissing vortex. The stairs groaned and swayed beneath their feet, and Xander pushed himself harder and pulled tighter on the hand in his.

They reached a landing lined with closed doors. Xander aimed for the front of the house and kicked down the last door. He tore through the empty dark for the window, already open a crack. The building shuddered and rocked under them.

"We have to get to the roof," he shouted over the roar. He threw up the sash and started to swing a leg through when it dropped with guillotine-like violence on his thigh. He wrenched it up and freed his leg, turning to scan the dark room for a stick or block of wood, when Cleo handed him a short iron rod clutched in her hand. He jammed the length of iron into the rotting sill and pulled himself out on the narrow roof of a protruding bay. Clay tiles crumbled under his boots and dropped into the hissing, foaming flood below, but an iron pipe, clamped firmly to the building where it joined its neighbor gave him a hold. Xander gripped the pipe and pulled Cleo out onto the ledge. From there it was an easy step onto the steeply sloping roof where it met the neighboring building. They climbed from the roof of the public house to the flat roof of a neighboring tenement. For a moment they stood breathing raggedly, clinging to each other.

The building shook beneath them as the dark tide surged on, breaking windows and sending objects slamming against brick and stone. Above them only the faintest pink tinged the clouds.

Xander turned and captured his wife's face in his hands. They were both shadows now, but he thought he could still see light in the green of those eyes. He kissed her slowly and deeply, a kiss to undo all the violence and terror of the flood below with his unspoken love. He had not lost her. He pulled her close, and she rested in his arms, his bedraggled bride.

Minutes later, she pushed free and kissed him again with fierce impatience. "I was afraid."

He nodded. She had been trapped in a hole in the ground.

"Afraid I would never have the chance to tell you I love you."

His throat closed around a reply, and he answered with kisses, until he realized the roar of destruction below them had subsided. He lifted his head and settled her against his side.

"What just happened?" she asked. "The whole world smells like beer."

They turned then to look below. Xander pointed up the street to the top of the rise. Even in the dim light he could see the change in the shadowy contours of Bread Street. Empty dark air yawned to the west at the top of the street where the brewery wall and three huge vats had stood moments before. "The brewery's tanks broke. There was enough beer in them to make a river."

"An accident?"

Xander shook his head. He didn't believe it was an accident at all. He didn't know how the tanks had been broached. "March planned it. A trap for you." Xander found it hard to speak of March. Rage choked him. The whole street had known something was up. That was the meaning of the closed tap, the empty houses, and Nate Wilde's signal. Everyone else would have a slim chance of escape. Only Xander's wife was meant to suffer an accident, to be drowned in a hole. He had almost lost her before they even knew what they had. Cleo shuddered beside him, and he fit her securely in his arms and held tight.

When he lifted his gaze from the drowned street, he saw more shadows like himself and Cleo. On an opposite roof a group of phantoms huddled around a tall youth in a long flowing cloak. They clung to his garments or pressed against his legs. His hands rested on the shoulders of a child not half his height. He looked steadily across the gulf between them, until he caught Xander's gaze.

Xander felt his whole self go still.

The youth leaned down to speak to the children, who loosed their hold on him with obvious reluctance. He came to edge of the roof, and the last light caught his pale face and fair hair above the dark garments. He raised a hand in salute.

"Kit," Xander breathed. He found his voice. "Kit!"

The shadow youth waved again, sadness in the gesture. Forgiveness or blame? Then he turned away, chose darkness, and with him the band of shadows disappeared over the edge of the roof.

Xander stood stunned by it; only his wife's hold kept him anchored to the roof.

He tried to bring his mind to order to understand what he'd just seen. All his dreams of finding Kit had ended in thumping hugs, mad celebrations, in that delayed supper of beef pies and porter, in all of the brothers together in their mother's house laughing at the world.

Beside him his wife placed a steady hand over his heart. "You found him alive."

Xander swallowed the pain in his throat. "He knew you were in the cellar?"

Cleo nodded. "We talked through the window. He gave me a broken rod to work the lock."

Xander took it in. "How did he know you were there?"

"The children were outside the house this morning when March took me. They must have followed the hack and seen me carried into the cellar."

Xander let out a shuddering breath that turned to white vapor in the wintry air. His chest ached. "Kit meant to save you. He tossed me an iron rod to break in the door."

"Xander, he comes to your house most nights. He hides in the garden and watches over you, over us. I thought at first that he was one of March's spies. I didn't suspect who he was until after your arrest."

Xander swore. "Why? Why doesn't he come home? You saw it. He's free now."

"But not safe. Yesterday your father came to the house to warn you that you have enemies beyond March, enemies who do not want you to find Kit."

"Always such fatherly concern for me."

"Actually, yes. He accused you of presumption and of being a dreamer and a fool, and I had to invite him to stand closer to the fire, he's so cold. He's haughtier than the prince, I think, but there was a moment."

Xander kissed the top of his wife's head. "Now you are the dreamer."

"Xander, your father remembers the dragons and goblins rhyme. Why would he remember that? It must be twenty-five years or more since he—"

"Abandoned me."

"Sat beside your bed. He must have done that once at least."

"I don't remember."

"Liar."

The tide below them began to subside. Voices could be heard coming from the court, and lights appeared in upper windows along the street. The snow had been washed away, and now every crevice, every cellar was filled with black pools of beer with its eerie hissing foam. Three women appeared from the court, holding up their skirts, wading through puddles. Each carried a pint pot, and stopped to fill it from the receding flood.

All of sudden Bread Street came alive again, men, women, and children intent on filling pots and mugs with the unexpected flow of spirits. No one paid any attention to the two on the roof. It was a while before Xander could speak.

"What I remember is that I have a different bed now, and a wife to warm it. Let's go home. Tomorrow I'll look for your murderous uncle and my living brother."

Chapter Twenty-three

❦

XANDER did not release his hold on Cleo, not down the treacherous pipe to the ground, not through the beer-scoured street of reeling revelers, not through a quiet conversation with four bewildered officers who did not know where Will was, only that he had not come to Bread Street.

As the search began for victims of the flood, the constable in charge told Xander to go home and wait for Will. Still Xander did not release Cleo's hand, not in the hack, not up the elegant lighted stairway of the house on Hill Street, not until they entered his dressing room. It was like their trip to the bank before his arrest. They were consumed with a barely constrained need to touch.

He flung open his wardrobe and pressed a man's brown silk wrapper into her hands. "Wait here." He kissed her nose.

He was off. She could hear him giving quiet commands, hear Amos hobbling along insisting that he could help. Then she was left to think and feel. Disjointed moments of the day crowded in on her mind. March had tried to kill her. His face and manner and tone in the hack came back to her. Waking in the dark cellar. The details of the fate he'd planned for her. She shuddered from memory, not from the chill of her soaked clothes, and the thought hit her very hard. *He killed you, Papa.*

Only Mrs. Wardlow pressing a cup of hot tea into Cleo's hands stopped the shudders. She helped Cleo from her ruined shoes and beer-soaked skirts.

"Oh, my poor lady, wot ye've been through. We must get ye warm and snug. Ye've found Master Kit alive. We are ever so grateful." Mrs. Wardlow beamed at her. Cleo had never seen the woman smile. She disappeared with the evidence of Bread Street and returned with jugs of hot water.

Cleo tried to name what she felt. *Gratitude.* Likely, Xander Jones felt it, too. She faced the idea squarely as Mrs. Wardlow filled a fragrant, steaming bath. Maybe that is what they would feel for each other. If their marriage proved valid, they would have gratitude and passion. It would not be a bad beginning.

Xander came and stripped off his clothes, and her sense of gratitude faded a little. She really did like him naked.

Without a word, he took her wrapper and helped her into the bath. In the light he examined her bruised jaw and swollen lip. He took over and touched her everywhere, washing her hair, reclaiming her from Bread Street and March with hands hotter than the bath itself.

"Is this gratitude?" she asked.

He looked up then, his eyes alive with silver fire. His mouth closed over one breast, and she felt his desire sink down in and spread through her.

She tugged his head up. "No, pay attention here. What is this?"

"Gratitude is the least of it."

"I should be the grateful one. You saved my life."

"At least twice by my count."

"You should be knighted."

"An overrated experience. Our prince's stays creak, and he's a mite heavy-handed with the scent and the sword, and not entirely sober. A man could lose an ear. Besides, I think I will go back to being plain Xander Jones." He returned his attention to her breast.

Cleo stopped him again by tugging gently on his hair. "I have a better idea. Where's my knife?"

His eyes grew wary. "On the dresser."

Cleo stepped from the bath and dripped her way over to his chest of drawers. She almost faltered, feeling his gaze on her, but she found her knife next to the jar of leeches and a piece of straw. The straw distracted her. "What's this?"

"Your gifts to me. Your gifts are hard to come by for a mere husband."

"Oh dear. We really should release those leeches."

"Not here, I trust."

She turned back to him, knife in hand. She took his breath away, rising from her bath in shining-limbed splendor. "You are aptly named, Cleopatra, never doubt."

She only smiled at that. "Kneel."

He stepped from the bath, and she spread a thick

towel on the floor, where he knelt before her, not such a bad position. He could lean forward and bury his face in her secret curls. "This is what you wanted all along. I remember you said I should kneel and beg you for money." He slid his arms around her and pressed his face into her curls.

After a moment she said, "You are interfering with the ceremony." Her fingers rested on his head, threading lightly through the damp black strands. "Tell me the words."

He pulled back. "Are you sure?"

"Yes, I rather like being Lady Jones."

"Then Lady Jones you shall be."

The words were hard to come by. Had he ever knelt before that assembly of shocked sycophants to receive the prince's whimsical favor? To kneel before his wife, to receive her favor was a vastly different experience. He would have to make something up, something that fit them.

"I swear by mouth and hand and heart and blade to serve you always, lady," he managed.

"That can't be right; are you sure?" She was dragging the knife edge lightly across his shoulder. She smelled of warm soap and herself, and her body trembled a little under his touch.

"I have a better oath to swear by."

"Do you?" Her voice was languid and dreamy.

He stood and scooped her up in his arms and carried her to the bed. The knife fell from her lax hand and slid to the carpet. He looked down on her, the princess he'd stolen from under the nose of a particularly nasty dragon. "I swear to love you forever."

She smiled up at him and opened her arms. "Oh, I like that oath. Much better."

Later from the depths of his bed, Xander spoke of his plan and the failed rescue of his brother.

"I thought I married you for your money, and that I could resist you and set you free." It was a confession that had to be made.

"Thank goodness I proposed to you. What made you get it right?"

Xander laughed and with a swift move pinned her under him again. "March. My whole plan was that March would act in the courts to dissolve our marriage, but every move he made to take you from me made me hold on tighter."

Again they mingled in love, a long, slow joining that left their limbs loose and entwined. But Cleo knew he needed to talk about the loss he had suffered as well as the joy he had gained. "Tell me about him," she urged.

"He's sixteen, just."

"How did he disappear?"

"I was playing the hero."

She heard the self-condemnation in his tone. "Saving the regent?"

He seemed to withdraw a little. "There was a mob around that yellow carriage of his, and the guards couldn't come to order. A wild fellow was waving a pistol. I saw the gun, and I . . ." He shuddered, and Cleo pressed her whole person against him.

"I shoved Kit in a doorway and told him to stay, but I think we were followed. We'd been to a boxing exhibition at the Fives Court in a huge crowd. Someone, maybe Harris, was waiting for the chance to take him."

"Who is Kit's father?"

"Daventry. He died at Assaye under Wellesley in India two months before Kit was born."

"Daventry? Wenlocke's son? His people did not help in the search?" She propped herself up on an elbow to look at him.

He was frowning. "You know, I think they may have delayed it. Will was still in France. There was a debate, in the Lords no less, about the prince's proposed knighting of a baseborn man. My father was opposed, as was Wenlocke. Until it was settled, I couldn't get anyone to act."

"What ended the debate?"

"The prince wanted his way, and his secretary, Clarke, had a line from Shakespeare that settled it." His rough, warm hand found her knee.

"Maybe you were meant to be a hero," she said on a little intake of breath. She believed it, but his hand was distracting, and she would have to make the point again later.

"Not a saint?" He shifted to kiss her throat.

She shook her head, letting quiet laughter fill her. "A saint would not slide his hand up his lady's thigh in that particularly provoking way."

It was dawn when they again spoke of Kit. "I did not expect him to grow so tall. Three years."

Cleo could feel the unspoken question eating at her husband. "It isn't that he's grown tall, but that he's not who he was." She laid her hand on Xander's heart and tried to explain. "You have been searching for a young boy. Kit is someone else. He doesn't believe that you want the person he's become."

Xander's person stilled under her hand. She thought he did not breathe, but neither did he shrink from the truth. "Who is he then?"

Cleo smiled at the note of uncertainty in his voice even as his mind worked at the puzzle of Kit's hanging back at the edge of his old life. That hesitation was the very thing that her fearless husband could not understand. He who could lean into a knife, or hurl himself at an attacker, or throw himself down a dark stairwell would not understand the self-doubt that held Kit back. With this she could help him. "Kit seems to have gathered a family about him. How many children were there do you think? It was hard to count shadows."

"Eight at least."

"You know what that means, don't you?" She saw it, even if he did not.

Xander couldn't answer, could only submit to the lazy stroking of her hand across his chest.

"He's like you. He looks out for those weaker and smaller than himself. He protects them. He's a knight of those streets."

Her words provoked a rueful laugh. "Which he's become because apparently he thinks it's more dangerous to live in a fine house off Berkeley Square than to be homeless and nameless on Bread Street."

"Perhaps it is. You and Will must find out why and who your enemy is, and truly bring your lost brother home."

Chapter Twenty-four

❧

The four investigators of the London Consistory Court faced a small assemblage of persons late on a dark November day. Though they wore neither robes nor wigs for the occasion, they sat on a dais befitting their position as men of probity and rank. The weather out was vile, a gale threatened, and their sober faces expressed a certain impatience to resolve the matter before them by teatime.

"Are all parties present?" Dr. Valentine, one of the two lay members of the court, surveyed the meager party.

Dr. Stephen Lushington, King's Counselor, rose from his seat opposite Cleo and Xander's side of the room.

"I regret, Dr. Valentine, that Mr. Archibald March, Miss Spencer's chief trustee, has gone abroad."

Norwood was instantly on his feet. "In view of Mr. March's absence, I believe we can move quickly to clear up any question of the validity of the marriage of Sir Alexander Jones and Cleopatra Spencer."

Lushington was plainly embarrassed. "Dr. Valentine, Mr. March is a man whose unassailable character and reputation are of such long standing in London that I encourage you not to act in haste. We have reports of serious conjugal irregularities in this case."

"Spies' reports," said Norwood. "March has left London under a cloud of suspicion regarding his involvement in the recent abduction of Lady Jones and in a number of deaths, including the death of the Right Honorable Lord Woford, four years ago, and the more recent deaths of Dick Cullen, an employee of Truman's Brewery, and Mrs. Lottie Greenslade, a resident of Number Forty Bread Street.

"In light of Lady Jones's present circumstances as a wife and under the terms of the original trust, I request that all funds bequeathed to her by her father must revert to Sir and Lady Jones for their management, and I further file a motion to amend the initial trust document, giving Lady Jones and her lawful husband, Sir Alexander Jones, joint guardianship of the minor, Charles Spencer."

Everyone spoke at once. Charlie cheered. Lushington began to sputter in protest. One of the other investigators began to ask questions. Finally, the chief investigator brought his gavel down with a bang.

"Mr. Norwood, from the beginning there has been cause to doubt this marriage. What do you now offer in support of its validity?"

"Why, Lady Jones is with child."

Again the small number of participants in the

little drama all had to have their say at the exact same moment, so that the deliberations of the four investigators at their table on the dais went unheard. When once again the gavel came down, the chief investigator spoke the following words, "We find that the marriage between Sir Alexander Jones and Cleopatra Spencer, hereinafter, Lady Jones, conforms to the criteria of both God's and man's laws and constitutes a valid marriage, entitling them to the rights and prerogatives associated with their status as man and wife."

I N a smaller room on the upper floor of the Brown Bear Public House, Will Jones found himself before his superiors. They'd rolled the big guns into place to knock him out.

A plain table and bench had been placed before the fire. The magistrate occupied one end of the bench, the chief the middle, and a clerk with a loose folio of papers, the other. A sergeant stood at the door. A few coals sputtered in the grate, and the windows rattled as the wind rose. Dark had fallen.

The Brown Bear was not known for the luxury of its accommodations, but a man who spent the night there in a gale would be warm and dry and well fed. With a few coins and the right smile, he could even manage to entertain a female companion in his bed.

In short Will's position was far superior to Kit's, wherever he was in London's shivering streets. That was a thought to keep in mind.

The door opened, admitting a burst of bright sound from the crowd below stairs, and one other man. Jack

Castle, a rising man on the force, took the chair next to Will, enduring a fierce glare from the chief. Will supposed Jack had a right to be there. He had, after all, found Will dumped in the yard of the Blue Ball, where he'd been dragged from March's club.

The magistrate leaned his elbows on the table and propped his wise and ponderous chins on his joined hands. "This hearing is in session. Complaints have been lodged, Jones, and inquiries made into your conduct as an officer of the law." His voice was weary and stern. The clerk dutifully scratched the words on one of the loose sheets.

Will did not blink or shift his gaze. This day of reckoning was not wholly unexpected. His injuries had nearly healed, and though he still felt a twinge in his ribs with any sudden move, his head was clear. In a matter of minutes he would leave the Brown Bear and start a new chapter of his life. His one regret at the moment was having Jack there. A man didn't want his friends to witness his fall.

"Have you anything to say for yourself?" the magistrate asked.

"March is a maw worm." No point in backing down now.

"We serve the public, Jones. Private quarrels, private causes are not for us."

"Murder seems sufficient cause for an officer of the law to interest himself in March's affairs."

The magistrate controlled himself with effort. "Unsupported accusations against men of consequence are not evidence at this hearing."

Especially not if the Home Secretary had anything

to say about it. "Has March been located?" Will's injuries had kept him laid up long enough for March to leave London.

The magistrate's jaw twitched, a tremor that shook his chins. "We are not concerned at this hearing with the whereabouts of Mr. March. We are concerned with a bill for damages to his club in excess of five hundred pounds."

Will's careless snort cost his ribs a sharp pang. "Shall I send my draft directly to the Home Secretary?"

The magistrate's head came up, and his fist came down.

"Jones, a small number of dedicated men hold back the tide of thievery and violence in this hoary old city. You seem determined to undermine every one of them by breaking furniture, destroying artwork, and generally offending peaceful subjects of His Majesty at their club. Furthermore, you put four men in jeopardy by sending them to Bread Street on a false trail, interfering with their duties, and wantonly ignoring your own by failing to bring in your brother."

"My brother was innocent, however. Is there anything else?"

A dangerous purple sort of rage seemed to make the magistrate incapable of speech.

The chief glared at Will. "Be grateful not to be taken in charge, Jones."

"Get on with it." He wanted the proceeding over.

"Rise." The magistrate managed through clenched teeth.

Will came to his feet. He sensed Jack standing beside him.

In a voice of iron the magistrate pronounced the expected sentence. "You are dismissed from this force. You will surrender your badge and staff of office at once."

Devil take it. He had expected a kind of relief that he had often imagined other men felt when sentence was passed. Instead there was a queer hollow feeling in his chest.

He took the black staff imprinted with the gold insignia of the crown, worn a bit from use, and put it on the table before the magistrate. He had carried it for three years. The sergeant picked it up. It didn't matter. Still his hand clenched around air.

"This hearing is concluded."

The clerk finished his scratching and gathered up the folio. With a nod from the magistrate, the three men negotiated their rising from the bench, pushing back from the table with a harsh grating sound. The sergeant opened the door, and they left without a word.

Will waited for the footsteps to fade. "Good night, Jack."

"You know this is not the way this ends," Jack said.

Will shook his head. "Take my cases, if you want."

"I've got my own now, you know."

The quiet pride of it threatened the perfect carelessness of the moment. He needed Jack to leave. "Best that you not know me again, Jack."

"Right. Not know you." He clapped his hat on his head and moved to the door. "I'll not know you whenever I hear something about March. How's that? I'll not know you when Bredsell's snatching boys out of the dock for that place he calls a school. I'll not know you when I find what Nate Wilde's up to. How's that? I'll not know you, all right."

The door slammed. *Thanks, Jack.*

Will had no trouble passing through the crowd in tap intent on keeping warm with ale and company.

The wind caught him as soon as he stepped outside, driving him back against the building. He pulled his greatcoat tight about him and leaned into the gale to bull his way up the street.

Strange to step into the London night as an ordinary man. That odd hollow feeling came to him again. Without his staff he felt weightless, as if the gale might blow him away the way it blew scraps of paper along the stones at his feet.

The streets were empty. The whole dark city huddled under the blast. But Kit was alive in it somewhere, lost to them still. The thought that had been lying in wait for him for days as he faced the inquiry now sprang. *If he had not gone to March's club, if he had stuck to Xander's plan, Kit would be home.*

Well, he had to live with that. He'd lived with worse.

Epilogue

❦

CLEO put her hand on her husband's shoulder, solid as ever under the fine wool of his coat as he bent over the letter he was writing. He lifted those smoky eyes of his to her, and she let her fingers drift behind his ear.

Around him, packing crates covered most of the library floor while the bookshelves stood empty.

"Wife." His voice was almost a growl, as he put down his pen and turned to catch her between his legs. His hands instantly tugged at her skirts, lifting the fabric above her knees, sliding under the silk along her thighs and pushing upward to cup her bottom.

"Are you sure about this move?" she asked him, leaning into his embrace.

"Yes. I'm just writing to my mother. Explaining. She'll want to be back in London now. Now that we know he's alive." His voice was muffled, his lips against her swelling belly.

"But you, do you want to give up this house?"

"We need a larger establishment for our expanding family, and you want your brother to live in his own home."

"I do, but . . ."

"Then we'll live at Woford House until he comes of age. You know I have another house for us."

"You do?"

"On Wimpole Street, perfectly respectable. I did have to promise Charlie one thing about the move."

"You promised Charlie?" She was enjoying the play of rough masculine hands on her skin and that deeper note in her husband's voice to which her being made an answering vibration. Her skin was, if anything, more sensitive to touch as her pregnancy advanced.

"I told him that I would not allow you to redecorate his house in the Egyptian style."

Cleo laughed and leaned down to steal a kiss. "I'm sure he was vastly relieved. You are a nice man, Sir Xander Jones."

"I wonder that you can say that to a man whose hands are wrapped around your bottom."

C LEO laughed, all the way to the bank with Roger, the newest of her footmen. She carried a parasol that Xander claimed matched the green of her eyes and that ended in a wicked point.

Xander had discovered an endless supply of footmen in soldiers down on their luck, and really since their duties might run to protecting the family from its enemies, Cleo could not object to either their size or their number. Besides, she thought Roger might make a strong impression on Mr. Meese.

Meese, of course, bustled out of his office to greet her the moment she entered the bank. She let him practice his bowing and scraping. Someday he might get it right, if he did not knock himself senseless against the floor. She was in no hurry. She strolled across the vast chamber, drawing looks and even stares from the gentlemen gathered there.

Meese made an especially deep bow at the door to Evershot's office. It was still Evershot's bank, but there had been a restructuring of the board of directors to include the first female member.

"Lady Jones, go right in; Mr. Evershot is waiting for you."

Meese reached to open the door, but Roger snagged him by the tail of his threadbare jacket. The fabric parted, exposing the shiny bottom of Meese's worn trousers. He backed away, and Cleo sailed past him. "Ah, Mr. Evershot, I believe you have some money for me."

AUTHOR'S NOTE

I am grateful to many wonderful writers of fiction and history for allowing me to roam the streets of London in my imagination, to the occasional airline for permitting me to roam in person, and to the Internet for virtual access to every corner of a city that Samuel Johnson said one could only tire of when one tired of life itself. Impressions from those excursions have shaped my own fictional London of the Regency period. It is a London defined by stark contrasts between rich and poor, light and dark, glittering West End palaces and unlighted rookeries. While my Bread Street is entirely fictional, I hope Dickens, Orwell, Dore, or Morrison would find its stones and people familiar. Any flaws in this fictional creation are my own.

LONDON, 1820

IT was a bleeding soggy night for a man to leave his bed to buy a virgin. Will Jones looked through his fogged carriage window at the white-columned portico of a discreet town house in Half Moon Street. If Jack Castle's information was good, deflowering virgins was just one of the depravities available inside.

Fistfuls of hard rain rattled the glass as Will swung open the door and stepped down. His foot met wet cobblestones, and a sharp twinge in his ribs stopped him cold. He covered the hitch in his stride with a gentleman's small vanities, tugging white cuffs from the fine wool of his black evening clothes and tilting his hat at a jaunty angle.

The pause allowed him a moment to observe the house closely. He had spent weeks in less-secure prisons. Cleverly painted wood panels covered the upper windows, and two oversized pugilists in footmen's attire stood guard on either side of the door. Still the place had its vulnerabilities. The top of the carriage matched the height of the portico, above which an iron railing connected with others down the block to the corner of Piccadilly, where late evening traffic still passed.

Over his shoulder Will offered Harding, his driver, a few words in French, shedding his own identity as he became the Vicomte de Villard with a West Indian fortune, an ugly wife, and a habit of collecting erotic prints.

The oversized footmen stared straight ahead as Will raised the door's brass knocker. A face as red and pitted as a brick appeared in the peephole.

"Twenty-five guineas." Brick Face had a rasp of a voice that could file metal.

"*Bien sur.* To attain a great prize, one must expect to invest one's silver." Will shoved the paper notes through the hole.

Inside, Brick Face took Will's cloak, hat, and gloves and grunted an order to wait. The entry hall gave no sign of vice, just the well-bred English comforts of a Turkish rug, mahogany console, and tall case clock, but somewhere in London, Archibald March, the murdering maggot who owned the place, was free.

Most Londoners knew March as the city's great benefactor, a man whose charities reportedly supported widows and orphans, the lame and the blind. Only a handful of people, including Will, his brother Xander, and Xander's bride, Cleo, had reason to believe that March was a murderer and a blackmailer who had killed at least three people and corrupted many more.

Coarse male laughter erupted from a room somewhere above, and quick steps sounded on the stairs.

The next moment the host appeared. Will decided
that the hall was an anteroom of hell after all.

He did not care to shake hands with Guy Leary, a
lean, freckle-faced felon with carrot-colored hair and a
cold glance that said he was up to any viciousness. That
he was in charge and not some well-preserved bawd with
a plump bosom and an ingratiating air spoke volumes
about the place. Will suspected the female employees
did not enjoy Leary's supervision.

"What's your pleasure tonight, Monsieur le Vicomte?"

"I understand an auction is about to begin."

Guy glanced at the clock and shook his head. "Sorry,
Vicomte. Auctions are by invitation only, to interested
parties known to this house. We can offer you other
delights, however."

"Allow me to express my interest in participating in
your auction." Will put a stack of notes on the console
next to him.

"I don't know you."

"You don't know Vicomte de Villard? I thought my
print collection had a certain reputation." He handed
Guy a flat package wrapped in brown paper.

With another impatient glance at the clock, Guy tore
off the wrapping and regarded the print. Closely.

"How did you come to hear of our auction?" Nothing
changed outwardly in the cold face, but Will caught the
change in tone.

"A friend took pity on me. I faced a dull evening with
my wife, and only my prints to rouse me. The prospect of

your virgin lifted my spirits at once. She is the authentic article? One may examine her to be certain?"

"One may not."

"But you do guarantee . . ."

"Do you want in or not?"

Will waved a languid hand. "Please. Lead on."

Guy spun abruptly and led the way up a curving staircase.

"Does this exquisite have a name?"

"Helen of Troy."

Will almost choked at the irony. Clearly Guy was a man who'd never had the benefit of a good tutor. Old Hodge would have set him straight about naming his virgin after the most famous wanton in history.

At the top of the stairs they entered a red and gold salon filled with gentlemen of various ages but a similar carnal bent. The air was stale with smoke and lust. Three young women dressed in cream silk corsets over lawn drawers as thin as tissue circulated among the more completely clad males, keeping every glass brimmed. Their presence in proper English undress among the fully clothed men gave a carnal kick to the gathering. It also gave new meaning to the practice of dress-lodgers, women so wholly owned by their employers they had no clothes to their names. With a nod Guy Leary summoned a dark-haired beauty with red pouting lips and empty eyes, who provided Will with a glass of brandy.

Over its rim Will surveyed the mixed lot of pleasure seekers. He recognized two members of Parliament, not of the Reform Party, one octogenarian lord, and where the talk was loudest and bawdiest, one of his own noble half brothers. His luck held. There were no officers present and no one who knew either Villard or Will Jones. Certainly his half brother would not recognize the family bastard.

The crowd was the sort he'd known in Paris after Waterloo and before the disappearance of Kit, his youngest brother. Some had lost a sense of the boundaries of civilized men, hooked on debauchery the way a man could be hooked on opium. Others merely came to be titillated. They would go home and pump their wives heartily while images of erotic excess danced in their heads.

For a moment Will felt Villard's identity slip away from him, and his old identity as a Bow Street Runner assert itself, but he was not here in an official police capacity. He straightened the diamond stickpin in the folds of his cravat to recover his disguise as Villard, refined connoisseur of decadence, a man superior to ordinary brutes with their vulgar zest for pinching bottoms and ogling breasts.

Chairs and sofas had been arranged to view a stage draped in red velvet curtains at the far end of the room. One of the hulking footmen brought Will a chair as Guy Leary mounted the stage and tapped a glass.

Conversation died, and men turned to the stage. The three corset-clad women, nearly indistinguishable in round-limbed, vacant appearance, took positions behind Leary. Most of the room's occupants watched them as Leary explained the auction rules.

Will studied the competition. They'd been invited, so they knew the girl behind the curtain was a virgin, not a professional, and they'd paid a steep fee to participate, as he had, so he had to assume that he was up against men with deep pockets and shallow consciences. Still, a lot would depend on the girl herself.

Guy paused. "Gentlemen, what am I bid for a night with Helen of Troy?"

At his signal the women drew back the velvet curtains to reveal a girl with tawny golden hair in a blue-sashed gown of virginal white, lolling on a rose and gold striped sofa, her head resting on one slim arm, dark lashes against flushed cheeks. She had the look of a girl who had stayed up too late and just closed her eyes for a moment. Guy would have done better to advertise her as the Sleeping Beauty.

It was hard to tell her age, but at least she was not fifteen as Will had feared. Except for bare feet, unbound hair, and rouged breasts, she looked respectable enough for a ball, innocence and sensuality combined. That wanton innocence hit him with an erotic jolt that could raise a cock in a corpse. He reminded himself that in such a place, the girl's appearance could all be a show. She could be a professional after all.

Then her eyes fluttered open, deep brown and instantly panicked. Not a professional, but a trapped, frightened girl. How had she fallen into March's net?

Her attendants helped her to stand. Their efforts had the look of guards restraining a prisoner rather than the three graces attending a goddess, but she would have done well for one of those Italian painters. She was tall and lithely built, like a young Amazon, and fighting the influence of some drug. He could see it in her dilated pupils. The narcotic would take hold and make her head sag on her slender neck, or she would shake it off and look frantically about. He wondered that she didn't scream or protest.

Men began shouting. A flurry of bids quickly reduced the competition to a pair of young bloods: a ruddy, flat-faced blond and a long-nosed brunet. On their feet, facing one another, the pair swayed from drink. Others in the crowd immediately made side bets on the outcome.

The flat-faced blond gave his opponent a shove. "Bow out, Milsing, you've been sailing on River Tick for months."

"I've got twice the blunt you've got, any day, Cowley." Long-nose shoved back.

Cowley staggered, righted himself, and giggled. "Here's a thought, man." He waved a finger in the air. "We could share her."

There was a general mumble from the crowd, not an actual protest, just a sense of grievance.

Milsing frowned. "Well, we could all buy shares, Cowley, but only one man goes first, you know."

It was time to act. Will Jones would pick up a table or a chair and break it over someone's head, but as Villard, he needed a more subtle approach. He rose slowly and hurled his brandy glass against the mantle.

Glass shattered with a satisfying ring. All heads turned his way. The sound seemed to penetrate even the girl's fogged brain. She lifted her chin, and her dark gaze met Will's in a brief moment of lucid consciousness. *That's right, sweetheart, you're leaving with me.*

Enter the rich world of historical romance with Berkley Books.

Lynn Kurland

Patricia Potter

Betina Krahn

Jodi Thomas

Anne Gracie

Love is timeless.

penguin.com